Inez Baranay was bor[n] [...] been a schoolteacher [...] scriptwriter, an editor and a journalist, she is also the author of three books: *Between Careers* (a novel, 1989), *The Saddest Pleasure* (stories, 1989) and *Pagan* (a novel, 1990). In 1992 she worked in Papua New Guinea for a provincial Women's Council as an Australian Volunteer Abroad. She is currently working on her new novel, set in PNG.

Also by Inez Baranay
and available in Imprint

Between Careers
The Saddest Pleasure
Pagan

IMPRINT

The edge of BALÍ

INEZ BARANAY

Angus&Robertson
An imprint of HarperCollinsPublishers

Arts for Australians
Australia Council

*Publication of this
title was assisted by
the Australia Council,
the Federal Government's
arts funding and advisory body.*

AN ANGUS & ROBERTSON BOOK
An imprint of HarperCollinsPublishers

First published in Australia in 1992 by
CollinsAngus&Robertson Publishers Pty Limited (ACN 009 913 517)
A division of HarperCollinsPublishers (Australia) Pty Limited
25–31 Ryde Road, Pymble NSW 2073, Australia

HarperCollinsPublishers (New Zealand) Limited
31 View Road, Glenfield, Auckland 10, New Zealand

HarperCollinsPublishers Limited
77–85 Fulham Palace Road, London W6 8JB, United Kingdom

Copyright © Inez Baranay 1992

National Library of Australia
Cataloguing-in-Publication data:

Baranay, Inez
   On the edge of Bali

   ISBN 0 207 168 997

   I. Title.

A823.3

Cover: A Dream, Bali, c1970. Pen and ink,
watercolour gouache and gold leaf,
47 × 61 cm. Collection of Philip
Bacon Galleries, Brisbane.
Typeset by Midland Typesetters, Maryborough, Victoria
Printed in Australia by Griffin Paperbacks

5 4 3 2 1
95 94 93 92

To my sister Christabel

Be not afeard: the isle is full of noises,
Sounds and sweet airs, that give delight, and hurt not.
Sometimes a thousand twangling instruments
Will hum about mine ears; and sometime voices,
That, if I then had wak'd after long sleep,
Will make me sleep again: and then, in dreaming,
The clouds methought would open, and show riches
Ready to drop upon me; that, when I wak'd
I cried to dream again.

WILLIAM SHAKESPEARE, *THE TEMPEST*: III, ii

[M]en will know they have entered the Kali Age when society reaches a stage where property confers rank, wealth becomes the only source of virtue, passion the sole bond of union between husband and wife, falsehood the source of success in life, sex the only means of enjoyment, and when outer trappings are confused with inner religion.

OMAR GARRISON, *TANTRA: THE YOGA OF SEX*

ACKNOWLEDGMENT

I am grateful to all my friends who, while I was writing this book, nourished me, encouraged my work and made me laugh; and to all those who shared their Bali experiences with me by being there with me, by telling me about it, by writing a range of books and articles over the past decades.

PART ONE

NELSON

ONE

Bali is known as a land of a myriad religious ceremonies, and this mania for ritual affects even the most irreligious tourist, and the most sacred and strictly observed of the tourists' ceremonies is to gather together to marvel at and worship and photograph the sky at sunset, on beaches, headlands and hilltops, and the most famous of these congregations is the sunset at Kuta beach.

Nelson Brodie was back in Bali. Her skin tingled, the fresh salty sea prickling softly as it dried. Far down to the south you could see where the airport was. Planes took off and landed frequently. She could see a large aircraft departing, lifting off the distant runway, its lights dimly aglow against the yellow sky. Her own plane had landed only a few hours ago. The long slow queue at Immigrasi, finding a bemo, getting to her room . . . that was all over. From now on it was all glorious. She had hurried down to the beach and straight into the waves. The afternoon had been clear and the sunset would be postcard quality spectacular. Cameras were ready. The swimmers came out of the water. Tourists shook out the sarongs they had purchased, patterns of old batik and the latest designs flapping all around her. The beach was a mile-long fiesta. Boys pummelled their way out of the surf, chased frisbees, rode motorbikes along the wet sand. Everyone faced the western horizon, the edge of sea and sky. Nelson lay on her towel and people came and squatted around her, setting down baskets, uncovering boxes and trays. She looked, she laughed, she waved them away. She was offered cold drinks bikinis sarongs watches jewellery wooden chopsticks

3

carvings of fishermen of birds of crouching dancers old-style paintings new-style paintings massage manicure pedicure hair-braiding *The International Herald Tribune* used books peanuts pineapples mangos bananas lollies hairpins T-shirts wrist-bands love friendship. It was only background to the immensity of actually being back here at last.

His writing on a postcard of a Bali sunset. 'I am love you. Come back Bali. Miki hope Nelson come back very soon.' A while ago now. You couldn't expect him to keep writing, the same thing each time, words that weren't needed. They knew each other's thoughts. Didn't need postcards. Then it was time at last for the final letter.

'Guess what!! I've booked my ticket to Bali! I've done nothing but work well nearly nothing it's really been worth it though. I still miss you *just as much*. Sorry I haven't written for a while but I've been so busy working. Here is my flight number and time of arrival. What can I say!!! If you are not at the airport I will go to Padma and see you there or at the Bungah Club. I'm bringing you those tapes I told you about. I can't wait to see you lucky I'm busy right up till I leave. Then I will be there with you and we will be together and I will love you in the flesh day and night.' She had written it as neatly as she could.

It had been like a beautiful movie. Miki was the greatest-looking guy she'd ever seen, the nicest she had ever known, the one who cared most for her. He was the one who was exactly right for her. Knowing him had made a million things clear to her—who she was, why she was born, what she believed, why she hadn't really been in love before. When she met him she was just nineteen. Now she was twenty.

She could work for a year and make enough money to come back, he had told her. He said he couldn't do the same. 'Work here for a year, make only a little bit of money. Only enough for stay here. I want to go to Australia,' he said.

'You will! If you want to, you will.' This, contrary to her normal scepticism, she had said with certainty.

'I want,' he said; 'I want.' She loved all his expressions: this one of grim desire, that one of angelic trust.

'Just believe in something,' she had told him. 'Believe hard enough and you'll get it.' Why deny it? She had doubted but had heard so many examples which proved this. She, for example, had for years and years believed it was time for something wonderful, something transforming and liberating, something she was not able or allowed to imagine. And look what happened, she hadn't even wanted to go to Bali, and it was practically only a coincidence that she did, but she went to Bali, and she met Miki. He was her proof!

TWO

The evening sweated its own heat, too; the air softened and darkened and remained warm.

The streets were abuzz with activity between sunset and closing. Shops and stalls side by side overflowed with brightly coloured goods: clothes hats bags shoes leather jackets cassettes . . . 'Look only, look please, come!' called the shopkeepers to all who passed their displays. 'What do you like? Special price,' they promised to all who paused.

Nelson enjoyed their calls as she wandered up the road from the beach, detouring along the curves of the main road, before turning back to the Pensione Padma. Her memory and the sights she saw were meeting and merging; she was thinking joyously I was here before! I remember this, this is new I think, I've seen that guy selling shoes lots of times, I've seen that lady in that warung, she was here last time, she's been here all the time, and now I'm back, and she's still here. All of life is in these streets. I'm here! she thought, here at last here forever.

The traffic was chaotic and noisy as ever on that crowded narrow road—bemos, motorbikes, bicycles, all cheerfully competing for right of way, my way's right, out of my way, right away, it's all honking and jostling. What's the big hurry? Everyone's in a hurry behind a wheel.

'No! I said no!' screamed an Australian female tourist. She and her companion were ablaze with anger and irritability. 'Leave us bloody alone!' they yelled. They were angry at the transport guys, who were always calling 'Transport? Transport?', their hands turning an air wheel. Even if you're walking along obviously not looking for transport they call to you. Some tourists get really shitty, won't answer them, or scream at them like this. Nelson didn't mind. It was like that before, and after she'd walked up and down that same bit of road enough times they'd recognise her and she never once got transport from them and still they'd yell at her, 'Hey, transport?' with that hands-on-wheel gesture. She was glad they were still doing it.

Groups of boys in jeans and leather jackets were lounging on motorbikes, those small bikes they have here. Nelson looked at them, all of them black-haired brown-skinned like Miki—if she should see him now! Longing as she was every moment for the moment, it was not time yet, and she felt a thrill of apprehension as the boys looked at her, in case he were there among them, and saw her in the random street, rather than at a moment dressed for and orchestrated by herself, a moment at which she would deliberately appear.

She got out of the way of a red-eyed, mangy dog with scabby pink skin. Her attention was diverted to some food carts that had been set up by the side of the road. The fruit slices looked good. 'Cholera carts,' sniggered a couple of blond surfers charging past her, all tight-muscled lumbering disdain. True, you were told not to buy cut fruit; apparently the germs here were especially virulent. Nelson went on her way again, then paused and watched a boy in a baseball cap serve some kind of soup—*bakso*—to five children who waited patiently for their turn and then squatted by the cart to slurp the soup. The children here seemed so independent. They were certainly very beautiful. She would have children like this. She had eaten food off a cart with Miki.

She turned, and suddenly hurried to find the alley that led to her room.

THREE

Nelson walked into the Padma just after dark. 'Hello!' they called, three people sitting outside the family rooms, chatting, animated and langurous both, eating peanuts from a paper cone. It was Ibu Saren, who ran the Padma with her husband, with Wayan and Belgi, two of the boys who worked there. 'Hello,' they called to her, 'where you come from?'

They called to her in English, and she answered in English. Some tourists in the cheap losmens insisted on Indonesian. They'd go *selamat malam* or something, and Nelson had heard the common greetings often enough to recognise them. But she would never try to say them. She hated tourists who tried to talk Indonesian, they sounded pretentious and condescending, and usually they ran out of words pretty soon. The people here speak English and they want to learn English and English is the world language and the words of the songs are in English.

'Hello,' they called, 'where you come from?'

'The beach!' called Nelson gaily, waving as she went to her room. This room. The room at the end. The *same* room. The room she had moved to after she'd met Miki. This room was unoccupied, waiting for her. If ever there was a sign! The luck, the good fortune, the assurance of it.

They hadn't even known they were keeping the room for her. She had written to Pensione Padma when she knew the date she would arrive, but this afternoon, although Wayan and Belgi had, gratifyingly, remembered that she had been there before, they knew nothing about the letter she had sent. Still, her room had been vacated that morning, and she took it as a sign.

It was still hot inside and she switched on the electric fan. She emptied her bag on to one of the two single beds. Losmens never had double beds. Nelson had found, last time in Bali, that two people in love didn't need any more space than that provided by a single bed.

She hadn't brought much stuff with her. She wouldn't be wearing the same things she had been wearing in the last months, working seven days a week in Sydney, three jobs, coming home to find out who was crashed out in the lounge room, totally out of it in the kitchen, playing loud music in one of the bedrooms . . . it was worth it, the room had been cheap and she only went home to sleep. That wasn't home any more. To think she had left that house only this morning! Already it was far away and long ago. Forget it now. She had earned her way back.

And enough to buy a few new clothes, the kind of clothes you wear here, cool and bright and cheap as anything. She took off her sarong and bikini and went into the bathroom, showered, washed her hair, shaved her armpits for the second time that day. When she was dry she sprayed herself with scent.

She would buy new, colourful clothes, the latest styles. The best clothes to wear around here are the ones you could buy here. First she put on her birthday present from her past housemates: boxer shorts in bright green silk. Miki would love them. He'd probably want them for himself. Then she put on her jeans. She would wear them tonight with this huge scarf folded then tied around her breasts. Or was her skin still too pale? She tried another top, then went back to the scarf. Then she added the dangly silver earrings she had bought last time. Miki had been with her, and his help in choosing them, his pleasure in their perfection, made them his gift to her.

There were footsteps outside and a cough, a call. It was Belgi. 'Hello,' he said, smiling, 'finish bath?' *Pinish bath?* That lovely lilting accent.

'Yeah,' said Nelson, standing at the door, fiddling with the scarf. 'Getting ready to go out.'

'You go with friend?' he asked. Nelson got an inkling that he had come to ask something, not just chit chat. But points were reached in roundabout ways.

9

'Yeah,' she said, 'meeting my friend later. Have to finish getting dressed now.'

'Oh, please,' he said and held out an Australian aerogramme. Wasn't that her own handwriting?

She took it and realised it was her letter telling them she was coming back on the 10th and wanted room number one again. 'This from you?' Belgi asked. *Dis prom you?*

'Yeah,' she said. 'That's from me. You found it!' He smiled at her with apparent great joy, a dazzling, beautiful smile, making her smile widely back. 'Glad you got it!' she said, her intention if not her expression sarcastic, handing it back.

'OK!' he said happily. 'Please finish now!'

Still smiling, inside her room, Nelson realised that she hadn't even considered that Miki—as if it mattered much— might not have received her letter. And here was another sign. Letters *did* arrive, he *had* got the letter she had sent him, he knew she was here, and he at this minute was setting out for the Bungah Club with the same sweet certainty as her own.

FOUR

When Nelson suddenly made a lot of money—a lot for her—
from being in a television commercial, she had thought it
would be the start of her savings. When she had a bit more,
she planned to go to New York, or maybe Africa.

'You got an *attitude*, girl,' her ex-best friend Grace Sanyo
had complained. She meant Nelson's obstinate passion for
reaching faraway places, places her favourite music came from.
'Asia-Pacific, girl, that's where it's at.'

Grace's mother had been a singer and then she married
Grace's stepfather, who was very rich. Grace, whose real father
had been Japanese, possessed luscious Eurasian beauty, always
enjoyed most of the attention and never revealed any doubt
about the inevitability of her brilliant success in modelling,
acting and marriage. She hung out with Nelson a lot in the
year after they'd both left school. Nelson had to take a few
scungy jobs to pay for acting classes, caffelattes in Stanly Street
and ecstasy for dance parties. Grace, who could ask for as
much money as she wanted, was getting paid really well for
modelling. For a while Grace had a boyfriend who was doing
a post-graduate degree in the ecology of communication, and
she would repeat everything he told her with an air of
authority. 'Evil is not a useful category', and 'Europe is now
irrelevant to Australia'.

Nelson only got put in the commercial through knowing
Grace. Once it was made, she had enough money for some
real choices, and once it was aired she had to endure the status
and embarrassment of seen-on-television. Then Grace broke
up with the communicating ecologist. He was saying rap
wasn't really music and ecstasy fried your brain and modelling
was an insufficient social critique.

'So,' said Grace, 'I go, get lost, hippy,' and Grace turned
her considerable charm into persuading Nelson into going to

11

Bali with her. As Grace pointed out, Nelson didn't have a serious boyfriend. (Nelson couldn't stand the boys who tried to get her interested and would stare in dumb, ignored wonder at guys who never noticed her.) In Bali, Grace said, they would lose weight, get a tan and have a ball.

A *tan*? What was this about a tan all of a sudden? All you hear everywhere is sun danger, and skin cancer, and factor 30 block-out, and you never needed a tan in Darlinghurst to discuss machiatto and cappuccino, the true meaning of paranoia, which DJ played the best music, whether marriage was just a piece of paper, if bad luck was the person's own fault.

Nelson used to wear all black clothes, her hair spiked, messed, jelled, hennaed and greened. Doc Martens on her feet, layers of raggedy black tights over her legs, layers of raggedy jumpers from Saint Vinnie's over a miniskirt. That look. She used to like winter, pallor, and black clothes.

But it had been clear for a while that it was time for a change.

A friend of a friend inherited her aunt's record collection and they went to listen to Grateful Dead, Frank Zappa, Cream, all in their early days. A friend of Grace's tie-dyed all their white Hanes T-shirts. Nelson had already let her hair grow out and just as she was thinking she was sick of wearing black all the time, this friend of a friend who lived in New York had a party called 'B(l)ack to Colour', which made them all consider the implications of entering a new decade. Nineteen ninety, tanned skin, bright clothes. It was the way it was going. A sixties kind of feel. But a different interpretation, they said, than in the sixties, which is when most of their parents were around, and had got certain things wrong. Then a friend of a friend just down the road threw the I Ching for her and it said, 'It furthers one to cross the great water'.

In Bali Nelson found that Grace simply dropped her whenever she found someone else she wanted to be with, and expected her to be available when she wanted her again. For a while Nelson was upset and then she met Miki and she found that the meaning and purpose of Grace Sanyo in her life was as an instrument of her ultimate karma, that is, being with Miki. Goodbye Grace. She played her flashy little part and she's out of this story.

When the three weeks were up, Miki went with Nelson to the airline office. If she changed her flight she had to pay quite a bit extra. That took every last bit of money Nelson had. She paid it. Three extra weeks. She then sold her bag her jeans her Docs her watch her mirror-ball earrings and her black denim jacket. She had her new Balinese clothes: bikinis, sarongs, a dress; together they cost practically less than any one of them would at home.

Nelson gave up shopping and drinking, and moved out, of course, of the expensive place with the swimming pool provided by Grace's package deal. She and Miki lived together in a room at the Padma in Legian, and spent a lot of time inside, the room's limited dimensions as huge and as tiny as any lover's universe. They ate cheaply at warungs, went to the beach for sunset, and were happier than anyone in the world.

FIVE

Nelson walked slowly all the way to the Bungah Club, along the main road, south from Legian to Kuta. Steady, not hurrying, deliberate; feeling purposeful, dignified, entranced.

Most of the shops were now closed, some closing, while the restaurants were filling and the night-time street stalls setting up for business. She loved the cheerful hustle, the lively racket, the traffic on its one-way race past her. Closer now to the Club she felt in her body a wave crash on a shore: an excited fearful feeling momentarily lift her and then leave her behind, floating.

Outside the Bungah Club there was the usual crowd of locals: little kids and older boys. The boys hung over the fence between the Bungah Club and the street, as if inside it was a show, an exhibition. The kids, selling trinkets and postcards, were crowding, clamouring, round an embarrassed white couple—embarrassed enough to make a purchase or two. Nelson hardly noticed them, and entered.

Same place, same as ever. A large outdoor space, bars, huge video screens playing music videos—that's good old Madonna up on the screen. A large circular bar, surrounded by bar stools, many already occupied, stood in the middle, a number of small tables with chairs to one side, smaller bars down the back. Although it was early for Kuta nightlife, quite a few people were already there.

She stood inside the entrance gate and watched for him. Which bar is he on tonight? And she sees him! Miki! Behind the bar! Miki, her Miki, and she watches him a moment, will she wait till he sees her? Will she go right over now? She stands still a moment, wondering if he'll see her before she gets up close to him. Now she'll go over to him. And then this is what she sees. A girl—white girl, maybe age twenty like herself—comes and leans over the bar and Miki is leaning over right back, their heads are close together, familiarity, they know each other, it's straight to the point, they are smiling nodding whispering making agreements making plans a quick kiss and it's obviously 'see you later then' and she goes. Walks past Nelson as she leaves.

It's OK, thinks Nelson, it's OK, a guy, he doesn't think I'm coming back, he thinks I'm not coming, he didn't get my letters, he's trying to . . .

She moved over to the bar. Miki had turned away to answer a drinker's summons. Another waiter approached to take Nelson's order. I want to see Miki, she told him. He raised his eyebrows at her. He called to Miki in Indonesian. Miki came over. For a small moment he didn't know who she was. The next moment was too late. Nelson walked out of there. Miki called after her. Not her name. 'You! Girl! Chick!' Finally, 'Nelson!', but she had gone.

Nelson walked, she didn't hurry she didn't run but in a split second she was out on the street. The little kids gathered closely round her, holding out woven cotton wrist-bands for her to buy, bright threads with words woven in the patterns: *Bali; Peace; Jiggy-jig*. Their jabbering pleas seemed to come from very far away. They suddenly fell back away from her. I'm hungry, Nelson thought, I'm starving, I forgot to eat. She walked across the road, dodging a bemo and some bikes. The smell of the food made her ravenous. She ordered satay and soup and rice, and ate them all up, sitting at a little table near a cluster of food stalls set up for the night-clubbing crowds and those who serviced them. She was left alone, while she ate, and ate steadily, looking at the way food, tables, light, flesh, fabric, feelings were actually all made out of the same stuff. That's funny, she thought, everything is actually the same as everything else. When she had finished eating someone would talk to her and she would find out what to do next and there would be somewhere else to go.

Six

Nelson paid her cover charge to the guy at the door and so did Gala. But the boys exchanged a handclasp with him and with a few muttered words slid inside. Belonging, a bond, brotherhood, that's what they had, the tribe of young men who made their living at the beach in Bali.

They understood each other and talked among themselves freely, unapologetically, leaving Nelson to watch quietly or to chat with Gala. She didn't mind. She liked it. In here you couldn't really talk anyway. The music was loud. Good too, good dance music.

Words weren't all that great anyway. Nelson had thought about this before. Sometimes it seemed that anything you could put in words was a lie: it was a lie because you could say it. The truest stuff you knew, it was impossible to say it properly, like telling your dreams. People who liked conversation mainly liked an audience for their opinions. Preferably one which agreed with them.

Gala had happened to sit next to her and talk and now was like her best friend. And this, she thought, this is my hardcore gang, my own live crew. They had never sat around and told each other about their childhoods and opinions and stuff, but they knew the places to find each other and which table to sit at when they got there.

Nelson liked this song and made it plain and France pointed to the dance floor and she followed him there. He lifted his arms and fell into a rhythmic twisting movement. There was lots of space on the floor, even though it was filling up. Next to her, two Indonesian girls in fish-net tights and high heels danced together.

Sputnik was the club where the Indonesians hung out. It wasn't just the prices that kept them out of most of the other places; you wouldn't want to go there. There were quite a few Australian clubs full of rude, raucous drunks, rough as guts: heavy metal music, wet T-shirt competitions, blood and vomit everywhere, you'd hear about it. Those people wore nothing but thongs and stubbies, night and day. There were places not so rough, like Coconuts, a disco and bar for tourists to meet. There was the Bungah Club, a bar, not a dance place, unique in its easy mix. You could sit under the stars and watch music videos. People were friendly, they drank and talked. Gay guys went there, and Indonesians, as well as tourists having early drinks before the clubs opened. Well, Nelson wasn't going there any more. Further up in Legian there were places favoured by Europeans, more sophisticated. Mali 2000 was the best. People dressed really well there and the music was so cool. Mali was good to go to before the dance parties started. There'd be a few every week, either at Arak-Arak or Three-Four, starting at midnight. Three-Four played such good music, and there were some really good dancers and really interesting-looking people. Music and dancing were the big things there, and no one hassled anyone. Soul music, sixties music, lambada, samba, cha-cha. The piss-heads stayed screaming at each other in Kuta.

The music took over, displaced all thought and led her body into its rhythms, this song and the next.

France took Nelson back to their table. 'Thank you,' they both said.

Gala had got her a Coke. They wouldn't necessarily have ever met each other in Australia. Gala was from Melbourne, for one thing, and not much like Nelson's Sydney friends.

'Where's Robbie?' Nelson asked her.

Gala shrugged. 'Gone for business.'

The three boys Gala—and now Nelson—hung with most didn't have regular jobs but they'd disappear from time to time 'for business'. Errands for business people, she guessed, commissions for introducing buyer to seller, casual stints looking after someone's shop. If anyone asked, they said, 'I do little bit business, this and that,' in those exact words, every time, a phrase-book formula.

Gala came to Bali frequently, with her Australian boyfriend who did business here. This was a guy she had been with ever since she was really young but they were only together when they were together. A factory made them consignments of clothes that they sold at the markets. Not markets like in Paddington but the big markets out in the Melbourne suburbs. Their stuff was not fashion stuff, more like mass-market stuff. Gala stayed on after the Australian boyfriend left, to go out to the factory every few days and see how things were coming along. You had to keep checking things. Things easily went wrong. Often did. The stories she could tell.

Everything else seemed so far away and unimportant compared to the places here.

At Lyn and Ktut's house they sat on piles of batik cushions on the floor. Dozens of bird-carvings hung from the ceiling. Wind-chimes tinkled in the doorways. Dropping in here took care of the rest of the day one way or another.

Suddenly, Robbie said to Nelson, 'Go with France. I think he is in love with you. He tell me. France must be your lover.'

What was Robbie, some kind of elder brother suddenly? Tall, theatrical, flamboyant, that was Robbie, leader of the pack. His parents were of mixed parentage: there was Dutch, Timorese, Chinese. He came from Timor or had lived in Timor or did some business in Timor. Or something. Nelson didn't want him telling her what to do. 'I only want to be friends. I don't want a lover.'

'When your heart broken,' Robbie said, 'better get a new lover. Take France.'

He took a deep hit off the bong and passed it to Gala.

'Leave her alone,' said Gala, surprisingly. Robbie had been Gala's boyfriend in Bali, or maybe still was; Gala herself wasn't sure.

There was something tough and knowing about Gala: it wasn't a pose; some quality she had in spite of herself. She might have seen some rough things. She wasn't easily impressed. Her suntan accentuated the pale blue of her eyes in her thin little face.

'Yeah,' said Nelson, 'leave me alone!' Her jokey tone might not have sounded jokey. It was strange here. At home she made people laugh by the tone of voice she used: sarcastic, funny voices, insinuated meanings, shared references. Different things were funny in Bali.

Different things were funny when you smoked this shit. She wasn't usually big on smoking but in Bali she had a very open mind. She had to remember that she was the centre of the universe only to herself. Or else you learnt the true meaning of paranoia.

Nelson kept watching Lyn, who was lighting incense sticks which seemed to accentuate rather than disguise the odours of buddha smoke. She had put on some incredibly cool music. Deeply tanned, platinum blonde hair tied up with leather thongs, very thin, leather bangles, silent, self-absorbed, married to Ktut, together in their Bali happy-for-life forever-young beach-chic. Why should Nelson be wondering about Miki, just because here is a girl actually married to this Balinese boy, he stayed with her, he waited for her, or maybe Lyn just never went away . . . But Nelson had had to go. Miki might have thought she wasn't coming back. She could—just—forgive him for having another girlfriend, if he hadn't received her letters and had stopped believing she would return, yes, just, although she had spent nearly a year being as faithful as anyone could be. But she could never forgive the way he looked at her—that fateful split-second, that taking a long moment to remember her, and then that flicker of panic. He didn't know how well she had got to know him by loving him. He would never be loved like that again. Thoughts of him caused her actual pain, so she banished them as they approached. She wasn't exactly thinking about him, rather he was an after-image burned into the screen of her mind. He hadn't come looking for her. She never went looking for him.

Think of something else. The bong was passed to her. It

was France. France was a small, thin fellow with a broad flat face and a quiet, intense manner. Sweet, really sweet for sure but being just friends was all she wanted, all she could imagine, all she could bear. France was from Lombok. That wasn't in Bali. Some girls try to get romantic with lots and lots of boys if they've been hurt but Nelson couldn't get into that mood at all.

The smoke-stained water cooled the acrid smoke she held in her lungs. She heard the chimes in the doorways, bells from somewhere, flute music from the hi-fi, a rasping breath: herself. She passed the bong to Agung.

Agung suddenly got talkative, and began to tell Nelson about himself. They were sitting at Warung Annette. Lyn, Annette— these were all Gala's friends. No, Gala didn't know everyone who did business around the beach, there were too many of them, hundreds; she didn't even know all the European girls married to Indonesians. Once you would have known everybody.

Robbie and France left. 'Business'. Annette came and sat with them. Annette was older, thirty-ish, an English girl with a serene upper-class air about her. She was married to Salim and was going to have a baby. Her stomach swelled under her lovely blue rayon overshirt. She and Gala gossipped quietly about some guy whose company had sent him out from New York to check on a large consignment that was late.

Agung was telling Nelson things all backwards. First he told her that all the girls he had been talking to were staying in Bali too long. 'Two weeks, three weeks, six weeks, like that,' he told her. Why was this such bad news? Well, he wanted to meet a girl who had less than ten days left here. So when he met girls he would ask first how much longer they would be in Bali. Nelson apparently was somehow meant to know that his Dutch girlfriend was coming back in ten days.

'Ten days,' said Nelson, 'what a long time.'

Agung mistook her tone and smiled at her. 'Long time,' he agreed.

'Yeah,' said Nelson; 'don't waste ten days just waiting.' He stopped smiling. She lightened up. 'Keep trying,' she said, more gently. Agung was really pretty: large almond eyes, hair growing longish, wearing a wide loose blouse, lots of silver bangles. Too vague and babyish for her taste. Definitely trouble or joy for girls she could easily imagine.

Annette was saying that the guy from New York found out that the late consignment was because there had been a lot of cremations recently: people had had to take time off. The New York office didn't know what it was like in Bali and sent angry faxes: first an ultimatum, then they cancelled the order.

Don't even try to work out who all these people are or remember their names. You never know who you'll meet again. Mostly you won't. It's the way things are here.

A woman had come over. 'Excuse me,' she was saying, 'you are Annette?' She was older—thirties, forties—and looked overdressed in tailored cotton slacks with a neat shirt tucked in. Annette was telling Gala that New York's Indonesian partner here had become furious, planted some dope on the guy and called the police.

The tailored woman had pulled out a photograph. Did Annette remember him? Annette thought he looked familiar but couldn't be sure. Why? 'Please try. He mentioned this place in his letters.' The woman spoke good English, with a European accent and a slight American twinge. 'He ate here. He came here for sure. He stayed in Legian Sunset Cottages.'

'When?' asked Annette. 'So many people . . .' Warung Annette was on the main road in Legian. It was a really nice place. You could sit at the tables out in front and watch the road, or in a courtyard at the back. They served houmous, pizza, curry puffs, french fries. The best chocolate cake, lemon meringue pie. They knew that tourists got sick of local food. They got passing trade, word of mouth, mentions in guide-books, regulars. Annette wasn't likely to remember everyone who came there.

'A year ago,' the woman said. 'More than once, maybe often. Because to mention . . .'

'I'm sorry,' said Annette, handing back the photograph. 'What happened to him?'

'Exact! What happened to him?' she repeated and held out her hand and said her name.

'Annette,' replied Annette, taking the hand briefly, 'and Gala, Nelson, Agung.' Greetings were murmured.

'So,' went on Annette, 'good luck with finding your friend. What happened to him?'

'I came a long way to find out,' the Dutch woman said as she tucked the photo away and left. One more of those people trying to find out something. Nelson thought she was meant to find out something too but had forgotten what. Agung was saying something about a letter from his last girlfriend. Gala was saying, 'I told him to be extra careful'.

Nelson had brought her novel with her, the one she had tried to start on the plane. She loved Thomas Hardy but she hadn't done much reading yet. She had also brought her Chinese notebook, a going-away present. She thought she might write a diary. She sipped her pineapple and banana juice and wondered how to start. She wondered if she might eat something. She wondered in a general way about not much at all, just wondering. She looked around her.

She was sitting alone at one of two single bamboo chairs next to the small counter at the back of Warung Kecil. On the counter stood jars of peanuts, krupuks, squares of yellow cake, cigarettes you could buy singly. It was a little place; the other people there sat on the chairs set in a row either side of a narrow table at the front.

After a while she noticed the posters someone had tacked on to the walls. Small, cheaply printed posters, more like handbills, black and white; with a photograph and the words, 'Have you seen this man?'

That's what those two people down there, Canadian backpackers, had just been talking about. She hadn't really been listening, but she'd heard. The photo was of a Dutch guy who had come to Bali to make a film about their religion. He had gone to some remote area in the mountains and been murdered. The police here had done nothing and the Dutch government had sent out some people to find out exactly who was responsible. They would never find out, as the body had been burnt and no one would talk.

Little Ktut brought the Canadians their drinks. Not the Ktut who lived with Lyn but it was no coincidence, most Balinese were called Wayan Nyoman Ktut or Madé. How the rest escaped this she didn't know. 'Hot tea!' remarked a girl in a pink sarong, red-skinned, wet-haired, the wet outline of her bikini showing underneath. She had just come up from the beach: too hot, she reported, to stay.

'The best drink to have when you're hot,' said one of the Canadians, 'is hot tea. The best drink when you're thirsty in hot weather. You sweat, you cool down, it quenches your thirst.' The girl did not look as if she believed it. 'Hot tea,' he said authoritatively, 'is best and beer is not a good drink. I like a beer, but hot tea if you want the right drink.'

Nelson opened her notebook. How did you begin a diary? Nothing had happened yet today. She could write about yesterday.

Where to start? First explain why she was here? Who was she explaining it to? You wrote a diary for yourself but could you tell yourself anything you didn't already know? So what was the use? Well, for the future. What would she like to remember? She looked around again.

Warung Kecil was not on one of the main roads leading to the beach, but on a narrow, winding side road, close to the Padma and a cluster of other cheap losmens. People who have travelled the length of Java, catching local buses and carrying backpacks, those who seek a touch of bygone authenticity, those who would never stay in hotels and eat in restaurants, those who would never pay one rupiah more than they have to, those who insist they are not tourists, and occasionally Indonesian boys who came to Kuta because its streets were lined with gold—they all come here for fresh juices and black rice pudding, fried rice or *kopi arak*.

The pink sarong girl said defiantly, 'I like the juices. I wish mine would arrive. I ordered it before you.'

An Australian guy looked up from his thick paperback and joined in. 'Iced tea,' he offered, 'is very nice too. If you trust the ice.'

'Hot tea is actually better, it cools you,' said the Canadian firmly.

'The ice is OK,' said the Australian guy's girlfriend, looking up from her own paperback. She had on a blue singlet top exactly like his. 'It says in the book the ice comes from a government factory.'

'Oh yeah,' said the guy scornfully, 'the book says! I wouldn't trust the ice here; you don't drink the water, do you, so you wouldn't trust the ice.'

Nelson kept hearing their stupid conversation that she didn't want to listen to. She wanted to think of a good idea for her diary.

'Ice is not too great for health,' declared the first Canadian. 'They eat hot food in a hot climate, chilli for the heat, that is actually very good for you, chilli on the food.'

'I wish my drink would come,' pink sarong complained. 'They are slow, aren't they? Oh here it is.'

'Isn't that right, man?' the Canadian said to Ktut as he put down the frothy juice. 'Hot drinks, chilli in your food, keep you healthy in Bali, hey?' Ktut looked confused. Did they want some chilli? He hovered uncertainly, then, as he was ignored, went back to the kitchen. 'Everyone ate local food before it became so touristy.'

'Lomotil,' the Australian girl was saying.

'Avoid the ice and you won't need it,' the Australian guy said bitchily. These two had been travelling together for too long.

'Shouldn't take it,' said the talkative Canadian. 'It blocks you up. You should let your body get rid of the sickness, let it out.'

'Yeah, and how long might that take?' said the bitchy Australian guy. 'Shit yourself non-stop you reckon; what about if you have to get a bus for eight hours. No thanks, I'll have the Lomotil.'

'Why do you shit—it's toxins,' the Canadian insisted. Suddenly everyone looked as if they had had enough of the subject—the silent Canadian companion, the pink sarong girl, the Australian couple. 'What you need is to eliminate,' he went on. 'Symptoms,' he was saying. 'Build up resistance,' but everyone began to talk at once.

Mum would have liked this, Nelson thought. Mum loved to talk about toxins and about nature cures and shit, and about how Kuta was great in the old days: 'No big hotels, Nellie, only a few losmens, coconut groves, paths through the jungle to Legian, no noisy pubs, no discos, only surfers and hippies, only a few of them and you lived with the people, no rip-offs no hassles.' Nelson's seen tourists, Mum's type, right here, who moan, oh Kuta is so commercial, Kuta is so spoiled and they want to go off to a village. What makes them think the villages want them, they probably don't, people like Mum think they could turn up in some village and live like the people there do, which probably isn't even the way Mum thinks, and Mum thinks because she went on Vietnam demonstrations when she was young she can go and be welcomed in villages, and in the villages all the people want is TV and video and the village-freak tourists all come to Kuta for pizza and new clothes and night-life.

Nelson likes Kuta as it is, both international and Balinese, a gorgeous gaudy blend, a spiced-up tropicana rave for the young for whom pleasure is proudly proclaimed life's greatest good and pleasure is a long surf beach banked by a buzzing little fantasy town where you shop eat drink and meet people without end, and everyone is suntanned pleasured pampered on holiday rich desirable and indulged.

SEVEN

If she thought about it, she didn't know what she was doing in Bali any more. So she didn't think about it. It was easy not to think. It was easy just to *be*. It didn't matter what time it was. A day went by and then another. It was always hot.

If she thought about it, Miki had changed her life but in an unforeseen, devastating way. She felt a pain in her breasts, her throat, her guts. That's what they call heartache. Nausea battling with fury. Banish, banish. If she were ever to become an actor she would know what this felt like. She would recreate this emotion and the emotion would create the posture, expression and voice of heartbreak. She would use it. She went into her room and shed a single tear. Relief, she told herself, because the pain would not damage her. Cold water! Out, go out, don't brood, so much to do.

If she thought about it, she would have to make plans. A long long future stretched out ahead. She had to decide something. She liked the future that had her and Miki together, where everything would work out: some business in Bali, one day a baby. That was closed off now. And business was a complicated thing. Gala had been in business for years and she, Nelson, would be just starting. And she wouldn't do it by herself, alone, there'd be no reason, there'd be no fun. And there couldn't be another Miki. Better just live one day at a time. The future was mysterious, but it was a long way off.

The present offered slow hot midday hours; you felt dehydrated and had to get up and drink a lot of Aqua, tea, juices. The night before! She'd never done alcohol so regularly, or the other stuff. You could go alone to Warung Kecil nearby and later to Warung Madé on the main road in Kuta where you might see some of the others. You could wander round the shops. You could go to one of the big hotels and use its swimming pool. Soon it was around four o'clock, a good time to go to the beach. The others were either at the south end of Kuta, just down from the main entrance, or right up at Legian, near the Green Sea. The boys rode their motorbikes on the beach. Once Nelson was on the back of France's bike—Robbie's bike but with France riding it—and Miki went by the other way. On his bike. That bike. The most stupid ridiculous thing was she hated to think Miki had seen her and thought France was her boyfriend. She should *want* him to think it, that'd show him! She did not, absolutely not, want to run into him.

They might all go to see Lyn and Ktut, have a bong before sunset, or after. Sometimes after the smoke Gala and Robbie would disappear together but they'd be back before long. Then Robbie might go away later and Gala wouldn't know if he were coming back or not. Relationships were different here. Nelson smoked because she was with them and this seemed a good place to do it.

She didn't smoke dope in Sydney. When she was fourteen, fifteen, she had. A lot, for a while, even at school. Teachers, kids, they all did. Then they had moved and that changed. Then dope got really expensive and hard to get, which was ridiculous for a herb, a weed, mild and harmless. Everyone knew it was because government, crime and business were united in wanting a society full of people addicted to stuff they controlled. Cheap, easy, quick hits that destroyed you. Kept the best stuff to themselves. Listen:

My homie got a year for an ounce of weed
While Bush sells weapons to the enemy
You got to be blind not to see

Here, in Bali, who knows? Nelson doesn't know. She doesn't live here. You have to be careful, that's what she does know. Don't do drugs with anyone you don't know really well. Don't make enemies. Don't believe in the authorities.

My heroes don't appear on no postage stamp.

27

She had listened to Public Enemy on her Walkman in the early mornings going to her cleaning job, saving her money for her return, one of many jobs, drudging for glory, her head full of the clear purposive anger of righteous rap.

Like the song: *black man black woman black baby; black man white woman black baby; white man black woman black baby* and hearing that she realised that was what it was all about; the song was *Fear of a Black Planet* and that's what people had, white people, most of them, not her friends but most people. She had learned so much, she realised. She had found out what she believed in. Satellite dishes in remote tribal communities and remote tribal music on urban airwaves. She was furious at anyone who didn't share this vision. One world for sure, that's what Nelson believed in, world music world peace. She had gone back to Sydney knowing so much more.

And there her main pains and pleasures had been the sense-memories of Bali, awakened by petrol fumes borne on hot sunshine, a brand of coconut oil, someone smoking a kretek: the clove-spiced tobacco sharpening both her sense of missing *there* and of being *here*, very far away. Between lay a vast island continent whose distant interiors—red deserts, purple mountains, a giant sacred rock—seemed more foreign and more forbidding than the outlandish jewel-bright tropical island she would return to. She would stare at Asians in the street: they were all so different; she could pick the Indonesians. Indonesian boys really made her look! A young Indonesian family—two little kids—lived two blocks away and she followed them home and then, feeling silly and compelled, detoured past their place to catch a glimpse of the faces, a whiff of their cooking, a sound of their language.

Eight

The reason Nelson went to Coconuts Club in the first place was to avoid the Bungah Club.

'Ignore him,' Gala advised. 'He mightn't even be there.'

But Nelson would not be persuaded to go. It was late at night and Madé's was closing. But Three-Four didn't open until midnight. 'Do me a favour?' Nelson asked.

'I'm meeting Robbie,' said Gala. Gala did not like to be asked for favours.

Nelson realised that if she wasn't going to Bungah, she wasn't going with Gala and if she had to go somewhere alone she'd prefer somewhere she didn't usually go.

Coconuts. She had been there ages ago with her old ex-best friend Grace at the beginning of the first time in Bali. At the door you got a blast of the loud music and the cold air-conditioning. It cost 2.000, 'But one free drink,' said the doorman, one of four in uniform black T-shirt with the word 'Security' stencilled on it.

Coconuts was one long wild party. Nelson watched a barman line up a number of clear drinks on the bar, and set them aflame. These Australian guys threw the drinks down their throats, flame and all.

Across from her, girls in bright make-up perched in a row sipping long orange drinks out of straws, peering around, as if waiting to be asked to dance.

There was a dance floor down one end of the long narrow room, which was divided in the middle by the bar. Seats elevated on tiers down the other end. Coloured lights flashed, loud music pulsated. INXS or some shit like that.

'You Aussies sure know how to have fun,' one of the Yanks yelled into Nelson's ear, gave the noisy room another admiring once-over, and ordered more zombies.

The two Americans were staying at Sanur but had heard

29

the night-life was livelier over at Kuta. Nelson talked with
them a while. You couldn't really talk in here, more like yell
in someone's ear. You wouldn't want to get monopolised by
these guys, though it was nice of them to buy the drinks.

Nelson went to the toilet. Maybe to get away from the
American guys, which was one foolish move, in retrospect.
They had looked a bit taken aback. When you try to remember
something, especially like this night, where you can't remember it all, it's funny how little moments emerge really clear.
That funny look on those guys' faces. It was because she had
said 'toilet'. Those guys, where they came from, they went
to the bathroom.

She remembered the bathroom. The toilet. There were a
few other girls in there including one really beautiful Indonesian girl in a gorgeous dress. That's a gorgeous dress! Nelson
exclaimed. The girl gave her a business card. She had a shop
somewhere. All the girls crowded round a mirror and checked
each other out. An Australian girl was telling her friend, 'They
all come and ask if you want to dance. I don't come here to
dance.' It was in there that Nelson had realised she was really
drunk. Midnight might have passed. It never occurred to her
to leave.

Nelson found herself back at the bar. She intended to keep
on drinking. She wanted to reach some boundary, exceed some
limit. All kinds of impulses were raging inside her. She wanted
to push past the crowds around the bar and hurl herself on
to the dance floor, where she would dance amazingly, like
Prince, like Madonna, like Hammer. Also she wanted to crawl
into the darkest furthest corner, where she would be invisible.
Also and also and also.

'G'day,' she hears. 'Wanna denz?' This hulking Aussie. But
the barman had reached her at the same time. She thought
she'd have a drink first. But she didn't want another zombie.
It ended up the Aussie told her some drink to have, and he
had one of the flaming drinks. Next thing, or several things
later, there were a few of his friends around her too. 'Where
ya stayin? Never heard of it.' They were staying at the Gone

Troppo. Really close to here, to all the bars. 'Top spot Bali, innit, if you ignore the filth the dogs and the natives.' She was surrounded. She could barely remain upright. The din in the bar reverberated in her head, making it all random, violent noise. As if all the sounds were channelled through a mixer programmed by a maniac. The Australian guys were talking to each other but had taken possession of her. A long time had passed. She had fallen into a black hole in time. She had had another drink. How many was that? A lot. The guys knew she was drunk. That wasn't good.

'We all come here for the one thing, right,' this gargoyle was spitting at her. 'Sun, surf and sex.'

She must not look at these guys surrounding her and blame them for the distant panic trying to get her attention but she must not look at the panic as it was only about looking as drunk as she felt must not feel that these (whatever, don't look) persons cause it . . .

'Where is he then?' one of the guys asked her. Where was *who?* They meant where was a male.

Where was someone to validate her. Escort her. Protect her. What a load of shit. But where was he? Who?

She tried to say something but she couldn't even understand her own words. She just could not bear to dislike these guys who were only being friendly, it was because she felt sick and that wasn't their fault. If she looked at them she felt sick which was an ugly feeling to have about anyone and not at all fair. So she felt the sickness and ugliness was in herself, awful to feel. She wanted so much to get away from them which would be so rude and to be seriously rude as well as ugly and sick was to be avoided.

She had a home to go to and would never be able to reach it.

She could have howled with misery, sitting on her bar stool.

But perhaps. There was something she had learnt once. In acting class. Expression creates the feeling. Posture elicits the mood it portrays. The psychological gesture. She would look at ease. She opened her mouth wide and forced it into a wide smile. She lifted her head and made herself laugh.

The guys looked at her.

A whole period of time fell into an abyss, a limbo. She would never remember it.

The guys were taking her somewhere she could lie down and get well and be safe and serene. Or die. At first it was like they were helping her. You'll be right, she heard, you'll be right. Are you helping me? The voice was hers or not hers. She was taken captive. She didn't know where she was going. She needed to be taken care of.

One sharp flash of clarity. They were not taking care of her. They had captured her. She could not understand their words, but understood their tone of voice.

She was hollow with fear, a sudden fear that combined with her drunkenness so that she was overwhelmed by it. Fear, the abyss, her captors, her helplessness.

NINE

'Bali is beautiful,' he repeated, 'but,' he said, 'it is not my home or yours.' Marla Cavas sat next to him taking notes.

He had sat her at one of the tables in the dining area adjacent to the bar. He could keep an eye on things and she could check out a typical Australian hangout. Video monitors were screening a film, and a dozen Australian men were gathered around the long U-shaped bar, in the dim light, steadily drinking and watching, or not watching, the video. In the middle of a glorious bright day in Bali!

'A lot of our visitors don't go to the beach,' he told her. 'They don't go anywhere. Blokes like these, they're anti-social, only interested in drinking, that's what they come here for.'

Rodney had been the manager of Gone Troppo for a number of years, a number he knew very well, to the exact fraction. He was leaving very soon, for good, and high time too.

The scriptwriter, he forgot her name already, had heard of him through that bloke, the director, from Sydney, who was a friend of hers. Rodney remembered him: nice bloke; he and his girlfriend had stayed over at the Tanjong Sari in Sanur but they were shooting the commercial around Kuta and Rodney had looked after them, had a few drinks with them and told them some of the stories about how his guests behaved. They'd told her.

But she was not here, she said, to write another 'Aussie yobbos wreck island paradise' story. She wanted 'background' for an 'impressionistic essay on the effects of tourism in the developing world'. She was living up in Ubud, doing research for something on Bali in the olden days, when the first Europeans lived here, a few artists in the thirties. She had thought of maybe linking that with what that all led to: this— Kuta and the Gone Troppo. Normally he would not have had time for her, but she had turned up while he happened to be here during a quiet part of the day, she looked OK, she was a friend of Kim's, he did have—just—a spare hour, and he had no further reasons to keep his mouth firmly shut.

'Bali is beautiful but it is not my home or yours. We don't belong here. It is very different here, more than most people realise. Here they believe in spirits, black magic. I don't, but here I'd say ninety-nine per cent have that belief. I do believe in mind over matter, the mind is so powerful it can make things happen. I've seen things, trances. Yes, in ceremonies, or it can just happen, different voices come out of them.'

'Hmm, there've been stories like that for decades,' she said. She'd done her reading, heard the stories. 'But I believe it's rare for outsiders to have first-hand experience,' she added. She was encouraging him to tell more. He recognised the technique.

'Strange things happen here,' he said, ' things you couldn't explain, and I don't advise you go looking for them.'

She didn't look young enough, silly enough or airy-fairy enough to be the kind who would want to go looking for witch doctors, sorcerers and spirit-raisers. The kind who were gullible prey for all those who exploited certain westerners' need for hocus-pocus. The genuine magicians and healers, Rodney believed, kept their secrets to themselves and their magic for their own people.

She was interested, though. 'Strange things?' she prompted. 'Do your guests get involved in these strange things?'

He drank some of his Aqua. She was sitting on the OJ she'd bought herself while waiting for him.

'Here's an example. One time we took a few of our guests on a tour to Candi Dasa. I was sick and couldn't go. Ask Mannie about it later, if you want, he took the group—works here, great guy, you should talk to him too. Two of the girls in the group met two guys from somewhere, and went off with them. We think these guys were taking a lot of drugs. Mannie and everyone are asleep, and the staff wakes them: one of the girls is having a fit, she couldn't breathe, they'd already spent half an hour trying to get her to breathe. And then the other girl has a fit too. They could have swallowed their tongues, died. Our driver, who is also a priest, ran out and went to the temple of the big hotel there and began praying, then he freaked out and said there were evil spirits around. There was a big panic going on, and these girls were still having a fit. Anyway he got some holy water and sprinkled it on the girls and they stopped their fit at once and slept peacefully. Next day they couldn't remember a thing. Now, I don't believe it but I know it happened. There are supposed to be evil spirits in Candi Dasa. The driver and Mannie went to find the guys and shoved them round a bit but they reckoned they hadn't given any drugs to the girls.'

'Sounds scary,' said the scriptwriter encouragingly. No, he thought, it hadn't sounded scary. Coupla chicks can't handle it and have hysterics. Jesus, the weird things he'd seen, people freaking right out with spirits and apparitions and spells. You recount one of these instances and it sounds like nothing, something easily explained, someone who couldn't handle booze or drugs or being far from home. It was the accumulation of these things, the way they'd keep happening, unpredictably. The mind was powerful indeed, his training had taught him that, and maybe the group mind here was powerful enough to communicate its collective phantasms to any visitors who were psychically vulnerable. Just what he *didn't* want to talk about.

Rodney shrugged. 'They didn't know it was holy water being thrown on them but it worked. I believe they hadn't taken drugs, but even so it doesn't explain what happened.'

'Lots of people do take drugs, though, I've heard,' she prompted. She looked to be in her thirties, with ash-blonde hair pulled off her face. Nicely dressed in a loose, light, red patterned suit that she hadn't bought here. Most Australian women went to the dogs with their presentation once they were here. She wanted to find the scary stuff, did she? 'So where do they get the drugs?' she asked.

'Narcotics? Used to be Regin ran it!' Rodney gestured to the reception area, to remind her that she had met Regin while

35

asking for Rodney. Regin was a thin, forty-ish Balinese in a leather jacket and with, unusually, a beard, showing grey hairs. His card said he was an assistant manager. 'Regin says it's not the little people now. Now it's run by the army and the government. Of course you can't say that, you'd be dead. The army runs the president too. The transport guys in red singlets? They're in with the army, and they're the pimps and they run the drugs. "Want woman?"—you hear them.'

'Is there—er—any opposition . . . ?'

'Once I thought I could stop it, now I know I can't . . . There's a streetseller that set up right ouside here. I say to him, politely, "You can't come here, I'm the manager and this is private." "I'm Balinese, you can't tell me," he says. I say, "I don't care, piss off." There are a lot of muggings because there are so many sellers. Now, my security guards here, they have the power to arrest. I said to one security guard, "Get him" but the streetseller just laughed and went off. The security guard says, "I can't, he's Javanese, he'll get me later." I've heard that so many times. The Javanese come over to control, and they psyche them out. They don't have guns, but they have the kris.

'I've had lots of martial arts training, and I've lost my fear. I say, "You want a problem, I'll give you one." No one takes it up. In Sydney I'm shit-scared, they've got guns and they're good fighters. But here, no one's taken me on. I'd be on my own too. But it is time for me to go.

' "You long time here," they say, "long time here, you," in that tone of voice. It's time for me to leave. I can't keep turning a blind eye. If I see someone doing something bad, I'm in there. The bad guys get to know me too. People here hold grudges.

'I'm not scared. They've got no heart. They have skill in fighting, but no heart, only if there's a hundred of them.'

'Is that the way it's always been?' she asked. 'These fights? Is it true it's because the Javanese are here?'

He sighed. 'Bali is spoiled, it's because of the Javanese—you keep hearing that, right? It's not that simple.

'The Balinese have become jealous and greedy. It's just like in Australia with the Japs, the same, the Australians are selling out to them, money will buy anything.

'The Balinese stood up against the Japanese against the Dutch against the Communists against the Indonesians, and they remained Balinese, still Hindu.'

'And now?'

'The Head of the Banjar just up here had a curfew, everyone had to be off the street, he wanted to clean up the streets. Couldn't do it. Now there's a brothel right next to his house. Because of money. People who used to care have been bought. I used to say to them, do something *now*. If they wanted to stop it they could, but now money is more important. The longer I'm here, the more I'm sad about it.

'My staff and friends don't want me to leave. I have good friends here, the chief of Immigrasi, the ex-chief, I was one of two westerners at his farewell. We have our temple right here—' he pointed to a corner of the area they were in '—and the offerings are always done. I do all the ceremonies, if someone's sick I look after them, I sponsor kids. An Australian girl here had a fund-raising for the street kids here—there are plenty of them.

'Why do the Balinese want what we've got? Yeah, why? I was pissed off with one girl staying here, all the guys she went with, all gigolos. "In Australia I can have an Australian guy any time," she said. "Why should I have one here?" That's what it is. And I'm intrigued by Asian girls, most white men are. So it goes the other way too, doesn't it?

'Most of the girls, Australian girls, haven't got a clue. There was an Australian girl waiting for a barman here, she had bought him a motorbike, she wants to buy land with him, she goes to all the clubs with him. She's being used, sucked in. She says, "I know Bali," but if she really wanted to be his girlfriend she would find out about his religion, his family, the ceremonies. Ninety per cent of the girls with Balinese boyfriends don't know.'

Rodney hadn't missed a thing while he'd been talking to

the aspiring essayist. He could see everything that went on in the reception area and the bar. The rooms beyond, set motel-style around the swimming pool, remained quiet. The blokes who'd caused the fracas last night had been pretty well sorted out. For now. They'd get pissed again in a few hours but it would be somewhere else.

And the writer was asking him about prostitution. As it was a well-documented feature of third world tourism. And she already had heard . . .

'Our guests—' he used the word with some irony, for guests seemed too genteel a word for the hooligans with tourist visas and white-supremacist fantasies '—our guests use the prostitutes round here, sure they do, even the really young ones, kids still in school. Everyone else does, so they do. We get some groups of schoolkids and they behave just like the footballers. They mainly treat our staff like shit. Like, "Where's your room, I want to fuck you". Yes, a lot. A lot of the prostitutes are just kids. On the street they charge 3,500 to 5,000.'

'That's two or three dollars!'

'Or there are clubs that are really brothels. They're all around here—check them out. Pussycats? Australian guy runs it. His partner is a government minister. Pussycats has never been raided. They charge the girls to use it to meet blokes.'

'Health checks?' she asked. 'Condoms? No? Not at all? Hmmmm. Is it true all the girls are from Java?'

'No Balinese girl would ever, ever be a prostitute. Most of the Javanese are from this one village; the girls are brought up to it, it's a way of life.

'Male prostitutes, some are transvestites, some of them incredibly attractive. They'd charge 5,000 upwards. Lots of drunk tourists so they get picked up. The gay scene here is huge. Now, because of money, there are many Javanese boys, younger and younger. And some Balinese. There are people high in the government who are gay, high up in the hotel industry—they're into little boys. It's all happened in the last three to four years. I was never offered a girl until the beginning of '87. Now it's humungous. Before, there was just the odd place, and you'd have to go there—Sanur, Denpasar.

'Nice guests? An Aboriginal group from Alice, brought over by their teacher. Everyone in the group was an Aboriginal apart from the teacher, who was Australian. Yeah, that's a funny thing to say, you know what I mean. At first they were really timid and shy, but they were the nicest, best group by far. They got on real, real well. They had never seen the beach before and our staff took them surfing. They gave us more than we gave them, we really learnt something. When they left, all our staff even went to the airport to say goodbye. That has never happened.'

Rodney looked at his watch. 'I said I'd give you an hour . . .'

'Yes,' she said, 'it's been just about an hour, you've been great.'

He saw that last night's culprits were out in the reception area with their bags packed. They'd belly-ached long and loud at first, but the guards and the police and Rodney himself sorted them out. He made sure they realised they were lucky that being asked to leave, no refund—read the small print, jerks—was all they copped. He could make a charge of attempted rape get them in a hell of a mess, he'd told them. Seen the jails here? Seen *Midnight Express*? They were too stupid to know.

Rising, packing away her notebook, she had seen them. Rodney didn't have to say anything but he did. 'Worse things have happened,' Rodney said, 'than what those blokes did, but I've had enough, and out they go. I could get them kicked out of Bali but out of here will do me.'

They had gone over to Coconuts last night, he told her. She had heard of it—one of the famous party bars. 'You should go there, drop in, check it out. Don't go alone. Australian bar, heavy drinking, pick-up joint. These two blokes come across this young Australian girl, who'd already had a few cocktails. Girls like the sweet mixed drinks, don't realise how potent they are. They give her a few more drinks, knowing she's past her limit.'

'She's there alone?'

'Apparently. She's got friends here, but they weren't around. This girl—we can find out anything, and I got the story—had been to Bali before, and got herself a boyfriend, a Javanese who works at one of the clubs, I know him. Better than a lot of the gigolos, at least he's got a job and kept it, and is an assistant to the manager over there now. This girl came back to Bali for him. It's happened so many times.'

'I think I know what's coming next.'

'You're right. She finds out to her great amazement that he hasn't been sitting here counting the days till she gets back. Unlike some of the others she doesn't hang round him, trying to get him back. She gets herself some new friends, drinking every night. Ends up in Coconuts last night, drunker than she's ever been in her life.

'These animals here drag her back. She doesn't know the type. I saw her after Mannie and the boys rescued her. Nice girl, but naive, a bit lost.'

'She was all right?'

'My blokes got to her before any real harm was done. My guard watches them drag her in, they had to carry her. If she'd been staying here he probably wouldn't take any notice. He gets hold of Mannie, who happens to be around. They go to the guys' room and hear what's going on, break in . . . My staff took the girl home in the car . . . We call some police in, friends, tell them to give the blokes a scare. These animals are standing around, right over there, and they turn to the temple and piss on it.'

TEN

Nelson lying on her bed in a very hot room. Heat. So much going on outside but outside was very very far away. So much to do out there. Doing anything, the very thought of it, was so enervating she had to just keep on lying there, and might not ever get up.

In the bathroom she had washed herself thoroughly once more. The shower wasn't working—no water from the taps. There was the deep, tiled tub—luckily full of water—so you could bathe Indonesian-style instead, and the broken plastic pitcher had been replaced. So she had thrown water over herself, soaped and rinsed, soaped and rinsed, until the tub was empty.

As she washed, she looked at the plants. The roof of her room did not extend over the bathroom, so it was an outdoor bathroom, which was lovely until it rained. Her bathroom, like her room, was in a row adjoining the others. As they all had open roofs also, you could hear everything going on in the other bathrooms. She had heard people washing together, chattering, laughing, or making erotic noises. Today she heard only someone two rooms along emptying their loose bowels into a toilet, groaning.

She stepped on something shiny on the bathroom floor. It was one of the earrings that she thought of as Miki's. Broken, wouldn't you know it.

Thinking of Miki didn't change the way she felt. She already felt as weak and tired as she ever had, and there was no space left for any other feeling. Only this weakness, and this cold calmness.

Perhaps she had never felt this before. Perhaps she had. Her memory was better left unstirred.

Clean and fresh, she wrapped herself in a sarong. She fetched the thermos of tea and a glass off her verandah, and then closed the door again. She left the bathroom door open and opened the shutters on the windows, so light entered from both ends.

Did light enter, or did light reveal light? She was lying on her bed, thinking about light. Then heat. With effort, she rose to switch the electric fan on, then lay down again.

She did not have to go anywhere. She had always enjoyed the few hours she spent each day after slowly waking, at a late hour, slowly getting ready to go out. Those other days, she would drink a thermos of tea, looking at the garden or reading a book, then go inside, wash and dress. Fresh tea would arrive, and she would drink a little more and eat a few sweet little bananas. She might talk to the boys here, or other guests. Those other days she'd eventually feel it was time to go somewhere. Lunch, shopping, swimming, meeting the others.

Today, the whirring of the fan and the patterns of light on the windows provided quite enough of active life. Perhaps she should shut the windows and the bathroom door again, darken the room, and sleep. No. She could not move off this bed again. Just lie here. Look at the patterns of light, just lie here, thankful for the calm.

And for the distance from her memory.

They had brought her home. The dark early morning, only a few hours ago. The guard and a boy on the staff from that place, that place. She knew but her mind would not say its name. Gone Troppo. They had brought her back here in a car. The gate to Pensione Padma was, as usual, locked. The high wall had shards of broken glass embedded in its top. When arriving back late after a night out, Nelson usually got in by climbing over a gate in the back. But the car had woken them and Bapak and Belgi had come out to open it. The guard and Pak had conversed rapidly. Nelson of course wouldn't know what they said to each other. She only said, 'Good-night,' and went straight to her room, leaving them to tell stories about her, if that's what they were doing. It was already morning. Soon a rooster crowed.

What had happened seemed so long ago, so far away.

Longer and further than other things. Longer ago than anything and more appalling.

She had heard of people leaving their body and that might be what was happening to her.

How far away could she go?

Better not go too far. Just so that she could hover close. Close to home. If she thought of her body as home, who was she? She knew that the mind and the body were one, this is something you had to know, it was the side you were on.

But if her body were there and she were . . . were . . . well, she was back in it now, in her body. If you concentrate on your body you inhabit it most certainly. She was lying on the bed again, body and soul. How had she just done it, could she drift away again?

Those guys had really wanted to hurt her. It wasn't even personal, not particularly, she wasn't *who she was* to them, she was just one of the people they could make their victims. That's what they were, guys looking for victims. Is that what guys were all about?

How could she think it? 'Cause there were good guys, gentle guys, guys who were real. Just like there were women who used people, women who made others their victims. She didn't want to go thinking feminist like her mum. Mum thought everything wrong was men's fault. She would never tell Mum about this. Mum thought Bali was hippy fairyland.

Those guys had known she was helpless. They would have raped her. In fact they had started to, taking her away with them, starting to get heavy as soon as she started to get concerned, getting really heavy as she became panicked. And terrified. And enraged. If it was rage, for it had turned to dull shock, threatening to make her rigid, helpless. She had needed to fight. How hard how long could she have fought? She would never know. Thank God.

She never ever wanted to have those feelings ever again. The next few hours had been horrendous and weird and long. There was so much violence going on. The guys who had taken her there were bellowing for a while. Then they shut up. Someone brought her coffee, and water. She could not make the effort to follow what was going on. A woman arrived later and talked to her, and then held her hand, and gave her some pills to swallow. 'You're all right, Nelson,' the woman said. 'We'll take you home now.' She heard that. She was all right.

It was nice lying here. She might spend a couple of days doing it. She didn't have to go rushing out all the time every day. Nothing wrong with staying in. She was actually rather sick. She would have to throw up. She wasn't going anywhere.

She woke again, later, but this time she was fighting, she woke fighting, not only through the fog of sleep but through a massive dark force pressing down on her, hurting her, making it hard to breathe, terrifying. She fought through sleep to save her life but this was thicker and heavier than the deepest sleep more oppressive than the stillest fiercest heat fouler than her own sick breath but she struggled, moaning with the effort, until she burst through and found herself once more in a plain little losmen room. It was very quiet. The fan had stopped whirring. The electricity was off. The monstrous murdurous force lay there close to her, its dark edges just touching her. Misery.

Love had left her. She had known love's clearest cleanest light, gentle and bright, promising eternal renewal. Lies, stupidity, treachery. Making her a fool, making her ill. She had believed lies but it was worse than that, she had believed the truth but it had turned into lies behind her back. Mockery, treachery. She had been wronged and it hurt because it was so unfair as she had meant only good but it was worse than that: more unfairly, she felt she had done wrong, committed wrong doing. She felt angry at herself and it was horrible.

And then last night she had been deliberately, viciously, directly wronged, actually deceived and attacked with the purpose of harm and there had never been a moment of any clear kind light to dazzle and disarm her, there had been nothing but her own stupidity, created out of her loneliness. Loneliness.

She was crying now, and having begun, it was as if she would never stop, she hadn't cried about any of it yet, now she was crying for all of it, crying for her stupid hopes and dreams that she had spent most of a year of a very young life on all for nothing, so that now she didn't have the faintest clue how to know what to do next, crying because she always knew there were ugly brutal males out there and you kept right out of their way and then because she was alone, and drinking, and in Bali and not knowing who was on her side any more, instead of being extra careful she had been extra stupid, wanting to think everyone comes here to be friendly.

Nelson wept and wept. She cried with a soul-felt desolation, crying with her whole body. There was no one to help her in any way at all. There was no one she could tell. What could she say, what could she ask for? Gala was not the kind to give her a hug and not judge her. Lyn was always stoned and totally wrapped up in Ktut. Annette was so nice but always busy with her restaurant and house and Selim. And she didn't know any of them all that well and they were the only girls she really knew. They wouldn't realise it was not like her to be stupid, that this kind of thing never happened to her. You really needed a girlfriend. If she had any real friends they were all far away.

Her crying had become a regular, hiccoughing sobbing: rhythmical, exhausting and now, at last, oddly comforting. She sobbed and sobbed, slowly sinking back through her misery into a sleep that would take her far beyond it, and remind her that she was young and lovely and the worst was over, over, over. When she woke, there would be time for a swim before sunset and that would be tranquillising and refreshing, and she could give herself an early, special dinner at Mali, enjoy being very relaxed and very tired, listen to the gentle music there and drink lemonade until she grew calm and sleepy, and she would come home early tonight and sleep again, a long healing sleep.

ELEVEN

Nelson and the others sat around waiting for the mushrooms to take effect. It was Gala's farewell. Gala was going back to Melbourne in a couple of days. She wanted to do some mushrooms before she left. She said they could give you a good trip or a bad trip. Gala got some friends together. They'd take mushrooms at Bongo Man, then go to the beach for sunset. It was going to be timed so they would be peaking at sunset time. Later they might go round to Lyn and Ktut's house. Maybe smoke a couple of logs, blow a few lines, depending what was available. They'd keep going all night, go dancing at Three-Four. That was the plan.

The other girl and Nelson didn't really talk to each other. They acknowledged that they'd seen each other round, when Gala introduced them. And there were three boys, all tourists. Gala said the Indonesian boys never did mushrooms, though the surfer guy here said they used them in their magic ceremonies like all tribal people did. The surfer guy and the guy with the ponytail, she kind of knew them from one time at Sputnik. The Asian-looking American guy, she had never in her life seen him ever before, or she would have remembered. Gala knew so many people! The other girl probably didn't like Nelson; for no reason, Nelson realised, because, for no reason, Nelson didn't like her. It was really weird, when you thought about it, how many opinions, thoughts and feelings you could have immediately not only about someone in particular but in fact *anyone* you had just met. But were they correct thoughts?

Stir It Up was the song. They were playing all reggae music here, that was their main thing at Bongo Man. Some rasta freak set up a litle bamboo restaurant in Bali where there was non-stop reggae and you could order mushrooms, which they sometimes had. A lot of restaurants had mushroom this and mushroom that on their menus—omelettes, soup—but here at Bongo Man the mushrooms were magic mushrooms if you asked for them.

Thatch, bamboo, batik, airiness, casualness, light, mellow. The good places around here were really good. They couldn't exist anywhere but here. Look at how you could roll down the bamboo blinds when the fierce afternoon sun beat in. Some people had left and now there was only their group in there, and a couple of boys who worked there, hanging out over by the counter, changing the tapes, coming to get orders for juices, strolling around in that casual, rolling walk of theirs, smiling broadly when people laughed.

Reggae really was so mellow, like just chill out and don't you worry 'bout a thing and you can get it if you really want and I want kaya now. Every kind of music probably had its messages.

Everything was a sign of everything else. Yeah. Maybe Nelson had read that somewhere. It felt like something really true.

Someone came up close to her. The surfer guy. 'You've been quiet!' he said to her. What an *amazing* thing to say! It was a question it was an inquiry it was a sign of friendship it was a criticism . . . ! Could he see what a really amazing thing he had just said to her? Nelson was laughing as she tried to say it back to him: 'You've been quiet!' and could not form the words, she was laughing so hard. Some of the others were noticing, they were looking at her, wanting to know what was so funny. As she giggled, unable to stop—*you've been quiet!*—the look on his face, the many many questions in that strange statement—she felt her face stretching and pulling and breaking apart into pieces. The guy who had spoken, his face was a kaleidoscope of expression—embarrassed puzzled amused; torn between conflict and complicity. Nelson gasped and giggled and laughed, and some of the others started giggling too, it was catching, and Nelson laughed so hard she fell down and was laughing with her face pressed against the cool smooth tiles of the floor.

'Hey, Nelson, take it easy, mate.' It was Gala beside her. Nelson took a deep long breath. A million scents arose from the floor and, carried on her breath, exploded their messages in her brain. An ancient tiled floor millions of years old kept a memory of every footfall, every sweeping, every event that had been trodden on it. You could breathe it in. Eventually Nelson sat up, feeling awed by the promise of an infinity of sensation.

'Nelson, how many mushrooms did you eat?' said another boy, the one with the ponytail.

She gazed at him, dumbfounded. The questions oh God the questions people asked, they had so many other questions and statements hiding in them, how many? Like if she said, like, five and a half, I ate five and a half mushrooms, then what? What fucking difference, what was he asking, why was she laughing her face falling apart breathing in messages off the floor seeing clearly that no one could say a single true thing because the meanings could be stripped away in layers forever . . . Nelson shook her head at the ponytail guy and he took it as an answer.

Then they all stopped looking at her and the music was loud and clear and insistent and moving.

After a while Nelson went to the toilet out the back. She passed by the counter, where the tape deck sat. 'Hi,' she said. 'Hi,' the boy said with a smile, a smile so glorious that Nelson laughed a little as she smiled back. His smile! Elemental, irreducible, a smile of smiles! Joy! Strangers were friendly! Humans loved greetings!

She went into the little room out the back and had a piss— squatting over the floor-level Asian toilet—and splashed her face with cold water. That felt so good she went on doing it for a while.

Behind the toilet was a small compound; it must be where the people who ran the restaurant lived. On the steps of a central pavilion sat an elderly woman playing with a baby. Nelson stood still and watched them. The woman wore only a sarong tied around her waist and an old looking kebaya baring wrinkled breasts hanging low. The baby crawled all over her, pulling at her fingers, her breasts, her mouth. It was a naked little boy, with a wide-eyed solemn face. Nelson approached them. The old woman looked at her. She had red stains all over her mouth. Nelson came right over and sat on the step below her. The woman remained entirely relaxed, playing with the baby, making little sing-song noises at it. She wasn't pretending Nelson wasn't there, she wasn't showing Nelson anything. She was just totally fine about it, it was OK with her if this white girl just suddenly turns up and needs to sit beside her for a while. The woman teased and sang to the little boy and Nelson relaxed on the steps and watched them play. The woman turned and spat out a stream of browny-red juice on to the ground below her. Nelson noticed spots like blood appear on the ground, and there were old dry blood-like stains, and probably she had seen stains like this before and never seen them made. Betel, old people chewed betel, but she didn't know what betel was. Betel nut? That sounded right. It got them stoned, this old lady was high, and so she didn't need to speak about anything. Nelson sat with her, her thoughts turning and dancing elusively. Once the boy who had smiled at her came out to see where she was, but she only noticed him as he turned back into the restaurant. Later they would smile at each other again. At the back of the toilets there was a pile of coconuts. There were green coconuts and brown coconuts and coconut husks. The pile formed the most awesomely arranged composition of shapes and colours, moving in rhythmical patterns, different colours and configurations asserting themselves in turn. It was better than any video she had ever seen.

'Nelson! We're going to the beach!' Gala had come around to tell her, calling from the side of the toilet.

'OK,' Nelson called, rising.

Nelson walked over to Gala. 'You coming to the beach?' Gala asked.

'Yeah. No. Yeah, later, I'll come later.' Gala looked at her uncertainly.

'We're just starting to feel it, but it must have hit you early.'

Nelson knew what she meant but it was too complicated to reply to that. Anyway her mind was occupied with the fact that she didn't have to go to the beach now. 'I'll see you there,' she said. It was a big beach but she knew the places to go.

'You OK?' Gala asked uncertainly. 'On your own?'

'Yeah, I'm very OK!' said Nelson, and they both laughed. 'Yeah,' she repeated, very relaxed and assured. 'I'm OK here.' This was no time to ponder even notice the complexities of simple questions.

TWELVE

It had been violently exciting, that road, multifarious, vivid, seen through supernatural prisms, her senses colliding, a synaesthetic clash: things vibrated with melody, odours borne on the hot rainbow air exploded in her brain as colours, it was affectivity to the power of intensity, without boundaries between object and perception, it was more than a lifetime compressed into the road from there to here, and she was trying to get away from it to somewhere safe; she had felt *oh no everyone can tell!* and then remembered, no, it's only paranoia, no one can tell and who gives a shit anyway. *No one can tell; who gives a shit* she repeated like a mantra of protection; a tripper's mantra. No one had called to her, not from shops nor from transport stops, she had moved swiftly, dodging people, dodging vehicles, as if each step were choreographed, perfectly executed, as if her movement was in perfect harmony with all movement, her movement created all movement, her movement was an effect of all movement. She danced along on the dazzling air.

Who could doubt that Chaos was another name for a sublime design?

Here! At last! She turned into the alley leading home. At once there was a different atmosphere. This little road was peaceful, subtle and leisurely, its colours muted, its many messages whispered in sinuous rhythms. She stopped for a moment and caught her breath. She was gasping, the sweat pouring off her. She had been running! Hurrying, rushing, all the way down the main road and the next one. No wonder no one had called out to her. She must have looked bizarre, hot and red and tearing along. Now she stood, panting, letting her breath slow down, all the pulses in her face pounding. She leaned against a stone wall, an absolutely fascinating, bewitching stone wall, a universe of variegated colour and texture. Eventually she looked up, hearing the whirr of bicycle wheels, who knows how long she had stood with her face pressed against the wall, there were three little boys on a single bicycle. Hello! they call. Hello! says Nelson as they pass her, flattening herself against the wall to let them pass. Hello spunky! calls one as they turn into the road, and he giggles shrilly, cheeky little bugger about eight years old.

Palm trees grew out of and protected the Pensione Padma. The arrangement of rooms was so perfect, the tourist rooms in a row here the family rooms in a row there those two free-standing bungalows those pavilions.

Inside her room, the smell of herself, her own smell, the faint odour off her clothes, off the breath she had breathed in here, the bright clothes thrown in gorgeous disarray over the spare bed. That was how she kept her room tidy, threw everything on to one bed, leaving the rest clean and bare. She threw herself on them, she could roll in them and wind them round herself and play among them, a beautiful pile of tangles, she tossed the clothes over her and around her, loving their many colours, their abundance. How good that she had gone shopping, how good she had chosen so rightly, how good that she had kept on living in this room, now so full of colour and assurance.

Outside, the sky showed pink above the palms. Nelson had spent a long time washing and dressing again. Everything could be played with and examined as if it were the newest thing, as if you were a baby. Then suddenly she didn't want to be inside any longer. The thermos on her verandah had been filled again. She twisted off its top and gasped sharply at the fragrant steam. She poured herself some tea. That speedy frantic rush was over. She was a baby staring at the tea in wonder, as if she had never seen it before; she was her own adult, her own protector, knowing to stop pouring when the glass was full, to take the first sip very carefully in case it was too hot. Nelson sat on her verandah, sipping tea. How still it was here. No one else was around. This was the first time she wasn't at the beach at sunset.

Everything bathed in pink light. There probably were songs about that too. 'Pink is the colour of your heart's desire,' Mum used to say, placing lumps of rose quartz on her mantelpiece. Pink light transformed whatever was right there into your heart's desire. The palm trees glowed purple and green.

From the family rooms came the young wife, Saren. She was wearing a smooth sarong and kebaya, a brocade sash tied around her waist. She held a round enamel tray. Nelson could see there were flowers on it, white jasmine. Saren crossed over to the central pavilion. Nelson got up and walked a few steps to see her better.

Saren went to a little open box or shelf placed up high on an outside wall. Old petals and leaves and sticks were in this box. On her tray, Nelson could now see, there were little square baskets made of yellowish leaf, tiny bamboo skewers pinning them in shape, each holding a bit of rice, banana, flower. Saren placed one of these squares, and some flower petals and some incense, on to the shelf. She seemed to be muttering something as she flicked water from a bowl, three flicks with a flower held between her fingers. She held some incense and waved it and its smoke carried her blessings heavenwards. Nelson watched, transfixed. Saren went around, repeating this procedure, and there were some of these offering shelves right here close to Nelson, and she had never noticed them. Saren didn't look at her nor greet her, intent on her task and as she came close Nelson shrunk back a little, to show she wasn't going to interrupt.

Nelson sat very still until it was quite dark. Offerings. Saren was putting out the offerings. She had often seen the dogs eating the bits of rice off those cut leaves, squares of bright green leaf, left on the ground, with a stick of incense, burning or expired, beside them. What did Nelson know? The Balinese put out offerings. What for? For spirits or gods or ancestors. Maybe all three. They did it all the time, they did it every day, they had been doing it all the time she had ever been here. She'd never thought about it.

The people of Bali had customs. They had ceremonies. They

53

had their own religion. They had wide-eyed dancing girls adorned in elaborate gold head-dresses; their hands bent right back; their picture was on every poster, brochure and guidebook. Nelson didn't read brochures or guidebooks. She wasn't going to go chasing after stuff she couldn't understand; it wasn't what she was here for. All the customs stuff was for old people who didn't know how to have fun. Featherhead flowerchild types dressing up, and dull academic types who were always studying something from the past. People always trying to prove other people were different from themselves.

On purpose she never thought about it. Miki had told her that tourists should stay at tourist places. International places. Kuta was for young people, people of today. It wasn't just because he had told her. Here it was a tourist place and the Balinese still put out offerings. Spirits and ancestors. How did it all begin? Why did everyone think their own religion was true? Could they all be right? Did knowledge have anything to do with it? To know, to be: there had to be difference, didn't there?

She remembered things she must have heard. The offerings on the ground were for bad spirits, demons. The ones placed on high were for the good ones.

Balinese spirits. Seen, believed in by the Balinese. Created by them. What did the spirits do? Maybe they looked like Saren, like dancing girls, like the boy who smiled, like that incredibly cool grandmother, like the funny kids on the bike. Living in their own country, doing their own thing, surrounded by tourists. It was really peculiar to think.

Then for a while she knew it all.

THIRTEEN

'Nelson, Nelson,' said the California blond, 'listen to me. Do you agree that we as human beings go into resistance sometimes? Do you? I know that I do. I hear the truth and I resist it. Hey Nelson, where did you get that name? I don't know any girls named Nelson.'

'It's an Australian name,' said Nelson spitefully. She didn't like him telling her she was resistant to the truth. She happened to be a truthful kind of person, which he obviously wouldn't know.

He had sat next to her, here at Warung Madé, and started this really personal conversation, asking her all kinds of stuff about herself. She was at one of the tables at the back, on the top level, a few steps higher than the counter. The benches down the front had been full when she came in. It was hard to know at what point he crossed the line. People often ask how long you've been here, how long you've got, if you've been before; standard tourist small talk, opening gambits, requests for information.

So that was OK. Then they introduced themselves. Buzz. That was his name. Buzz. No one could be called Buzz. It was as though he'd made up his name from some American prime time sitcom with canned laughter and cute little kids uttering cute little one-liners, very wise stuff, and everyone all wisecracks and Hey Mom, Hey Junior, Hey Buzz, Hey Honey. Americans! Some girls would think he was gorgeous if they liked that type. Very blond hair, very blue eyes, square jaw, tan skin, good body, sure of himself, about twenty-five. That thing about this kind of guy, American; they could make all these wisecracks but not laugh at themselves. He was pretty earnest.

She was looking for something but she's looking in the wrong places he told her. Suddenly, just like that. How would he know, she asked, affronted. That's something he knows, he said confidentially. He didn't know, she said, starting to bristle at the way he was zeroing in on her. He wasn't trying to pick her up, she didn't think, she didn't get that vibe off him at all. But he was trying to get under her skin, make a connection. She didn't know what he wanted. Yet. That's when he said she was resistant.

This was his first time in Bali, and up to now it had been amazing. Let's talk about him, she decided, stop him making these sly remarks about her looking for the wrong things or whatever it was he said.

He told her he had been in Candi Dasa with the group he had come over with. And he wanted to tell her about it.

'I have a feeling,' Buzz said, 'that it is no accident, me sitting next to you today. Let me ask you something. Has this trip turned out the way you expected?' He looked at her intently.

Nelson laughed, not because it was funny.

'No? Is that right, it's different from what you thought? Am I right? You know why? Know why that is? Because you came here for a different reason from what you thought.'

'Sure,' said Nelson, sarcastically, 'and you're going to tell me.'

'What are you, resisting again? Hey, how about another drink? Let me get you one of these. No,' he held up a hand, 'let me. I want you to try one of these. The taste is great though the concept is weird.' He had to write down the drink order. They wouldn't take your order unless you wrote it yourself on their order pads.

Nelson didn't want to leave. She didn't mind this bullshit all that much. Though everything the Californian blond said sounded like something she'd already heard—predictable in instantaneous retrospect—she had never actually met anyone quite like him. Anyway, she had nothing else to do. Even though the seats down the front were emptying, and that was where she usually sat. Down by the road.

Buzz kept telling her things. 'I had everything. In quotation marks. Rich father—he's a producer in Hollywood; I did OK with girls, I could surf pretty good, I got into the college I wanted. But I didn't feel good inside, you know what I'm saying? I didn't feel good about myself. I did a lot of drugs for a while, flunked out, got into some real heavy mess-around. If you had seen me three years ago, I wasn't the same guy. I won't go into details now. I was real skinny, real sick. Just imagine someone looking to get dead. Then I met the man. I met Hermann and I turned it all around. I gotta say I was the one turned it all around, but I owe it all to Hermann.'

The drinks arrived. Down on the bench seats, Robbie had arrived, tossing his long scarf around flamboyant as usual. He was probably looking for a new girlfriend. Gala had left. The last time she saw Gala was when they parted in Bongo Man, going off on their separate trips. Nelson wanted to meet some other girls to be friends with. France was down there too. And a boy she had seen before, sleek black hair to his shoulders, beaded headband, she wouldn't mind talking to him if she got the chance. If she didn't want to listen to California bullshit any more she could go and join them. But she stayed where she was. Anyway, he had ordered her this drink.

'Hermann learned a lot from the Native Americans,' Buzz was saying. The Red Indians: wow! Nelson got interested. The Red Indians were some of the interesting people in America (the blonds were not).

'You know Don Juan, Carlos Castaneda's Don Juan? You've heard of him? OK. Hermann spent a long time in the desert with an Indian sorcerer who told him more than Don Juan ever told Carlos.'

Apparently, Hermann had not been resistant like Carlos, and soon was setting out from where Carlos left off. He was already a psychologist who had explored human potential to the limit that western psychology offered. With the sorcerer, he had learnt to fly like an eagle, burrow in the earth like a snake, become as tiny as a mosquito. He travelled in the past and the future, communicated with spirits and learnt to see into people's minds, hearts and destinies. Then he came back to the white man and set up a personal development seminar. That's where Buzz came in.

'I am no longer effect,' said Buzz, 'I am cause.'

Cause? Effect? Which was she? But she couldn't work that out at once, as Buzz was saying that Hermann had had a dream and as a result brought a group of his graduates to Bali. They booked out a set of beachside bungalows in Candi Dasa. 'CHandi Dasa,' Buzz explained, 'not Kandy Dasa, which it looks like.' There they had done an amazing workshop. At the end, they had had a Balinese-style ceremony.

A ceremony? Did they all wave incense smoke to heaven with flowers and holy water? Did they make offerings to the spirits? How did they know what to do? She didn't ask, she only kept listening.

Initially, the plan was that after the workshop they would go their separate ways, explore Bali, maybe even further, but what had happened had yielded such power such bonding such enlightenment that they had all, spontaneously and simultaneously, made a commitment to creating a new workshop. Hermann would stay on. They would each go to whatever part of Bali their inner self led them to and find two people to come up to Candi Dasa and take the next workshop. This was to happen within a week.

'Five days from now,' said Buzz, 'you could be starting the most amazing, empowering adventure of your life. In fact, you could start it right now. I bet you've got questions. Let me hear your questions.'

Nelson stared into her drink as she stirred it with her straw. She didn't really like avocado juice.

'People usually say, I've planned this and that, I've got to get home, my schedule is set, the money's a problem. You haven't created those smokescreens, Nelson. Clearly, your way is clear.'

Nelson had already told him she was four weeks into a two-month visa and didn't have to hurry back for any job, boyfriend or school.

'Here is someone,' said Buzz, 'I want you to meet.' A tall

woman in a bright blue knee-length T-shirt dress and a blonde ponytail was on her radiant way over to them.

'Candy,' he said, 'this is Nelson.'

'Nelson!' she exclaimed, sitting down. 'You're going to be a Gladiator, I can tell.'

'Hey,' Buzz protested, 'I haven't mentioned the G-word yet.'

'Isn't this a beautiful guy?' said Candy to Nelson. Candy looked like she must have ordered her nose and teeth out of some catalogue.

'Gladiator?' Nelson asked.

'Nelson is interested in coming to the workshop.'

'Am I?'

'Are you?'

Nelson shook her head, mystified and slightly irritated. These two people were older richer and more everything than she was and they were acting as if it were just so important to them what she decided. 'I'll need to know more! How do I know if I really want to go?'

'Ask for a sign, Nelson,' said Candy. K-andy not Ch-andy.

Nelson looked up at the ceiling and then out to the road. A momentary blur as she refocused her eyes, adjusted to the glare outside. Riding by on his motorbike, that was Miki.

FOURTEEN

'Isn't it good to get away from Kuta!' exclaimed the woman pressed up against her. Nelson gave a half-hearted sign of assent. Rather than argue. She had never wanted to 'get away from Kuta'. It would have been all right with her if this thing she was—terrifyingly—on her way to attend had been held at Kuta. Why couldn't they? Candi Dasa is the exactly right place for it, Candy had promised her, she would see.

The tour company's bemo providing an express service from Kuta three times a week left at eight in the morning. Nelson had packed up her things and left the Padma in a daze, stupefied by what she was doing and by the early hour.

The woman on the bus kept on. Kuta was noisy, dirty and 'incredibly touristy'. It was expensive, so expensive you may as well have stayed at home. (Home was a suburb of Perth.) She was not impressed with the beach here. They had better sunsets in WA and much better beaches. The things you bought at Kuta were really bad quality: colours ran, fabrics tore, shredded, shrank. The place was full of yobbos, yahoos and hooligans who made you ashamed to be Australian. The locals were rude, greedy and forever trying to rip you off. You got hassled on the beach and hassled in the street. The woman gave Nelson many examples of this kind of thing all the way to Sanur, where they picked up another couple of passengers to cram into the already crowded little bus. Everyone was quiet after that, as they made their slow way to the north-east coast.

Nelson thought that the complaining woman really had had the tiresome experiences she had tiresomely recounted, and yet that didn't make her right. She could only see things a certain way, her own. Was that because of the kind of person she was? Or did she turn to ceaseless complaining because of what had happened to her? Nelson had an idea that this was the kind of question Buzz loved to answer.

Nelson had been pushed away from her window seat by the newer passengers, and it was uncomfortable to try to see out. There were paddy fields and villages. It was a long ride. Hours. She closed her eyes and dozed uncomfortably.

The bus finally stopped in a parking lot outside a large losmen with many rows of rooms. Candy was waiting to meet them, her teeth gleaming and even, looking fresh and happy, wearing wide batik pants and midriff-baring green T-shirt. It turned out that three of the other people on that bus had also come here for the workshop—two Dutch girls together and a red-haired boy, solo like Nelson.

There were rooms available right here for only 5,000 a night. Very basic, the rooms, but it was only a place to sleep. They'd be spending most of their time at Bee-Lin Bungalows. They were to take rooms here and then come along to the Bee-Lin, five minutes' walk away. At low tide they'll be able to walk along the beach to get there, Candy promised, but now, take the road.

The red-haired boy waited, and walked with her. Philip, from Australia. Nelson, from Australia. Sydney. Sydney, too. Then they fell silent. The Bee-Lin Bungalows were set in a garden—lawns and paths and trees—and surrounded by a high wall. They went to look at the beach first. You had to go through a gate down the other end. They stepped on to a stone wall, which divided the hotels and losmens crowding the shore from a narrow strip of sand which now, at high tide, was covered over. The water was blue, clear and still like a lagoon. A few people were swimming or snorkelling. Sunbathers lay on top of the wall. The beach was divided into several small bays by large, ugly black T-shaped jetties lying flat in the water. Further down, brightly coloured little boats were pulled up high on the sand.

'These are fairly new. They had to build the wall and those jetties,' Philip explained, 'as the beach was eroding. Unplanned development. There wasn't a single building here five years ago.'

A large pavilion surrounded by flowering trees was full of

graduate Gladiators and their new recruits. Nelson felt rather awkward. She could hardly believe she was here. It wasn't her kind of scene whatsoever. Most of these people were older than she was, late twenties, thirties, some even older. Another generation. Who had problems, being responsible for the world being in a mess: poverty, racism, the environment, making wars, telling lies, being cruel. People older than Nelson had been too much into money and the ones older than them too much into sex.

As she registered, she listened and learnt that the current occupants of the Bee-Lin—elderly Dutch people—were off on a day trip, so the Gladiators had commandeered the restaurant for the day. It was going to be the meeting room; they'd have it all to themselves and take their meals there too. Arrangements had been made. The Dutch group had booked the entire place for a week, and the American group had had to move out as soon as their first workshop was over. Most of them had left Candi Dasa for a few days, to see more of Bali and to seek out the unknown people who were meant to return with them. They were coming back from their recruiting expeditions and staying at various hotels and losmens. Tomorrow the Gladiators were going to move back into the Bee-Lin.

'Hi-yyyy!' said a beaming Gladiator with her hand outstretched. 'I'm Annie.'

'Nelson,' she muttered, feeling awkward. Shaking hands with another girl; these Americans!

'Welcome, Nelson, I'm glad you came. Who was your sponsor?'

'Uhh . . . Buzz. And Candy.'

'Oh grrr-reat. They are such good people. How do you feel about the workshop?'

'Uhh . . . I don't know . . .'

'Perfect!' Annie beamed at her. 'It's so great not to have expectations. Hermann Hesse is a true Master.'

'Which one's him?'

'He'll be here later today. He went all the way to the top

of Mount Agung! The most holy mountain in the Far East,' said Annie with immense pride. 'He is going to be coming back just, ohhhh, with just so much to give! Nelson,' she said, 'I'd like you to meet . . .' Two other Gladiators had joined them. Nelson's mind instantly went blank. Was she expected to remember all these names? 'Nelson knows Buzz and Candy!' announced Annie rapturously.

'Grrr-reat,' said the girl.

'Don't worry, we all wear name tags for the first couple of days,' the guy said, a thickset dark guy; did he read minds?

'Hey, I'm going to leave you now,' said Annie. 'I'm so excited that you chose to be here. You will be giving yourself a true adventure of the spirit.' She flashed her mega-watt smile once more and targeted someone else. Annie had meant to be reassuring of course, but Nelson felt sick.

'Go work the room, Annie,' said the guy after her. 'Let's get you a drink, Nelson. Don't be worried, this is the best thing you ever did.'

'Hermann Hesse is a great teacher of the spirit,' the girl assured her.

'Hermann is an amazing human being, full of power and compassion,' someone else told her. Nelson had fallen into a kind of trance, a social trance. She could hardly believe she was part of this bizarre scene. If she were here, she had no idea who she was any more. 'Grr-reat,' someone said, though she surely had not spoke aloud. 'To know not to know, that is the start of your wisdom.'

'Hermann is a great spiritual teacher.'

'Hermann is a highly evolved being.'

'Hermann is a charismatic healer.'

'Incredibly psychic, wise and funny.'

'A real guru.'

'An avatar, a holy demon, a wild angel.'

FIFTEEN

When you became a Gladiator you became an initiate, you became nobility. You knew yourself to be as brave and clear and in control as those legendary champions of a great empire had been, warriors of single-armed combat, glorious charioteers, celebrated archers and unbeatable swordsmen. The Gladiators were the fittest, freest men of their time (and our time which now included women too). Gladiators were rewarded by monarchs, idolised by the masses and esteemed by their peers. They had to be on guard constantly against the erosion of their powers by egotism, complacency, or laziness, for if any insidious tendencies blunted the sharp edge of their skills they died. Today's Gladiators lived by the same *credo*.

When you graduated as a Gladiator from a Hermann Hesse workshop you had such a new, deep, amazing sense of yourself that you felt reborn. Your life was just beginning, whatever age you were, a new life that you newly created newly empowered to fill with satisfaction success prosperity love: as much as you dared. You understood that your individual life was a spiritual choice for a very special journey.

You forgave your parents and yourself and anyone who had ever wronged you with a forgiveness so real and so astonishingly grateful—yes, grateful, for all apparent wrongs were gifts to the enlightened—that you were united with the divine light and it was better than any high you ever had before.

You acknowledged that the story of your life so far was all your own choosing—yes, you had put it all there, every bit of it, from birth and even before that, for you, not a human ego but a soul with a mission, had been looking for the right environment to bring you to the lessons you needed to learn and had found your earthly parents for this purpose. When you became a Gladiator you saw that those people were just

64

right for you in this life whoever they were and whatever they did to you, yes even if you had been the victim of parental crimes from misunderstanding to abuse you came to see that these were all your own soul's choices made out of love and honour for what your soul needed. You know how as a small child you think: these ghastly people in my house, they can't be my real parents; my real parents must be a king and a queen and one day I will find them. You know when you endure the conditions of your imperfect daily life because you feel it's only temporary, just a stage, and one day you will wake up and be a princess in a castle. This was true in fairy tales and as a Gladiator you would discover for yourself the mystical truth of this knowledge.

Having experienced—not only been told, not only understood but experienced—all of this you then accepted that the story of the rest of your life would also be your own creation. And you would choose!

When you do a workshop with Hermann Hesse you get to know your psyche. It is not only your own mind, though it is hard enough to know your own mind. It is your larger self—mind, soul, connection to the entire cosmos. Your psyche is like a satellite communications dish and like an ancient mystery play. You learn to know your psyche and you draw a design for the character of your psyche and then the maskmakers come to make a mask. Did you notice the masks on the walls? Those were masks depicting the psyche—each one a Gladiator's. It wasn't just a type of face that you constructed. You found a range of objects—small as a feather, large as another planet, concrete, abstract, whatever—which had special meaning to you, to your psyche, and these objects became part of the design, the head-dress of the face of the mask of your psyche.

It is the most amazing thing that this workshop is taking place here in Bali because if you think about it there's nowhere else on this whole planet where it could possibly be. And it was all because of this dream that Hermann Hesse had, as you already know. Dreams are full of information and guidance if you access them properly, which you learn with Hermann. Hermann can program his dreams to solve problems, attract what he needs, take him to realms beyond, all kinds of stuff. All this can be learnt. Hermann had a dream about Bali, a place he knew nothing about; he only knew the song *Bali Hai*, you know the one. *Bali Hai* was written about *this* Bali and they put it in the South Pacific so that too many people wouldn't all go there at once before it was time and also for esoteric mystical reasons having to do with these grids that are on the planet that are like the chakras in your body. Anyway for a long time people have known that Bali is a very special mystical place and as soon as Hermann had this dream he gathered together a group of people who had studied with him and told them he was offering an advanced course in Bali. And everyone who was meant to go found a way to be able to go and it all fell into place. And they read up on Bali and found it is just *full* of an amazing spiritual culture and Hermann said the culture had been psychically protected in isolation until now, the twentieth century, when it was time for all the spiritual cultures to kind of feed into the world community. It just so happened that one of his graduates was a travel agent, which was perfect.

So it all worked out, Candi Dasa, and the Bee-Lin with its new, comfortable beds and clean American bathrooms, and the maskmakers and the gamelan. It is all included in the cost of the workshop. You design your psyche mask and the Balinese maskmakers come and make the mask which you wear at your graduation, and a gamelan orchestra comes to play and we all dance to the gamelan, amazing, it's not like our music at all. The Balinese have special masks for their own ceremonies so they would be right into this, some of their masks are sacred, and the native Americans use masks, and some places in India, and all kinds of places that have tribal people, so they are a very primal thing. Because masks aren't only in our sense of covering up, something to hide behind, that's not it, masks are also to reveal, to actualise; whether a new part of yourself or a whole other being: by putting on

66

the mask you *become* what the mask is and it's such an empowering thing. And this is only a tiny glimpse into what Hermann can teach you, as he can read the meanings in the shapes of clouds, the sounds of the wind and the motifs traced on the bark of a tree.

It's a lot to think about, Nelson, but don't try to understand any of it, understanding is not the point, it is an experience, as you'll see, and tonight it all begins.

Sixteen

When everyone returned to the Bee-Lin restaurant that night, things seemed disrupted.

The Dutch group had returned from their day trip earlier than expected and without having had their evening meal. They were to leave Candi Dasa early the next morning to depart from Bali at Denpasar and continue their guided tour to points of cultural interest in the Far East. Apparently they had not found Bali to their satisfaction. They gathered in the restaurant to reiterate all the horrors they had endured. The air-conditioning had not worked on the bus, and then the bus had broken down and they had been left in the sweltering heat to wait for another. The Indonesian guide had not pleased them, and they were going to have him sacked, as well as making sure they were refunded some money in compensation for their sufferings. This Nelson gathered from the aggressive remarks they made in English to the Bee-Lin staff, whose fault it clearly was not. Among themselves they spoke Dutch. They were all really old, Nelson observed, didn't know how to have fun, and had no business travelling in the first place.

And then they came back here and found their restaurant crowded with people trying to have some kind of meeting. During their week's stay the restaurant had been open to the public, but tables were always kept reserved for the Dutch group. That they were not expected to eat here this evening did not seem to them an excuse for their not being promptly accommodated. The staff cheerfully placed small tables alongside each other to form one long table down one side of the restaurant for the Dutch group.

Nelson realised she was glaring at them scornfully, and went on doing it, then decided to ignore them. She stared at the masks, peculiar masks crowding the wall, occasionally glancing around her, trying not to catch anyone's eye. These were the people she was going to share the coming week's experience with. She had been told that each of them had been chosen by her Higher Self to be there for her, each to reveal to her an aspect of herself. Bullshit. They must say the same thing to everyone and it didn't make any sense. Trying to get to her ego, that's what they were doing, she reckoned, to suck her in, but here she was, already sucked in. Well, then, she wished they'd get down to business. Because now she was very curious to learn to fly like an eagle, cast spells, travel through time, be invisible. She was nervous about designing a mask, though, but would probably get some ideas. Maybe she could make Miki fall in love with her totally. Or she could discover a way to get her revenge on him. Hmmm, that was a new thought! Where was the famous Hermann Hesse?

She became aware that the Dutch group was not the only reason that the Gladiators were huddling into groups, muttering, and looking . . . worried. They seemed to be divided among themselves and it was now way past six pm. Punctuality was one thing Hermann was very big on, Nelson had been told, punctuality, exactness, honouring your commitments. And Hermann wasn't here. It wasn't long before everyone knew what was up.

Hermann had not returned from the magic mountain. Two Gladiators had decided, in the face of some opposition, to take a Balinese guide and go to someplace a few miles away where he set out from.

This was interesting. Nelson stopped trying to hide and joined a small but expanding circle including Philip, the red-haired boy off the bus. 'He should have been back early today for a session with the graduates,' a thin, bearded man was saying. 'He's never not shown up before, apparently.'

'He could have been hurt,' a woman suggested, 'climbing the mountain.'

'It's easy to send messages, there's even a telephone at this place, or send someone, easy enough.'

'There's no phone up that mountain, I bet.'

'They'd send someone.'

'I didn't think grand master gurus could get hurt!'

'He's probably taken all our money and run off with it,' said a girl. A few people laughed nervously.

'Can you fill me in? He went to climb some holy type mountain, right?'

'It's a volcano.'

'It erupted in 1960 something.'

'Or was that the other mountain, Mount Batur?' said a confused guidebook freak. 'It was a punishment from the gods, the people weren't doing all their ceremonies.'

'Too busy chasing dollar.'

The red-haired boy stood next to Nelson. Neither of them had spoken. They looked at each other and remained silent.

'How long's he been gone?'

'Do we get a refund?'

'We paid a *lot* of money to be at this thing, a lot of money, and I am not impressed.'

Gong, gong! A bell, clanging through the hubbub. 'Welcome, everyone.' It was Buzz. People fell silent. 'Welcome. It is great to have you here. Congratulations on choosing an experience that will enhance your life path. Tonight we're going to do something a little different than planned. Each one of you knows at least one of the graduate group, but we're going to introduce you to all of us. After that we'll initiate a process that'll let us meet all of you.' He went on to say that each one of the graduates would step forward and share with everyone something about their experience of becoming a Gladiator. The first would be Annette. The group applauded as Annette came forward—they sure did a lot of applauding. Some of the new people applauded too, others folded their arms. Annette, thought Nelson, now I know two people called Annette, both in Bali.

'Hermann Hesse is with us tonight,' the new Annette announced portentously. She paused dramatically. 'If none of us can see him it must be because that's the way he wants it! He may not be here in his body, but his *energy* is very

70

strongly right here in this room. He doesn't have an attachment to being in his body, so why should we?'

She hadn't quite finished her sentence when the lights went out.

Darkness, chaos. Gasps, murmurs, giggles. Black holes of silence and terror. Mutterings.

Some people went outside. There was no moon. Tomorrow there would be a new moon. The new moon was the right time for beginnings.

In a little while someone brought along kero lamps, hissing softly as they threw off a bleached-white light. Only two lamps. One was placed on the Dutch table, adding to their aggravation no less than unrelieved darkness would have done.

'What? Did you hear? What are they saying?' The news was passed around the little groups gathered in the dark. Power failures were common. But they have their own generator here. They waited for the generator to restore the electric lights. It usually took five minutes. It was much longer than that now. A few people had produced pocket torches, flashlights. They shone them around, as if they were searchlights, then just held them, pointed downwards.

One of the kero lamps went out. Gasps, sounds of attempts to revive it, sounds of impatience. Drops of rain were reported, denied, then felt by everyone standing outside.

Beyond the Bee-Lin's perimeters, other lights appeared, soft and at a tantalising distance. The common electricity supply was off, but a few places had got their generators started up or had lit a score of lamps. *Other* places.

This had been going on too long. Now no one could find any of the staff. They called, they searched, there was no one to help. After a while people put out their flashlights. The darkness had blackened. No one was in charge. No bell rang.

Suddenly, a steady drizzle began. Flashlights were switched on again, to light the way back to the rooms. Some rooms were nearby, others farther. Tomorrow was a better time to start.

SEVENTEEN

Coming back to Kuta took a lot longer than leaving it had. They took the public bemos and there were several changes. At every change drivers would descend on them. 'Charter? Charter?'

'No charter,' they would say firmly. 'We're taking the public bemo.'

'Where you go? Kuta?' How did they know? 'Kuta, OK.' The drivers haggled. 'Twenty thousand only. OK, fifteen.'

The public bemos cost them a total of 2,200 rupiah each. Philip knew exactly how much they should pay for each section. He had it all written down.

She glimpsed other bits of Bali out of the open back of the inevitably crowded little buses. Once in a while she wondered, in an abstracted kind of way, what it would be like to get out. Alight here, at this market, here, outside a stone wall enclosing a village, here on this open stretch of road with bright green paddy fields in all directions. Here. Wherever here was. And then what? Did anyone speak English out here? She wasn't going to do it. She'd feel totally ridiculous. If she got off it'd only be to take the next bemo out of there.

No, she wouldn't go wandering around the countryside.

Some pretty wacky things went on out there, if she believed what she had been hearing. There were sacred sites, places of power, springs of holy water and a volcano which frequently rumbled hints of displeasure and erupted when gods were displeased. Sorcerers could turn into animals. Witches cast spells, concocted love potions and protective amulets. (Did witches and sorcerers get aboard the local bemo, like this old lady with her baskets full of fruit and that old man with a rooster in a cage?) Hermann Hesse had seen too much. Alone he had gone to the magic mountain and walked far into its volcanic depth. When he transmogrified into an eagle he

72

wasn't able to revert to human form. People repeated this with a straight face. Another theory was that this was impossible, as he would have come and shown himself even if he were an eagle. Others felt what had actually happened was that he had gone into some kind of time warp. Or perhaps he had run away with all the money. People paid a lot to do the Gladiator training and he had made it up only for the money, they said.

Philip sat quietly beside her. He had been her companion in Candi Dasa. This is what happened when you went to foreign places, you spent time with people you'd normally never meet.

He was there when she went to get the latest news that second morning in Candi Dasa. Apparently the graduated Gladiators had decided to encourage the recruited people not to stick around the Bee-Lin but to investigate various activities. You could get a small group together and charter a bemo and go to see some ruins, some old palace, no thanks. Or an ancient site with a pool of holy water. There was nothing to do there but to look at it. Or there was some village not far away that was different from all the usual Bali villages.

Nelson and Philip agreed that it was nice enough right here, the beach, the restaurants, even a few shops. Candi Dasa was a much quieter place, a get-away-from-it-all place, somewhere for early nights and lots of reading.

Philip was OK. Nelson gathered he'd been to a posh school and had rich parents. He was twenty-one, and taking time off from university to travel around the world for a year. He didn't say what course he was doing. He seemed a still, inward kind of guy, sort of funny-looking with his red freckly skin and red hair. He was maybe gay, she thought. There wasn't anyone else around she wanted to hang out with. Philip was OK.

About this training thing they came for, he said, 'I've always steered clear of all that. My mother did *est* and left my father.'

73

But Philip met a guy at his hotel who was a Gladiator and he had said something personal that really got to him and somehow Philip had no reason not to go with him. 'I'm still very curious to meet Hermann Hesse,' Philip told Nelson.

'Do you think he'll come back?'

'Maybe he never existed,' Philip said and they had laughed a lot. No explanation for his disappearance was more bizarre than any other.

Nelson swam in the shallow still waters of the strangely divided beach. It was quite a change from the surf. She hit her toe on some rock and scraped her hand on some coral. Later she and Philip found a place to eat. They were ravenous, they had grilled tuna, avocado salad, fried rice, chips, juices and fruit salad. They only talked about immediate and present things: the sea, the food. They were often quiet. Once in a while they'd say 'What *happened*?' and laugh at it, puzzle over it. In the afternoon they went to the unique village. They walked along the road, the still, glittery sea glimpsed between buildings on their left, revealed in full panorama as the road bent to touch the sea wall and then curved sharply inwards again. It was really too hot to walk far. Some boys ran over to them a little further on. Philip worked out a price with them, then he and Nelson got onto the backs of a couple of motorbikes and were taken up a really steep road shaded by bright green leaves. The strange village had a carpark and stalls in front. You could only get bottled drinks and they had one each. They cost more than usual. Inside the walls, there were these long houses set in rows, with wide, paved spaces in between and jungle growth beyond. There was hardly anyone around. An old man was making marks on strange little objects, little slats held together by thread so they stacked up and you turned them like pages. These were actually books, and the marks were an old form of writing. Philip bargained a little and bought one. The old man asked his name and wrote it on one slat in strange lettering. In this village people wove patterns into cloth with pre-dyed thread, it took years to make one and they were precious. They were the original people of Bali and only married among themselves.

'Let's get out of here,' said Nelson. All she could think was, why should I be here staring at these huts just so I can say I've been here. I feel really stupid. 'They should only let in one film crew,' she said, 'only once, look at the whole thing, and we could see what it was all about much better than this, on television, better than sticking our nose in.' Along with dozens of others every day, people getting off tour coaches, snapping cameras, clustering around their guide.

'These people need to live,' Philip said. 'They want tourists, they get money from selling things, big profits from those drinks.'

Nelson got momentarily depressed at the thought of wanting busloads of groups coming round as if your village were a zoo just so you could sell them some Coke. 'They wouldn't make that much off those drinks,' she said.

'This stuff,' said Philip, meaning the old style book he'd bought, the cloth they wove here, 'that represents a lot of money for those people.'

Nelson didn't know what she thought. Maybe they could sell their queer old books down at Kuta but why should they have to travel all that way to do it? So she just said, 'Yeah, you get a lot of coconut for a dollar round here.'

The motorbikes took them all the way back, and they went snorkelling with hired gear. Gazing at fishes of extraordinary electric colour darting in and out of alien gardens of coral, to the hypnotic sound of her own breath, Nelson forgot everything in a bliss of wonder.

The ruins and holy waters were reported within earshot to be sufficiently curious and photogenic but let those other people get hot and bothered, you should either have fun or take it easy. Philip was easy to get on with on that level. Apparently as a mere child he had once been forced personally to view several great and famous sites in the world and became predisposed to go right off the idea of travelling that way.

Though he might, he said, look back on it all with appreciation one day.

The graduates had been meeting and debating all day, going off on search parties, contacting authorities. When people came back to them in the evening they didn't make speeches, only said it's all off for now, take this number and leave your address. There was a theory going round that Hermann had been kidnapped by the CIA, who wanted his power for themselves.

That night, Nelson felt exquisitely exhausted, and fell asleep over her novel in the plain little cement-floored room. There was another day of snorkelling, and lazing about. She read many chapters, and she and Philip read over lunch.

She was to meet Philip for dinner but he found her earlier. He had got a guy to drive him up the road going north. The reason he wanted to see it was to check out the development potential. Philip remarked that his father said that if Philip thought of a good idea for a business in tourism development, his father would give him the money to get started.

'What course were you doing?'

'What? Creative writing.'

'I didn't know they had that at university,' she said.

'Oh, at university I was doing law but I decided to change to economics.' Was there a life where all these things added up? Nelson supposed so, as here was Philip. By that evening she was bored with Candi Dasa and they agreed to leave straight after breakfast.

The final bemo change was in Denpasar, the big bus station. A few other tourists got on for Kuta. She and Philip started talking, after silent hours. He thought he might go straight to the travel agent and leave Bali tomorrow: back to his original plan. He told her the name of his hotel. Nelson said she might visit later. She might too, if she couldn't find anyone she knew; it'd be something to do.

She'd been away for three days. It seemed like a long time. The Kentucky Chicken place on the road to the airport was a welcome sight, and turning into the roads around Kuta full of familiar colour and life made her feel bright and fresh at once, or maybe only reminded her of those feelings.

There was this really strange thought she couldn't help persisting with, that she would run into Miki and everything would be different, everything would start all over again.

They got off at bemo corner. Goodbye Philip. People are always coming into your life only to leave soon after and you notice that most when you're travelling.

EIGHTEEN

There was no room available at the Padma. She could hardly believe it. 'All full,' Wayan reported. 'Oh no,' said Nelson, lingering and loitering, 'are you sure? Is anyone leaving today?' It couldn't be right. This was her *home*, this was where she lived. Maybe if Saren came out, or Belgi? 'Sorry,' said Wayan, sitting as if patiently prepared to wait as long as it took her to believe him and leave. 'Where can I go?' Nelson asked eventually. 'Many losmen, many hotel,' said Wayan gesturing beyond the glass-barbed fence.

She had said she'd be away for at least a week. It didn't make sense but she felt wronged. She felt as if she were being kicked out of home, stupid. It was so hot and her bag so heavy. Oh well, better go find a room. Sitting around didn't help. Wayan didn't offer her any tea.

She went to Warung Kecil first. Little Ktut wasn't there today. This whole place, all of Bali, this was what happened, you never saw anyone you counted on seeing. She didn't, after all, find herself talking to someone and asking them where they were staying. She had her drink and left, then realised she should have left her heavy bag there and come back for it when she found a room but it was too late now; the bag got lugged.

Finally there was a room at a place on the other side of the main road, far from the beach. It wasn't particularly nice but by now she was fed up, hot and tired and irritable, and it would have to do. The boys who worked there, their manner was sly and unpleasant. 'Alone?' they said, sniggering; she didn't like it. The bathroom wasn't all that clean and there was no thermos of fresh tea. They only served tea in the morning.

She needed to wash and lie down. Tomorrow she'd find a better place. Of course, she should have thought of asking Lyn or Annette.

At Warung Annette, there were very few customers, occupying only one table. A guy, bright pink with sunburn, looking very pissed off, came from the back, saying, 'Let's get out of here. I can't get anyone to serve us.' The table of people all got up, grumbling. 'That's not unusual,' a woman said, 'it's either no service or they won't leave you alone.'

'I'm going to write to *Daily Planet* about this,' another woman said. They left, and there was no one at the tables out the front.

Out the back, there weren't any customers either. Two boys were lounging around as if they'd been doing it for hours. She thought they recognised her. 'Hi,' they all said. 'Where's Annette?' Nelson asked.

'House.'

Nelson went through the back fence. Usually either Annette or Selim were on duty in the restaurant. Nelson hoped Annette was all right, sometimes girls got sick when they were pregnant. Agung was there, sitting on the verandah. 'Where you come from?' he asked.

'I went to Candi Dasa,' Nelson said, approaching.

'Why you not tell me? I want to go with you,' said Agung. These boys! It was no good being suprised by anything they said.

'I didn't see you to tell you,' said Nelson. 'Sorry,' meaning to be sarcastic but not sounding that way. 'Is Annette home?'

'In house,' he confirmed, 'but having problem.'

'Oh no. Is she all right?' Nelson wondered if they had good doctors here.

Annette came out. 'Thought I heard someone!'

'It's me. Are you all right?'

'Oh *I'm* all right. But is Agung all right? You OK, Agung?'

'I'm very OK,' he said.

'I have to get back,' Annette said, meaning to the restaurant. 'Was there anyone there?'

'Not really. Those two boys who work there.'

'I just sent them back, they came running here after me.'

'Some people were leaving, they didn't get served.'

'Shit. What a day. Agung, do me a favour, stay here, OK? It'll be fine, I promise you.' Agung looked alarmed. 'I've got no one else here, Agung. One of the boys or me will come over to see you in a little while, OK?'

Nelson went back to the restaurant with Annette and heard all about it.

The house staff had had the day off to go to some family ceremony. Selim was planning to stay at home. There always had to be someone at the house as there were so many robberies these days. Annette was going to stay in the restaurant. Then they got the news. Lyn and Ktut had been busted and taken to jail.

'What!'

'Yes. Robbie came over to tell us and Agung arrived at the same time.' Annette retained her air of serenity somehow.

Once in the restaurant, Annette swiftly went to the three tables where new people were seated, took orders from them, and gave instructions to the two boys, who seemed as cheerful about getting back to work as they had been earlier about neglecting it. She returned to Nelson.

'Robbie just went out to the house and quietly told Selim. But Agung came in here freaked out, and went on about the police being after him, and the boys heard it, and they panicked. Madness!' said Annette calmly.

Selim had gone with Robbie to see what he could do. They would need a lawyer, and a lot of money. Annette had returned to the house to get rid of everything. 'We don't have drugs,' she said, 'especially now'—meaning the baby—'but I got rid of all my Bach remedies, my homeopathic stuff, everything, aspirin, herbs . . . Imagine trying to explain to the police what they were! Of course if they want to they'll just plant stuff.'

'Jesus!'

'Yeah, then Jesus won't be any help. They know we were pretty good friends with Lyn and Ktut, but they don't know we weren't into what they were into.'

Agung wanted Nelson to go to his place with him while he got his things. It seemed to be a losmen only for Indonesians. Agung left her to wait while he went to talk to the family. Nelson watched some ducks waddling across the yard and wondered where they swam. She left with Agung and it turned out that where they were going to was her place and he was going to leave his stuff with her. He had two airline bags, Qantas and Jetset Tours. They had to find her a new losmen and the sniggering boys came out and stared. Agung talked to them a while and Nelson was left out. She felt bitter, furious for a while, sick of it all. What were they saying, and why was Agung telling everything to people he didn't know and she didn't like? Let him stay and talk. She was going to go to sunset, feel good in the water.

An Australian guy had agreed to buy this tiny bit of hash from a guy at a warung and the cops were hiding, watching, and he got seven years. He was still in jail. He had paid huge bribes to the lawyers like everyone did but his lawyers hadn't passed it on to the judge. The Australian government was worse than any of them as far as helping its citizens if they got busted here. There was a man who had a house near here, he had a great life, then one of his servants planted some dope in the house and now he was in jail while all the boys he had employed were happily playing in his house. In the jail here you needed a lot of money as you had to pay for your own food and everything else. It was better in all ways than the jails in Turkey but worse in most ways than any jail in Australia. Once you could do whatever you wanted to around here but as usual some people spoiled it for everyone.

Before you could visit anyone at the jail, you had to get a particular letter from the Australian Consul, over at Sanur. Nelson had to get a charter bemo and it cost a lot. At the Consul's office she waited her turn, then presented her passport and asked for her prison visit letter. The receptionist took her time. She had to go see someone inside some office behind her to get the letter signed. Finally she called Nelson's name. 'So,' asked Nelson, 'all I do is take this, and I can visit . . .' She didn't really want to say 'my friend'. The woman nodded dismissively. She was Indonesian, with permed hair, a silk dress, long red nails. 'Can I go any day?' Nelson asked.

'Only on visiting days,' said the woman with disdain.

'What days are visiting days?' Nelson asked.

'Tuesday and Thursday,' she admitted, turning to some papers on her desk.

Today was Thursday. Tuesday was a long way off. 'Any time?' asked Nelson.

'Eight am to noon,' red talons said icily, as if Nelson were being unreasonabley demanding. It was now after ten.

'Would you tell me please,' Nelson insisted, not daring to be rude, 'how I would get there?' She had an idea that it was her right as a citizen to know. 'How much would I pay a bemo?'

The woman looked at her blankly. 'I really wouldn't know,' she said. 'Don't you have a car?'

I don't have a car, you stuck-up bitch, Nelson thought but instead turned and flung herself out of there into the heat and on to the unfamiliar main road. Eventually a bemo did stop and took her to Denpasar, where she chartered another bemo to the jail. She was taken to the wrong place and had to walk in the heat to find yet another bemo. Hearing where she was going, the driver, a young man in a grubby blue T-shirt, boasted that he had done time for big trouble with the police. She didn't know how impressed she'd have to be to get him to shut up. Lucky it wasn't far. She persuaded him not to wait for her. By this time it was nearly noon. They wouldn't let her in, because remand prisoners—that was Lyn—were only allowed visitors on Wednesdays and Fridays. She felt she would suffocate on her fury, irritation, and the astonishment that she had coped with so much on her own. 'Well,' she asked one of the uniformed men hanging out the front—those were *guns* in their belts—'how do I get back to Legian?' She had an idea that the beach wasn't far and she could walk all the way, paddling her hot swollen feet in the cool water. And get sunburn, sunstroke, collapse on the burning sands and die and rot. One of the uniformed men told her to wait and one of them would take her to Legian for 8,000 rupiah. On the way the uniformed guy who was driving her, a prison officer she guessed, said he drove his bemo round Kuta at nights to make money. He kept saying, 'You smoke buddha, like your friend? I know many police in Legian, many police in Denpasar.' This was the creepiest moment in the worst morning she had ever had. He was playing with her but what game? She told him lies, that she was staying at a big hotel and leaving Bali tomorrow. He said the ride would be 10,000. She persuaded him to drop her at bemo corner in Kuta and it took ages to get back to Legian.

They had been watching Lyn and Ktut's house for a couple of weeks. Annette was glad she hadn't been there for a while longer than that. Not that she ever went there much. Most of her and Selim's social life was at their own place, if they had any; they worked hard she said.

Why were they watching their house?

They'd made some enemy. Someone would want what you had. People got jealous. What they didn't see was that you worked hard for what you had. Everyone thinks they can have a business. Love Bali, want to come back and have a business, that's what they think. People come and say, it's the Javanese spoiling Bali, but the Balinese all want to be good at business, and if they don't work as hard they don't do as well, but they might not ask why, they might blame someone else.

'But Ktut is Balinese,' said Nelson. Selim was from Java. She couldn't figure out why it mattered.

'Just because Ktut was Balinese didn't mean that he could have a good business or that he couldn't. They had quite a nice shop, selling the kinds of things they liked, like those birds, but a shop takes a lot of time, someone's got to be there, or they close down. They were still into just having a good time,' said Annette, who, Nelson realised, was ten years older than Lyn. She remained apparently undisturbed. No harm could come to such composure.

The shop wasn't making money but they didn't go broke so of course everyone knew what they were doing. You can't be too careful round here. Some people knew that Lyn and Ktut's house was being watched and so they kept away. Of course they were the ones who had reason to know. Meanwhile other people have been going there, and anyone who's been regular is being watched too.

'Oh shit!' said Nelson. France had gone. Robbie was leaving. Gala had left before all this happened.

'I'm not saying get paranoid,' said Annette. 'They wouldn't be interested in you, you don't do business.'

'Does Agung?'

'Agung has got a big fat mouth,' said Annette bitterly. In a funny way, Nelson was relieved to hear her say it, confirming she wasn't just being stupid about not liking his habit of telling everyone everything. 'He should clear out too.'

'He said he's going back to his village. He said I could go with him.' She wasn't going to though.

'Might be an idea.' Annette sounded like she didn't want her round, thought Nelson resentfully, and after this hideous fruitless morning she had endured mainly to please her.

'I don't know,' said Nelson. 'He said they're going to do some special dance there?'

'Oh they're always doing a special dance out there,' said Annette humorously.

'A trance dance? What's that?'

'I don't go into that side of things very much. But they do have trance dances, though I think it's only done for tourists now.'

'He said it purifies everything, all the people.'

'They have a fixation on purification, everything's got to be purified, we have to get the priest in all the time.'

'I'd like to get purified!' Nelson said with vehemence. They both laughed.

'You should go then! Actually that would be a really good idea, Nelson, no kidding. Get out of Kuta, see some real Bali, it wouldn't be a tourist thing with Agung.'

Real? Nelson sighed heavily. She hadn't wanted to get out of Kuta this time either. She wanted to be living at the Padma, with friends to meet every day, go swimming, go dancing, no problem. That was the kind of real she wanted to see more of. *What* 'no problem', though? She had her whole future to work out. In three weeks she'd have to be leaving the country— to return home or to go to Singapore to renew her visa. Or keep travelling. They say Thailand is really nice. But she'd better get a ticket home from *somewhere*. And stop spending money like she had been.

'Bali's cheap once you're away from here,' Annette encouraged. 'Just take a break.'

The next thing she knew she was told to leave her room. They were kicking her out. They said, 'Police looking for you.' She could see they were lying. It was because Agung had blabbed. They thought she was in a gang of drug-sellers.

She took her bags and Agung's bags and waited for him at Annette's. 'We're on the next bemo out of here,' she told him. 'Where's this village of yours? Do they have a spare bed?'

PART TWO

MARLA

ONE

The procession to the temple went past them in the rain. The gaily coloured offerings shaped into pleasing pyramids for happy gods, carried on the head, were covered with plastic sheets, or an umbrella, or a big flattened straw hat or a large banana leaf held aloft. Marla, with Carlo beside her, sat damply on the narrow pew at the tiny warung on the road to Sayan, watching in silence. The gongs of the orchestra were also protected but some of them managed to add some ringing notes. As the last of the pageant filed by, Carlo looked at her with a gesture, wordless but so eloquent. How splendid, how divine, what perfection, what grace, oh these people!

An hour ago, Marla had gone over to the Hotel Campuan to leave Carlo a letter. There he was, picking up his mail. He flung open his arms when he saw her. 'Marla!' The letter she carried began with a reminder of who she was, where they'd met. But he remembered her. 'The girls told me you were going to be here,' she said. Their mutual friends in Bondi. 'I came to get this,' Carlo said. He had picked up a sheaf of mail at the desk. The hotel was the first place he had ever stayed in Bali and his mail was still sent here. 'I never come here!'

'Well,' she said, 'I was sitting over there on the other side of the river and I thought the girls did say get in touch with Carlo and suddenly I thought I'll go now.'

As he was on his way. They smiled, recognising that that was how things worked here, and they loved it. They loved this, they loved here. They sat on a bamboo sofa covered in large printed cushions. The far side of the shaded lobby opened on to dark palms, streaking the intense light with cool shadows. The brightest light casts the darkest shadow.

Carlo was a dancer; his movements were fluid and expressive, given force by the drama of his huge black South American eyes, his high-pitched energy, his enthusiasm. He was not so much dresssed as ornamented in heavy Indian jewellery, pants of woven fabric, a multi-coloured shirt, a beaded shoulder bag, a black velvet pillbox hat with gold embroidery. He had acquired this silver bangle when he had been to India, and hung out with a tribe in the desert in Rajastan. He had been raving about it at the party in Sydney where Marla had met him.

He had also worked with Australian Aboriginal people. 'These people here,' Carlo told her, 'are like the Aborigines. They have a very Aboriginal belief.' Spirits and magic and community and ancestors and so on. 'They can tell at once if you're racist, they understand body language so well. They're like the people in India too.'

He had come back to Bali to live in a house in the rice fields—his words: a 'house in the rice fields'. A house in the rice fields was one badge of authenticity for a white native. Marla was 'only' in a bungalow in the Katak Inn. Carlo was clearly just that bit more the white native than she. He kept insisting he was not a tourist. That's either the first sign, or the ultimate delusion, Marla thought.

Eventually they had wandered outside, as a drizzle began, and sat at the little warung further up the hill—a single pew in front of a little stall. They both liked warungs even more than hotel lobbies.

'I love it in the rain here,' said Marla, 'everything's so soft.'

'Yes! I love the rain! You're the only other person.'

'I love things I don't usually love: rain, the early mornings, just sitting.'

'I love the way you *sit*!'

'*Kopi pahit*,' Marla ordered.

'What's that?' Carlo asked her.

'Without sugar. *Pahit* means bitter.'

'What's sugar?'

'*Gula*.'

'I want *kopi* with *gula*,' Carlo said to the woman sitting inside the stall. She smiled back at him. 'You're good. I'm no good at languages. Can you speak Balinese too?'

'No! God! Indonesian's hard enough and it's meant to be easy. Balinese is really complex.'

'I'm going to learn it.'

'I love the coffee here; it's such good coffee.'

'I love this,' said Carlo, taking a peanut cracker out of one of the glass jars. He smiled at the woman again. He loved the jars of snacks, he loved it that you helped yourself. 'I love these smiles.'

Marla shook her head in an excess of agreement. She took a kretek out of an open packet in another jar, raising her eyebrows at the still smiling woman.

'You do it too!' said Carlo. He did it: raised his eyebrows; Bali's ubiquitous gesture: an expression of greeting, questioning, affirmation, amusement. He had his own packet of kreteks; lit hers and one for himself. 'I love these. I gave up smoking in Sydney.'

'I don't smoke but I smoke kreteks. They're actually worse than ordinary cigarettes apparently, it's really rough tobacco.'

But the cloves scented the air and left a sweet taste on their lips. After the procession passed them, the rain reduced to a drizzle again; the air was steamy. A row of bemos that had been held up by the procession lurched along bumper to bumper. A flashy big car was trapped in the middle of the line.

'I sometimes think what it must have been like in the thirties, being here,' Carlo said. The thirties were the Golden Age for the foreign residents and culture-entranced visitors of the area. Reading about those days had given Marla the inspiration that was changing her life here and now.

But all she said was, 'I just got back from Singapore. I had to renew my visa. Two months I've been here, two months! I packed all my things, took everything with me to Singapore.'

'Did you think you wouldn't get back in?'

'Not really.'

'They can look at your passport, see a lot of visas, they can refuse to give you one.'

'I only had one visa before, for here.'

'I know why you took everything to Singapore. I had to leave here to really think about here. Everyone said, what about going somewhere different next time? One year back in Sydney, three jobs, and it was only for one thing, to come back here.'

Marla nodded. 'When I was in Singapore, two days, I wanted to really think about it. There are so many places. And I was supposed to be on my way to Europe.' She laughed. 'That's where a lot of my mail was sent.'

'Only three places: Bali, India and the central desert, the only places I want to keep going to.'

'That's what I thought. You don't really have to go somewhere different every time. I need to be here.'

'Isn't Singapore the pits!'

'So clean! So orderly!' Marla laughed. Carlo shuddered with distaste. 'I had a dream,' said Marla, 'in Singapore. It clearly said I should come back here.'

'The dreams!' said Carlo. 'The dreams you have here!'

They had more coffee, another peanut cracker, smoked another kretek. Some children splashed gleefully in the muddy ditches beside the road.

This was a place for dreams and strange states of mind. Carlo said he had been drawing and all these very strange energies were vibrating around him. He had picked up his rosary beads. 'I love my beads, they are so symbolic.' He thought Pak was a leyak. Penestonoan is known as a magic village. Carlo had been down to the village with Pak and they looked at him like this. Carlo mimed looks askance—fear, suspicion.

'Oh,' said Marla, 'magic!' Then fell silent, unable to choose among a dozen things to say. This was a place for magic. *Sakti*. You would hear any number of stories of magic, of persons with much *sakti*, who were called leyaks. There was a white guy who studied the magic and turned himself into an animal

92

and couldn't turn himself back. His friends and followers thought he had just disappeared.

This was a place for art and creativity. 'Here,' said Carlo, 'the creativity! The creativity!' It was all around him and inspired him. He would draw and paint for three days, not going anywhere, not sleeping, painting all night. If the frogs are croaking it means everything is all right. The frogs were croaking at three am and then everything went quiet. It was so eerie. Pak appeared with a white towel around his head. Carlo had never seen that before.

Marla only said softly, 'Here, at last, I feel I can do some real work of my own.'

'Of course you can! I only really started doing my drawings here. Come over and see. I never ask anyone to the house. Come over. This place is just so full of creativity.'

Carlo could not know how much it meant to her, to begin to find a new direction. The path itself was as much a new venture into a long-supressed creativity as her tentative new project.

This was a place for boys, all these beautiful boys, such a temptation, but what for? The boys came and slept with him, Carlo told her. That's the custom, here, boys sleep together.

Marla stuck her tongue out, a babyish jealousy. Carlo got to sleep with the boys, but, he explained, it had its drawbacks. Here. Where you are extra careful, extra cautious, because you're not quite sure what's going on, and you don't want to be like those—

Carlo gestured to Sayan. 'Have you met . . . ?'

'The White Rajahs.'

'I've seen boys coming home crying after they've been used by those people. I don't want anyone doing things for my money. I give them money, I give all of them money.' One of them, especially, so beautiful. So flirty. Boys and sex and not doing it.

'Not doing it is my main thing,' said Marla. She was forty and the world had changed. 'Now that I'm forty.' She told everyone her age now that she was forty. 'I like hearing about it though.'

Carlo said, 'It's like, one, two, three, four, five, six, seven, I want to sleep now. Sex is not like it is for us. Boys sleep together, and they do it, but they're not gay. The sex is frustrating if you're really into sex.' He didn't do sex with them, he said. Although he was tempted, tormented. The boys are beautiful but perhaps it is Pak he is in love with.

This was a place where westerners were very rich. The boys at Lola's—you know how expensive it is there—got 40,000 rupiah a *month*! 10,000 a week! Less than 10 dollars! Watching tourists spend more than that on one meal! And they have to work all day and then sleep there at night as security. Tourists don't realise just how poor people are. Tourists haggling over a few cents, when everything is so cheap anyway. 'Where,' said Carlo, touching his beautiful rayon shirt, 'can you get a shirt for ten dollars?'

'Did you pay ten dollars for that?' asked Marla. She thought, you paid too much; you could have got it for 10,000 rupiah.

They talked about shopping, and travelling, and communicating, and the stages your life went through. Carlo did most of the talking. This was a place for listening; it was for Marla. She was a good listener.

Down the road they parted. Marla walked back to her home. She stopped on the bridge and looked over the railing, down to the river. Some people in traditional dress, a priest in white, had gathered on a bank. Not from the earlier procession. There must have been a small cremation, perhaps a child's. They were setting afloat a brilliant little raft, a little golden barge, to be swept along by the river eventually to reach the sea where all human ashes must be taken.

TWO

The Europeans started to come to Bali in the 1920s, and the 1930s was their golden age.

Not the Dutch, those monstrous colonisers; they had come much earlier, they had invaded and exploited the rest of Indonesia and came late to the island of Bali. In Bali they found not submission but opposition: the extraordinary, glorious, shameful *paputan:* a steady procession of white-clad Balinese, led by their nobility, marching in solemn, unflinching procession into vicious Dutch gunfire, falling in serene bloodied defiance, an affair so profoundly disturbing that the white rulers had to devise an unaccustomed policy of co-existence and caring administration for this tiny island in their vast empire.

The Europeans who came to Bali in the thirties came as individuals; they were anthropologists and artists, leading the way for the early tourists. The tourists disembarked at Singaraja and were driven south to the hotel in Denpasar where they viewed some dispirited dancing in the heat of noon and bought some hastily contrived souvenirs.

The artists and anthropologists came and they soon left the hotel in Denpasar to go into the villages to live among the people and many of them stayed and built their own houses up in the mountains and out by the sea. The artists and anthropologists of the thirties did the work that all those who followed could only repeat, confirm or embellish.

Margaret Mead with Geoffrey Bateson were to provide the data for a changed civilisation's new convictions that our beliefs and behaviours are not absolutes but the products of custom and conditioning. Colin McPhee came and studied the music, and wrote an enchanting account of his life, in which he neglected to mention his wife Jane Belo who came and studied the trance dances. Doctor Goris sought Bali's own scholars of language, custom and religion. Hickman Powell wrote of the paradise he found in the most exotic location on earth. Popular novelist Vicki Baum wrote her best book, full of clever, knowing details of Balinese life. Miguel Covarrubias, that gifted Mexican, wrote the textbook on Balinese culture that remains the standard work. Muriel Pearson, inspired by Hollywood images of 'paradise', came, changed her name to Ktut Tantri, and eventually helped the nationalists fight against the Japanese. Such stories! There were others. They came and settled and celebrities visited them.

The greatest of them all was Walter Spies.

Walter Spies created Bali as we know it, as we see it.

His spirit was linked to that of Bali, and Bali's spirit was most clearly linked to his. All who knew him said so. He was made for Bali, and Bali for him, they said. To this distinction many were to aspire.

Saint Walter. He was amazing and aristocratic bold and benevolent creative dedicated *engagé* enlightened fascinating famous gifted historical influential intellectual inspiring just judicious kind lucky musical noble original pioneering popular persecuted queer rich successful talented vital wise extraordinary and young when he died, too young, yet who is to say when a life is completed?

A celebrated son of the salons of Europe he dreamt of an Orient and knew his real home was in an unimaginable elsewhere. He came to this faraway land where he chose to stay among its people. In the Sultan's court in Java he studied the entrancing music of the gamelan and devised a notation for it, even tuned a piano and played it with the gong. He turned his back on the white overlords, refusing to be one of them, although he accepted their honours, for it did not occur to him to despise colonialism itself, only that it was too often brutal, too rarely enlightened. But his admiration was reserved for the brown-skinned people he found here, and his admiration was unreserved: their beauty, their delicacy, their natural aristocratic grace, their artistry, the harmony of their lives, the richness of their culture.

What a life!

He went to Bali and found that finally he was at home. His early painting might have prefigured the style and subjects he would adopt and invent. O cycles of destiny!

Once upon a time Walter Spies had been patronised and now he became a patron. The boys came to him, and showed him their traditional drawings of mythical beings and he suggested they look around them and paint their own world and it all began. Balinese paintings—his and theirs—showed, in layers and layers of a disarranged perspective, scenes from village life: farmers and buffalo in the rice fields, women pounding rice in the compounds, priests conducting rituals, dancers performing, ducks and geese filing through the markets, all the separate scenes linked into a resonant unity. O Eternal Time!

This style of painting soon became known as 'classical'. He gave Bali's artists their own lives as their own art's subject; it became his subject too. It was a synchronicity, a synthesis, a symbiosis of influence.

Walter Spies painted dark dense palms, glowing mountain tops enswirled in mystical mists, the farmer and his buffalo stepping evenly their way home, a perfect Zen no-hurry pace, walking that same way for the length of one paddy or for miles or forever. Saint Walter painted Bali so that everyone else could see it: its intense shadows, multiple horizons, the pathways of time in a single complex moment, precision, detail, highlights, the eternal presence of Gunung Agung, the sacred mountain by which all direction is defined.

He made his first house at the *campuan*—the confluence of rivers—just beyond Ubud. Later he had to move further away, to avoid the consequences of his increasing fame near and far. He had become one of the famous attractions of Bali. The house at Campuan became the site of the Pita Maha, the Saturday group of artists, sharing, learning, controlling and distributing their own work.

While the other whites built their own houses and new hotels by the beach at Sanur and Kuta, Spies established the area of Ubud as the centre for the arts and the artistic and the lovers of arts, and it became known as the eternal centre of artistic life.

Some Germans came to make a film in Bali and Walter Spies was doubly qualified to assist, as he had worked with the great film-makers of Berlin in the twenties. For this Bali film he rearranged and developed the Kecak Dance. This became the famous monkey dance of Bali with its haunting chorus *tjak-tjak-tjak*, a monkey chorus of chattering, obedient rhythms as the monkeys agree to follow Hanuman to leap across the sea to Lanka and rescue Sita from wicked Ravana *tjak-tjak-tjak*. It was Saint Walter who added the Ramayana plot and the enlarged chorus to the old dance. The Kecak dance is today called a 'classical' dance of Bali. Spies' creations usually resulted in a renaissance of authenticity.

And people kept coming; they came to Bali to create, to be created, to create Bali. They came and wrote of beautiful bare-breasted maidens, timeless villages in a lush paradise, a place of amazing harmony disturbed only by occasional manifestations of wicked witches who were defeated by noble barongs, and of *guna-guna* the love-magic practised there. All the world knew that Bali was the enchanted isle of the world's sweetest dreams.

And there was another thing. They came because of the beautiful boys. They loved the boys, many of them. Walter Spies loved the boys. Imagine a far eastern symposium where elegant speeches were made about love's superior place in these boys. And no one minded, why should they? No one was hurt, it was no one's business, and amongst these people, it was said, homosexuality was but a pastime for the young unmarried men and nothing to make a fuss about. Until the grim events of the outside world caused grave fusses of all kinds, there was war, there was defeat, the Dutch, the Japanese, and a severe moralism came into force. Walter Spies' homosexuality had never been an issue but suddenly it was a crime. He was imprisoned for a while. And then, not long after, as a German national in the time of war, he was interned, then put aboard a ship which was torpedoed by the Japanese and that was his end.

No, he never had an end, he went on forever, and the Europeans' experience of Bali could never start with a blank page, it could only be a palimpsest, layering over the foundation layers that were the life of Saint Walter.

THREE

Here Marla lived in a bamboo and thatch hut. Sometimes she remembered that once she had thought that many other things were necessary for a good life, a comfortable life, and was amazed. Here she had only the simplest furniture. Cold water. And it was, well, you did fall into that old cliché, so say it, Marla: she felt it was paradise.

The idea of paradise was an illusion she did not intend to be deceived by. Knowing, as she did, that it was a construct imposed on this place to support false ideologies: colonialism, orientalism, tourism.

But here! But this!

The bungalows of Katak Inn were set in a spacious garden on a hill by the river. Stone pathways and stone stairways wandered through carefully tended flowering bushes and trees. Banana flowers, violently exotic, huge and mad and red, hung in front of her door. Each morning someone would come to sweep the room and place a fresh hibiscus flower in the pretty little jar on the table on the deep verandah. At night she sat there with the lights off and looked at the fireflies and listened to the river. Occasionally a tjetjak called, first its wind-up whirring sound then its several cries, which she carefully counted to discover her luck. Often someone would play the *angklung* that sat in the main building below and its clear notes and rushing gong rhythms floated to her on the dark scented air. She woke at dawn and slowly stretched her body in classical asanas to the gentle sound of sweeping. Gusti or Gusti Ngurah or Madé swept the pathways, and the stone steps that reached her bungalow, which was at the furthest end. When she emerged, they brought her hot water with lemon and ginger. Sometimes they peacefully sat with her a while. Across the river was a steep, bare hill, on which she would see a procession of tiny, distant figures make its single file unhurried way down to the banks, loads carried on heads, a timeless motion. The sublime freshness of the mornings! It was always the first fresh morning of all creation.

Every third day—there was a three-day week among the various weeks of the Balinese calendar—the local market was held at Ubud and often she would go there as soon as she was awake, steadily climbing the uphill road, to wander among the fruit and vegetables and spices where the peasant women squatted and cheerfully bargained for their best prices. They had all been there before dawn. Marla would buy a kilo of rambutans, a handful of mangosteens, a paper cone of peanuts, causing the women to laugh at her in a good-natured fashion when she bargained in Indonesian. At a stall of gaudy household goods she'd buy some incense and some hairpins. She'd squat by a seller of fresh sweets, watching the little cakes being made, and poured over with palm sugar and sprinkled with coconut, and she'd buy a few *lak-lak*, wrapped in a banana leaf. She would sit at one of the warungs—just a counter and a pew—for some hot fresh strong coffee, and with the next coffee a fresh hot fried banana, eaten with her fingers as she sat happily surveying the colourful busy market and exchanging greetings with those who sat near her, usually farmers, who stared at her with frank and benign curiosity. These people!

She tried to imagine their thoughts.

How strange these white people are. They are very clever and they don't know anything. They come into the market and they look around them as if searching for something. Don't they have markets where they come from? They stare at the most normal things in the most peculiar way, mangoes and cloves, they ask what is this? Then they ask how much, but they often mean nothing by it. Why would anyone start to reach a price if they don't want to buy? White people don't seem to know anything about prices. If you are friendly and offer a good price no one would refuse, they begin to argue.

If you tell them some very high price, just to open things up, to get a good long friendly bargaining session going, they'll open up a wallet and hand over the money! It is said that over in their country everything from houses to bananas has a single fixed price, always the highest price, and the tourist people pay it without discussion. It must be a grim business over there, buying anything.

The tourist people don't seem to have normal human needs. They leave their families to come here. Parents leave their children and children leave their parents. There are wives and husbands who leave each other to come here. They leave the places of their ancestors and they leave their temples. There are men and women who are already old and not married. They feel no shame, if you can believe it.

And rude! How rude the tourist people are! We laugh and laugh at their many kinds of rudeness. They can't answer the simplest greetings in a polite manner. The women show all parts of their bodies in the public street. They have so much money but they dress as if they were beggars. They insist on staying in places where each and every sleeping room has its own bathroom but they don't know about cleanliness. They spend half a million, a million rupiahs to leave their rich countries and come here on an aeroplane. Can you imagine so much money! Some of them come here many times. Then here they become so mean and stingy it would embarrass the meanest one in any village. And the ridiculous things they spend their money on. They like to pay a lot for food and they like to pay a lot for clothes.

Why do they come? Do they know why they come? It must be that in their country they don't have beaches or markets or temples. It is said that in their country they don't have ceremonies, they don't cremate their dead. They are clever but stupid.

Soon the sun was high in the sky and it was another blazing mid-morning; the shops were opening, those of the permanent market all around them and those of the streets. Other tourists were wandering around, their aggressive cameras shooting to pieces the picturesque remains of the early market.

Back at Katak Inn, Marla went down to the spring to bathe. The men went at one time, the women went at another time. Marla joined the women or went alone later in the quiet hours. A bathroom in heaven! The spring was below and out of sight of the bungalows. Further below, you could hear a tiny branch of the river rushing to meet itself. Bright jungle greenery all around. Pure mountain water gushed into a stone platform, never-ending, bountiful. If she was alone she took off all her clothes. If she was with the women she would crouch modestly with them in her panties and wash herself under a sarong.

She felt beautiful. She was forty years old and she had been set adrift from all the anchors of her past, all their securities, all their heavy weights. She was carried on the winds and tides of outrageous fortune, and would continue thus until they forced her back on to some sober, rational shore. One day. There was purpose enough in her present.

On the large table on her verandah sat her books and notes. She wrote her journal for the past day, added to the new work, and planned her program for the present day. Today she would spend a few hours reading at a small private library in Ubud. Tonight she would eat at the markets up there, and go to the dances at Peliatan. Such pleasure, all of it!

She enjoyed the buy-your-ticket nightly programs of dances for tourists, as much as the temple festivals she had attended, carefully attired in traditional Balinese costume, to please her hosts. All the dancers were a delight to watch, and occasionally you would see a special dancer, blazingly alive, the spirit of dance.

She had sat among the kneeling rows of worshippers, to join the *puja*, her hands outstretched as the priest came to administer water and rice. As the gong rang in her ears and the grains of rice blessed her face and the holy water dampened her head and the incense filled her breath she fell in love with the gaudy, unreasonable religion in which belief and ritual did

103

not illustrate one another but were inextricable, and to which solemnity and piety were unknown.

And it was there, in a moment of being outside herself, unrecognising of the self she had been, that her inarticulate prayers were answered. She felt—she felt she was *given*—a sense of purpose. She knew, suddenly, that *here* was not to be only a passing curious sojourn and she didn't even have the photos. It wasn't anything like the way she had made decisions in the past—lists of pros and cons, goals and outcomes, payoffs and compromises, even a careful allowance for intuition and lateral thinking. No, this was more like a revelation. Its message took hold, it would not be shaken off by examination or scepticism. Here! was the message; Here and Now! was the answer and her question was work.

She would stay here to research and write a screenplay about Bali in the 1930s. That was it. The inspiration. She let herself trust it. Easy. The signs were benevolent, bountiful. So she stayed on, reading and dreaming about that golden age, making her plans for more research, going to talk to people; and when it was time to go to Singapore she acted as if she were free to continue or to return knowing it was already decided for her.

She sat at her table and inhaled the fragrant air, listened to the stillness, watched the garden grow and thought of all the delightful things she could do, and of the marvel of being inspired with purpose, a project, a work.

If she knew she were going to die tomorrow, this is where she'd be. If she were sure to live forever, this is where she'd be.

FOUR

Once upon a time another life had ended. Or, another incarnation within a single life had ended. It took a while to sort out the mess, and then one thing was clear. Marla had to go away, as far away as she could. She had to make a break, to start over. Leave it all behind, that was the best idea. She'd go back to Amsterdam, there were old friends and a good chance of a job. She'd have a holiday on the way.

Everyone she knew had an opinion on the subject.

Why Bali? Why not Thailand? Why not Malaysia? You want an Asian country, a good hotel, a good beach. The Maldives? Kerala? A stopover before Europe, for R&R. Rest and Recreation. Get a good rest, get healthy. Swim and read and eat and sleep. Recovery and Reinvention. There are so many places. Thailand. Club Med. Bali? Well then if you've decided on Bali. There'll always be people who say not Bali. There'll always be someone. Lots of people hate Bali. Some of them used to love it and hate how it's changed. Some of them just hate it. But Mike says it's become even better. Sue and Zosha had a good time in Bali. Bill and Megan liked it. Susan even said she'd go back. Don't even think about Kuta, you would hate it. Nusa Dua maybe, but it is all new, large hotel resorts, not for you if you're going to want to do some sightseeing. Here are some addresses. This guy is the manager of a tourist place in Kuta, check it out, he's got some stories. These are some good restaurants if they haven't all changed by now. You remember Carlo, get in touch with him, he's been living there for a while. You want a small hotel, unique and stylish, interesting history, interesting people, right on the edge of the beach. Look at this brochure. This will be perfect. Sanur, on the east coast.

On her first morning in Bali Marla woke early. She could have stayed in bed longer, she could have stayed in bed all day, all week. She was exhausted, she was on the verge of total breakdown, getting here had taken up every last bit of her last reserve of strength. It was so early that there was only the faintest hint of approaching light outside. She rose and she walked out of her room down to the beach. It was fresh, it was lovely, it was perfect. The sun rose swiftly through a pink horizon. The nacreous sea of the dawn turned as cystalline as the soft clear air, as lucid as the message that said: here! A voice from the innermost and the outermost: here!

Marla stepped onto a painted wooden boat and a thin old man, wiry and strong, took her out on to the smooth still water, out amongst the reefs. He called sing-song greetings to other boatmen, fishermen, and grinned and chuckled at Marla.

They observed the capture of a huge turtle. Its flesh would later be consumed in soups and satays and its shell would make trinkets and ornaments to be purchased. Marla felt no horror at the turtle's fate; simultaneously she was ready to make a vow never again to eat the flesh of animals.

This time next week . . . How strangely that thought stopped there. She couldn't help it: setting goals, making programs. That was how she functioned. She went over check-lists in her mind: things to do today, exactly where I'll be in exactly a week, exactly how much time for this and for that. Suddenly, today, it no longer worked. These thoughts refused to be thought. There was no panic, no anxiety. She couldn't think of her timetable and it was all right. She was going with the flow and it was all right. She was going to let whatever happened happen and it was all right. This was a metamorphosis no less peculiar than if she had woken up as a cockroach. And it was all right. Perhaps she would go back to her room and find herself still sleeping there.

As she did not recognise herself in these thoughts and sensations it occurred to her that in less than a day—she had arrived the previous evening—she had achieved the purpose of her journey: to start her life over, to reinvent herself, to become a new person. The gap-toothed old boatman grinned at her as he steered the boat among the reefs in the clear blue water. They tried to make conversation but the limits of his English had been exhausted by agreeing to take her in his boat for an hour. How long was an hour? He grinned even more when she paid him and she let herself fancy that his humour was angelic pleasure that she had been guided to this island. Though she did suspect that what she paid him was exorbitant by local standards.

She would cancel her flight to Amsterdam. She thought of the bag of heavy, suitable-for-Europe clothes waiting there to be claimed by her. Letting go, that's what it was all about, letting go. That afternoon she bought a map of Bali, and a book about Bali, and a teach-yourself Indonesian language book.

She had not regretted it.

She had hardly known she was seeking, yet she had found.

When she returned from the shops, a sleek, plump, safari-suited Balinese man with huge gold rings on his fingers, accompanied by his comically contrasted batik-shirted thin unadorned brother, were chatting with the manager of the hotel. They all smiled at her. As if they'd been waiting for her.

The next day she went up to their small hotel, in a village near Ubud. The sleek man's wife, Sari, was a lovely woman of Marla's age who spoke fluent English and French. She had been a celebrated legong dancer in her day. (Also, Marla eventually heard, one of Sukarno's mistresses.) Now she taught dance to her own daughters and other little girls of the district. Marla sat with the women as they prepared for the temple. She was their guest at a three-day temple festival; it was full moon. 'What should I wear?' Marla asked. She had been reading her book and knew that she should wear a sash to the temple. 'I will lend you,' said Sari, and fetched a cloth, a kebaya, a long black bandage-like cloth and a pretty sash.

Marla bathed herself carefully, put her hair up and wore extra make-up. That, too, she learnt, was part of wearing ceremonial clothing. Preparation was part of it all. She was lucky to be brought here, shown this, allowed to learn these things at once.

Marla could not decide anything, plan anything, control anything. Realising that, she sat for a while, adorned in her new costume, in a stupor of amazement. Was this not her worst nightmare: no control, no plans, no power to decide? But to be here, treated this way, was lovelier than any fantasy. What a place! How many words were there for enchantment?

FIVE

The enchanting area around Ubud, then, would be her new home. Marla told Sari what kind of place she wanted to stay in and was sent to the Katak Inn down near the river. The furthest bungalow, the one she would have wanted, had just been vacated. She moved in and realised she had found her life's work. She would write a screenplay for a feature film.

When she had met Tony Liotta, way back then, she had just enrolled to do a weekend seminar on screenplay writing. Tony took her, instead, on a long journey into an alternative future, and many years later, when it was all over, and she could count her losses, then turn her back on them, when she was able after all to look ahead and make new plans, then, here in Bali, she finally turned her attention to all those dreams about writing, visual, dramatic writing: film. She had grieved and angered and wept over ten lost years; it was time to start life again.

A feature film, then, about a woman who was part of the Europeans' golden age in Bali, the 1930s.

That was the idea, that was the revelation, the inspiration, the game to play. You can't live here and not *do* something, that's what they often admitted in the colony of creative foreigners around Ubud. Tourists scurried around with scripts and theses and scholarly articles; with canvases and drawing pens; with percussion instruments of the gamelan. You breakfasted to the sound of wails and cries practised by the students of several forms of Balinese dance-drama. In these parts, if you stayed, you had a project. The screenplay was Marla's project, precious, tender, guarded; in these parts, ideas that take hold grow as luxuriant as the jewel-bright vegetation.

Who was this woman? Why did she come to Bali and why did she stay? Marla thought about her as she walked around.

109

Imagined the woman as she ate and shopped and sat; dreamt about her as she drifted to sleep. Was she American or European or even Australian? Not the latter. She was probably European Marla decided probably Jewish. She was privileged by birth marriage or accomplishment, so she could travel. Her name was Laura or Michaela or Miriam. Marla would have to know more about the world she left behind. Laura was, say, aged thirty in 1935. Or in 1930. Or aged twenty-five, or forty. She would have to think about this.

Her notebook filled with questions about Laura, with tentative answers, hypothetical information, provisional histories, lists of dates. Married? Yes she had been married, oh yes. She was alone now. There might have been something that revealed that their life was built on a lie. 1935, 1939, 1929. The stock market crashed in 1929. He had played with her money, without telling her, and lost it all.

Laura, then, was on a cruise ship that stopped in Bali. It was only going to be a stopover. Something happened and she did not get back on to the ship. Was this something a voluntary action or was she made to miss the ship? Was it possible that Laura had found herself in a single day unaccountably and compellingly reverted to an earlier self, a freer truer self?

Laura would meet some of Bali's celebrity residents—Mead, McPhee, Covarrubias and, especially, Spies. They would be support characters for her. Perhaps she already had an introduction to one of them and this person's life and work became Laura's inspiration to stay. What about Jane Belo? The one who had studied the trance dances of Bali. That's what Laura would do. Laura would not be based on Jane Belo though. Jane Belo was married to Colin McPhee who never mentioned her in his book about Bali. Laura's marriage was over. Marla was the one to decide every last little thing about Laura, because she existed only in Marla's mind. What fun, what spooky fun.

Laura decided to stay in Bali. Was she habitually impetuous or did this decision mark an astonishing out-of-character

110

departure? If it *were* a decision. Some odd mission might have made her stay. She, like so many of the others, became enraptured by the perfection of the life here. Laura, then, spent time in this area, around Ubud. She saw the houses the others had built and built a house of her own.

Laura needed to work. What kind of work did a woman do in Bali? In those days. She was not an anthropologist, not a musicologist, not a painter. Was she perhaps a business woman, who built a hotel on the beach as Louise Koke had done? Did she write novels, like Vicki Baum? Was she led to quite a new life as Ktut Tantri had been? She'd meet all those people, that'd be fun to imagine!

Maybe she became politicised, here. She would have to observe the Dutch in action. She would have to observe the beginnings of mass tourism. She might join those who got to know some local chiefs and begin to plead with them to consider the wisdom of the old ways; the false gains, the treacherous benefits of the new imports from the west.

Consider, chief, she might say, as some of the artists had said, your new American motor car, which will be a heap of rust in four years, has increased your expenses by fifty per cent, for which you had to sell pigs and coffee and copra, and which gives you no advantage at all. Nor do you need that iron roof, your thatch is cooler, lasts longer and costs less. If you keep buying imported goods Bali will no longer be one of the richest lands on earth but one of the poorest and you and all your people will have to work for a living, nine, ten hours a day, for a mere pittance.

Laura might join forces with a group that some of the residents then had begun to call for huge import duties and to encourage traditional industries. 'Bali for the Balinese'; that's what some of them had been saying, even back then.

Marla walked around trying to imagine the Bali of the old days. No hotels, no shops, no electric lights, no fleets of rented jeeps, not even motorbikes. The books of the time deplored the new fads for bicycles and flashlights! What was Laura's attitude to 'progress'? Could she see where it might one day lead? What happened to her? What was the central drama of her life? This would be revealed. It took time. Marla had enough to be going on with. There were many books to read. It was daunting—all those scholars who had made a study of Bali their life's work: anthropologists, historians, ethnographers, film-makers, musicologists, sociologists, and all the combinations. Whole libraries were made up entirely of material on Bali, surely the most studied, examined and theorised bit of real estate on this planet. Marla looked through all the books in the private library, and borrowed photocopied articles from the journals of the world, those in English anyway, and felt apprehension and exhilaration at the thought of all there was to know.

Rather think about Laura than herself!

Was she thinking about Laura in order to avoid thinking about herself?

Why should she think about herself? She had done too much of that already. After it was all over, she had needed help. And all those years of weekends on the self, the growth of the self, the development of the self, the knowing of the self. Enough of her self! Laura would be a better, more worthwhile focus. None of the therapies and theologies had offered her this: the therapy of fictional character.

Laura did not leave the island of Bali. The island held all she wanted. *All torment, trouble, wonder and amazement/Inhabits here*. Bali was her brave new world.

SIX

'They're running away. They're running away from them-selves.' Marla was watching an extremely self-assured blonde woman from San Francisco speak about the foreigners who made their home in Bali. How would she know? She seemed so sure. Patti was not on any old vacation. She travelled with purpose. She was networking. She was part of an international organisation. Ecology, development, poverty: those were its interests. She was here on business: she wanted Bali in the network. 'I'm getting into the banjars,' she announced; 'if structures exist, we work with them.'

Above her head, tacked on to a post, was a photocopied poster, with a smudgy photograph and the words 'Have you seen this man?' They were all at Ibu Suci's little warung, on the main road before the bend before the bridge over the river, close to the narrow road leading to the Katak Inn.

Patti was announcing that she knew this really special guy who was telling her all about the myths and legends of Bali. 'We use existing stories,' she said, 'and rewrite them . . .'

Marla sat drinking a fresh young coconut. Ibu Suci served big helpings of black rice pudding with fruit salad to Patti and her audience. Here at Warung Ibu Suci Marla sometimes talked with other people who came by; sometimes she sat alone and watched them, and listened, and made notes, and wondered if Laura would have heard anything like this ever.

'He was anti-Semitic.' Patti was talking about Joseph Campbell, the myths and masks-of-god man. A Canadian healer and natural therapist—she'd given Marla her card—begins to argue; she still thinks his work was great work. Patti won't be argued with; she is adamant that certain women have done greater work. Myths, heroes, archetypes, communities, networks: that's what they're talking about here at Ibu Suci's today.

113

Then Carlo walked past and saw her. 'I never come into Ubud,' he says, 'but I came today.' He sat down next to her. 'Is that good?'

'Good? Don't you drink a coconut every day? You must! It's the best thing,' said Marla happily. She had had some interesting talks with the Canadian healer yesterday, but she hadn't wanted to join in today's competitive New Age conversation, but she did feel like talking and suddenly here was Carlo! 'I have one every morning. One of the girls working at Katak Inn brings me a coconut every afternoon too so now I have two.'

Carlo pointed at the coconut and at his mouth and then put his palms together in *namaste*. Ibu Suci smiled tolerantly. She understood his sign language as well as the usual orders in English. 'Do you eat here? I eat at the house,' Carlo said. He thought it was more authentic, of course, to eat at the house you lived in, the house in the rice fields. Marla didn't mind being a bit touristy. He loved being fed at home. She loved to wander around following her whims and eating at several roadside stalls.

There are so many things they love. They love the food. The rice in Bali is the best rice. They love eating rice every day, just like a Balinese. If a Balinese doesn't eat rice, they feel they haven't eaten. They have a saying, 'Have you eaten rice today?' Carlo and Marla cannot understand why anyone says they get sick of Balinese food. It is the best food in the world, all their favourite things. Marla could absolutely live on rice, papaya and coconut. Carlo could absolutely live on rice and this dish they give him over at his house, spiced chicken in a peanut and chilli sauce. They love the way the Balinese just take their food and go and sit alone and eat it. They think tourists are totally weird—eating time is conversation time. Marla and Carlo wish that everyone would shut up and eat, and then talk. 'Dinner' and 'party' just shouldn't go together. They love eating with their hands in the traditional way: how good food tastes that way! There are all these European style restaurants now in Ubud. They have been to this one, that one, once, once is enough. People go to the one in Monkey Forest Road to get German bread. Why don't they stay in Germany! People go to the one by the lotus pond near the temple to see and be seen. Stay in Paddington! That was holy land, the lotus-pond restaurant, Carlo told her, and the locals hated it being a restaurant, so the new owners took over and put in all these notices saying that as it was holy land they were going to serve only vegetarian food.

Carlo and Marla paused simultaneously to watch a lovely young woman in a simple cotton dress and thongs, a very pregnant young woman, a serene, graceful beauty, walk past them; they observed her rolling motion, that beautiful way they walk, these people! The woman noticed their admiring stares, and smiled back at them.

Carlo's ever-expressive gestures told of the heart-stopping natural beauty they saw every day. They both basked in the nearer satisfaction of their craving for beauty.

'You look beautiful, you always do,' said Carlo generously. He was as ever amazingly adorned in a huge shirt of billowing golden gauze and numerous beaded accessories. 'That gorgeous thing you had on the other day. And this is so smart.'

'This, get this, this is Indonesian department store boutique fashion! I got it in Denpasar,' Marla confided with pleasure. She was dressed in a full skirt and overshirt of blue-and-white stripes, with pockets all over it. It was crisp and gay and oddly stylish and not in the manner of most tourists.

'Don't you hate the way tourists dress here?' said Carlo, lowering his voice. Opposite them sat some tourists in the tourists' uniform of shorts, singlet.

'I can't believe the mentality,' said Marla, 'like, we're tourists so let's get slobby; it's so hostile, really, it's so ugly, these people would smarten up a bit if they were going to see the great monuments of Europe . . .'

'No they wouldn't, it's everywhere, they dress like this everywhere.'

'And at the temples! You've been to the temples, to the ceremonies, you prepare carefully, you wash and dress, and

115

put on the special clothes and it's all part of going, and it's wonderful, and you see these tourists, oh the awful things I've seen.' They had a good old moan about the awful things they'd seen. 'Isn't this a good old bitch session?' Marla sighed voluptuously. 'Almost makes me homesick.'

SEVEN

What luck—it was Cherry sitting next to her. They had both cunningly grabbed the front seat next to the driver on the charter bus to Kuta. 'Carlo,' they said simultaneously as they greeted each other; they had met at Carlo's house one day; they'd turned up at the same time to look at his drawings. Carlo was being extra dramatic that day and they'd had to be a good audience for him, so they hadn't talked much. 'Aren't his drawings good?' said Marla.

'I actually really like them a lot.'

'All the incredible detail, the Balinese influence.'

They settled down to a nice long talk in the relative comfort of the front seat. Cherry, a Chinese-American, lived in Bali half of every year. Today she was on her way to stay with some friends at Legian and to do some shopping. Marla was going to have a look at Kuta, at the shops, stay overnight. She hadn't been there yet. 'Never appealed to me, what I heard of it,' she said.

'Kuta is good, too,' said Cherry. 'I like my dose of Kuta once in a while.' Marla regarded her curiously. This was an old Bali hand, a long-time regular, who had studied the rituals and attended festivals, who had known Bali before the major escalation of tourism. Cherry probably had the right attitude, Marla decided; she would try to see Kuta without prejudice.

Cherry chuckled as she glanced back. They had left Ubud at last and were turning into the road towards Denpasar. 'My favourite sign in Bali is on a restaurant down that road,' Cherry said. ' "Suckling Duck"!' It took Marla a split second, then she laughed too. 'Suckling Duck!' she repeated in delight. One of the celebrated feast dishes of Bali was suckling pig. You'd see signs saying, 'Delicious suckling pig here special order twenty-four hours notice'. The owners of Cherry's restaurant had made a false analogy for the roast duck they

117

served. 'I tried to tell them why you couldn't have suckling duck,' Cherry grinned.

'I love it,' said Marla. 'It'd be a great title for something about Bali: "suckling duck" '.

'You write, don't you?'

'Oh well I'm trying to. It's a new thing, though I wanted to write a long time ago.'

'It would be very hard to write about Bali.'

'It would be.' Then she admitted, 'And it is, but I'm trying to.'

They lit kreteks for each other, shielding the flames from the gusts of air coming through the open windows.

'When did you first start living here?'

''Seventy-two.'

'Ubud? It must have been different? Fewer tourists, less business?'

'Just a bunch of us temple groupies and we all knew each other.'

'Tell me how it began?'

In 1972, Cherry told her, she was spending time with some tribe people in the north of Thailand and smoked a lot of opium until she thought it was too much. She went to Penang for a break, and although she had left her luggage and stuff in a hotel room in Bangkok, 'it' started there and she knew she had to go on, in the other direction.

In Djogjakarta she went to the station to get a ticket for the train. She was seeing auras around everyone. The station was the usual hustle and shove and lines and waiting; she saw some westerners get really angry and upset; she saw their auras red and heavy; she saw clearly they were creating this experience for themselves.

She arrived in Bali, went straight to Legian and straight into the ocean and into the waves; she let the waves break over her and carry her, she gave up all control, she didn't struggle or swim, just let the waves do what they did, until she was thrown up on the beach. 'Like an empty seashell,' she said.

It went on like that for three months, this clear perception, this extraordinary state she was in. She saw a woman at the beach, come to sell something, she knew what she was thinking, that she had not sold anything and had no money to return home. Cherry gave her money, she gave all her stuff away.

One day someone drove her to Campuan and suddenly she said Stop! She got out of the car and there was a little statue with a flower behind its ear as if to say: this way! Up the stairs, there was another, as if to say: keep going! A man sitting there smiled as if to say: what took you so long? And that is the house she's been returning to ever since.

It used to be really quiet there, but now she hears traffic passing all day long.

Six months of the year she works in San Francisco, giving classes in creativity.

'How do you teach creativity?'

'We return to childhood—games, drawing, painting, mud pies.'

'Wow. And six months here. Still. Do you feel . . . what you felt at the beginning?' That clairvoyance, that enlightenment.

Cherry said, 'You have to deal with the everyday world, even here. Immigrasi.'

'There's this tradition, isn't there, of foreigners coming here that way . . . sort of being called here,' said Marla thoughtfully, thinking of Laura. 'I wonder if it still happens, what happened to you. People come here and still have that experience of being transformed, don't they?' Marla probed. She loved persuading people to tell stories.

'I saw a woman the other day. I hardly recognised her. I met her at Lola's the first night she arrived. She was real plain looking, very schoolmarmish, a woman from Nova Scotia, looking very uptight and anxious. Then she calls out to me from this warung—the one on the way to Carlo's? I hardly recognised her; she looked free and happy, and she was sitting and laughing with a bunch of people. I said, God, you look beautiful. She was transformed, actually radiant. She says, "I see myself reflected in their eyes, they are my mirror . . ." '

It was like magic, you could say. Speaking of magic, there were many stories about that, too.

There was a woman that Cherry knew. She met a man from Lombok in a restaurant. His wife came over to talk; she said she could not have children and so wanted her husband to have another wife and it should be her. Cherry's friend laughed it off. The man came to see her, he said she would be cared for, he was very insistent. She told him to go away. Then she had hot burning sensations all over her body and awful dreams where the man would appear, beckoning her. This went on for weeks. Finally she was taken to a dukun who took one look at her and said, 'Shit! Lombok magic!'

Now she's happily married to a Balinese and has two lovely children.

'Lots of girls get with Balinese guys,' said Marla curiously, wondering if Cherry would reveal any such episodes of her own. 'Kind of you can see why. Are there ever any Balinese girls with tourist guys?'

There was this nice, gentle, naïve guy from Australia and he really wanted a Balinese wife. He courted this nice shy girl from Penestonoan—bought her and her family all kinds of things. A house. They kept asking for more, and he gave them everything they asked for. On the day of the wedding she disappeared. The family swore they knew nothing. Finally he left Bali. She reappeared. And finally he came back and courted and married a girl from another village.

As they smoked and told stories and bumped along in the little bus, the road unfolded its images before them. Like a back projection in a movie about a couple of white women gossiping on a bus in Bali. The towns they passed through, the market places, the stone walls sheltering compounds, the banyan trees, the green fields, the roadside emporia and billboards and the displays of goods: statues, baskets, fringed umbrellas in brilliant colours, the outskirts of Denpasar.

At an area bright with awnings, banners and rows of

hulking tourist buses, camera-laden tourists were being shepherded to the entrance of a theatre, where, the billboards proclaimed, the famous trance dance of Bali was enacted at ten am each day.

'Pseudo places,' said Marla. 'Pseudo events. I've been reading about it.' At Warung Ibu Suci she had met someone who was doing a degree in Leisure Studies, majoring in Tourism. 'Pseudo places define the tourist world, and finally eliminate places entirely and then the true like the real begins to be reproduced in the image of the pseudo, which begins to become the true.'

'Right,' said Cherry.

'But that's one thing I haven't seen, a genuine trance dance. I've seen a bit of swooning and muttering at the odd ceremony, a bit of shrieking and spasming, but not the whole ritual thing.'

'The best place for that . . . but you'd have to go and stay there.'

'I'm going on a trip around Bali soon, I can go then.' Marla unfolded the map she always carried in her bag.

Cherry took out her pen. 'Here,' she pointed. She circled an area in the north-west. 'The palace is in the middle of the town. It's a tiny town, just a village. You can stay there. You can order a trance dance if you pay for it, but stay there and ask around, and you'll find out when they're having a real one.'

There was no time for more; their bus had stopped at the company's office in the middle of the main road in Kuta and Cherry leapt off the bus and disappeared in the jangling swarms.

121

EIGHT

'Not for ten thousand or whatever they're pro'lly gonna ask,' said the girl behind her.

Marla snapped out of it. She had been gazing at the horizon of the sea. It was too hot to be lying on the beach. Besides, she didn't care for the incessant pleas for her patronage. She had been tempted to accept a pedicure, but did not want to play the part of the white lady who was there to be waited on and served, all her pleasure anticipated—so she would hand over some of the money everyone now needs. Her pampered toenails were a sign or a symbol of a system she appeared to control, a system that now controlled everyone. Fuck that. After she refreshed herself in the tepid, flat surf she left the beach.

The Green Sea Café and Bungalows was perfectly situated, beachside. She took a room there for one night and then sat at the café on the edge of the sand. The two Australians behind her had sloped in off the beach in their skimpy wet swimsuits and had lain themselves out around a nearby table. Their aggressive remarks had been directed towards a youth who had come in later, trying to sell the newspapers and magazines he carried under his arm. He had stopped at the table, apparently wondering if the couple discussing something he held intended to buy something from him or not. They themselves didn't seem to know.

'Whatd'ya reckon it's worth?' The aggrieved voice of the girl. Marla sat sideways on her seat so she could look at them.

'How much is *The Australian*?' demanded the young man with her. The newspaper seller glanced down to see which one he was being asked about. 'One thousand,' he replied.

'What's the *real* price?' the man sniggered with considerable hostility.

The boy did not answer; he did not understand the question; he only hesitated, still unsure if there was going to be a sale.

'No, thanks.' The Australian waved him away. No thanks; he meant he was not going to be inveigled into the purchase of a newspaper whose 'real' price was maliciously being concealed from him.

A thousand rupiah was sixty cents, thought Marla; the cover price on the paper is fifty cents. Imagine the chain which brings you *The Australian* or *The Sydney Morning Herald* all those thousands of miles. A guy off the aeroplane sells it to someone at the airport who sells it to the beach guy. If the first guy doesn't pay for it they all make twenty cents. Or it would be a diminishing scale of profit, and the guy at the bottom also gets to deal with westerners and their idea that bargaining is about a 'real' price; that the game is for one person to conceal the real price and for the other person to guess it. The idea they have that it's a competition. Even a duel. The idea that someone wins. If they guess at, or below, the real price, with enough conviction, they have 'won'. If the seller convinces them the real price is higher and they agree to pay it, they have lost.

'Rip-off merchants,' the couple agreed. The bewildered seller shuffled away. Marla was glad he hadn't approached her. She was horrified to think that the world where you could buy that day's Sydney newspaper—and many morning editions were read in the afternoons—could be so close so easily so fast. Close this close to the airport: usually she didn't even get a chance to glimpse that day's Sydney newspaper let alone be asked to buy it. If she had wanted it, she'd have paid the asking price.

Of course, every culture has its share of fixed prices. And its different share of movable prices. Marla was quite getting into the whole thing of bargaining which seemed so right for here. Here, bargaining is about communication, and to draw the procedure out is a delight. Not that she wanted to have to do it in the western world.

The price is the price is the price. The price you agree on

is the price of the thing, what could be more real? If you have agreed to it, it is the price you have agreed to. How then can you go home and complain you were 'ripped off'? If someone else paid less, it was because she agreed to a lower price, and at that moment that was the price of the object she obtained. It is not the same object, however similar, and was not purchased at the same moment as yours. They don't tell you this in *The Sydney Morning Herald*.

Quite involved in such thoughts, it took Marla a moment to realise this guy was coming towards her, and knew who she was, and now she recognised him too. 'Tim!' she said as he said, 'Marla?'

'God,' they said, 'what are you doing here!' And they laughed a bit, recognising that their shared memories were flashing around each of their minds.

She knew Tim from the days when there was practically every kind of weekend workshop. At least, *certain* personal growth seminars but definitely not certain other ones. They had shared a series of advanced courses with this one organisation.

'Whatever it's called now,' said Marla.

'I haven't kept up with all the name changes,' said Tim.

'It was good at the time though.'

'Didn't we have the same rebirther?'

'Your rebirther and I sent you to that Rolfing thing; I'm sorry about that.'

Tim had eventually made a commitment and lived with the guy in Adelaide and got qualified as a primary school teacher. Now he had the career but not the lover.

'I honestly do sometimes wonder,' he confessed with bitter apostasy, 'whether you can have it all.'

Marla laughed a bit, and Tim lightened up and revealed that his annual holidays in Bali were a whole lot like having it all. He kept coming back here, he had been coming since even before he knew Marla, he had first come on a stopover to Europe in seventy-three and had a stopover on the way back in seventy-five and had brought the ex-lover here in eighty-three and now it was just *fine* to come here alone again, just totally fine. Marla obligingly guessed exactly what he meant.

'You mean it's still you guys having all the fun?' she complained. Apparently so. Marla said it was different for her, like only that morning she had had this electrifying eye contact with a barman.

They ordered more juices, and Marla told Tim all about how incredibly cute this barman guy was and all the remarks and hints and regrets they had exchanged.

'Why didn't you?' asked Tim.

'I couldn't have a one-night stand.'

'Stay another night, have a two-night stand.'

'I'm not what he wants. I'm not going to hang around and be a girlfriend. What it is, it's like I can see the whole thing exactly from start to end so there's no point. And don't smirk like that, I know it's different for you.'

Tim told her all about it. The year that Tim had first come he had taken mushrooms on the beach at sunset. The second time he did that was the last time: they're not called blue meanies for nothing; never again. But he returned to Bali over and over, and always to Kuta, or actually Legian now. 'The Australians in Kuta,' he said with a shudder. He didn't mean the likes of himself. He meant Australians who travelled in packs, swilled beer in particular types of bars, dressed in thongs and stubbies and singlets, gross and big-bellied, that kind of Australian, the kind that took over Kuta.

'I heard all about that scene this morning,' said Marla. 'But it's not all like that, is it?'

No. There was Kuta chic, Kuta gay, Kuta sophisticated. Up Legian way and further north. There was the part of the beach where the foreign business-people gather, if they can get away from the fax. Tim saw someone speaking into a cellular phone the other day. Things do change fast. There's a part of the beach that's a bit of a beat. Just guys. Not his scene really, though he has met the odd someone that way. There's the part where the Italians hang out; they get the clothes and the tan in two days and look like they've always lived here. A lot of the sellers on the beach don't say hello and goodbye any more, they say 'ciao bella'. Tim says it too. Some of them say 'Arigato'. Tim goes to the part of the beach where the massage ladies sit together, giggling about the weird western bodies they are paid to stroke with oil, the big dicks, the bared tits. 'Ciao bella' they all call to him and he to them. 'They all say, Tim's back!' Tim told Marla proudly. He felt he had a special place in Bali because the beach massage ladies let him sit with them, and greeted him cheerfully, and he would remind them he wasn't a mere tourist but someone who came here every year and that they knew him and he would have a massage from each of them, one every day, in turn. They teased him. 'Where is your wife?' they would ask. 'Gone,' he always told them, 'gone.' They all sat around screeching about the different sized cocks on the tourist men on the beach. 'Apparently we have a greater variety of sizes than they do,' Tim said.

'This is your part of Bali,' Marla said.

'Some people say it's just like Oxford Street and you could look at it that way, but it's got the beach and massages and shopping and it's all so cheap.'

'Oxford Street,' repeated Marla. 'Huh. I can't tell you how different my life has been since then. The whole eighties thing. Australian yuppie princess, that was me.'

'I know, I saw you that one time. I was a so-called mature age student and you were . . . what was it called?'

'An organisational consultant,' said Marla, saying the words with wonder.

'In your business suit with shoulders out to here. Briefcase, filofax . . .'

'Hard work and serious money.'

'Stockbroker boyfriend.'

'More your highflying entrepreneur. Banks threw money at him, and he forgot he'd have to face the debts. Or face himself. Or me.'

'What happened?'

'October 1987 happened. He'd been doing funny things

with my money. That was the end of the eighties and the end of . . . him.' She couldn't help the grim, troubled tone that came in.

'Well,' said Tim after an awkward pause. 'You look younger now than you did last time.'

'In this punishing sun, yet? Thanks, dear. We're both in good shape, actually. My tits sag.'

'I'm going bald.'

'But you can't tell. In either case. I used to wear things like this so long ago.'

'We're just old hippies basically.'

'Speak for yourself.'

'I was speaking for both of us.'

Marla said, 'I relent. I have been thinking, I feel closer to an earlier me. I didn't know how much I missed her.'

Sunset was approaching. Tim was staying close to the Green Sea, the Pensione Padma. He knew all the places. He went out every night. He would show her round the night-life of Kuta.

'If you don't mind going on the back of my motorbike.'

'*Mind?* I will adore it, warm wind in my hair and all.'

'Sorry but you'll have to wear a helmet. I heard that they made helmets compulsory because Suharto's son owns the helmet factories.'

'Am I glad I ran into you. I want to go to all the good bars. You know all the best ones, I know you do. I want to go to that place you said you danced till sunrise. I want to drink too much and see cute barmen. I never do that, and seeing as I'm staying the night. Are your places totally unconnected to the Aussie yobbo scene? I just heard this most awful thing this morning. I was *dubious* about Kuta and this was the worst.'

She told him how she had gone to interview a guy. These friends of hers had given her his name. She thought she'd interview him for something she was thinking of, well, of writing, don't ask, it's this new and tentative thing, writing. The guy runs this package deal place and the kind of people who went there, well, they had some weird idea of fun. Gone Troppo.

'I've heard of that.'

'It was mid-morning and there were all these guys in an indoor bar, getting pissed and watching videos.'

'Keeps them off the streets.'

'The guy I interviewed was great, though. He was like this tough martial-arts street-wise been-around guy, really nice though, and he's had enough and is leaving, so he told me a lot of stuff. Shit,' said Marla, 'horrible stuff.' He had told her that only last night this young Australian girl had been raped or practically raped but attacked anyway by these yobs that stay at the place, and from what he said they were typical. These same guys had then pissed on the temple.

'They had a *temple* at Gone Troppo?'

'Tim dear, there is a temple everywhere. Look.' She looked around. She got up. She pointed—politely, not using her finger. 'Come here. See that? That is a temple.'

'So you know where the temples are. I know where the boys are.'

In her room that evening, Marla put on a pair of red sequinned slippers she had bought that day, good for dancing. She wanted to dance, and it was good to have a gay guy to dance with. Was that a bad sign? She honestly didn't want to get a boyfriend.

No, she wouldn't be able to hang around and be a girlfriend. Which is what you did for the kind of guys she liked to look at. It's all so obvious: these boys are so pretty and so good at pleasing and they want a white girlfriend—the status, the money, she'll leave—but you think you're the only one and it only happens to you: that's romance. The boys of today who are into white girls are so contrived in their artless grace— the groovy clothes, the charming lilt to their phrases. Anyway, I'm an older woman, I'm set in my ways, I need to be alone sometimes. And it's always, either they're very young or

128

they're married. And sex—they keep telling me these boys aren't really into sex—well, I don't want to do it with anyone who isn't really into it.

'I mean,' said Marla to herself, 'that's the most banal story: went to Bali and had the romance.' Laura would not be going that way, she decided. Or perhaps. That was something to think about. Was there any romance in Laura's life? Why hadn't she thought of that before? Stories *mean* romance to some people. A movie must have a love story. Already Marla was looking forward to going home to Katak Inn and being close to Laura again. She would imagine the different kinds of romance Laura might have and choose one. Ship's captain, French artist, Balinese prince, Hollywood star . . .

Laura's story anyway would not be the cliché, the 'I had my tropical romance' story that's told too often: there's a guy who hangs around; little does she know, but one day he offers to give her a massage . . .

I suppose, she said to herself, even to begin to think of this is a good sign.

The sequins were already spilling off her slippers on to the tile floor. She would dance till her feet were quite desequinned, leaving bright little red dots scattered like a crazy mosaic, like chaos, like drops of blood.

NINE

It was early evening and there were lots of people in the streets of Ubud. Many of the shops were still open, and a lot of the tourists were wandering around, shopping, choosing a place to eat, lining up at the various venues where the nightly dances were held. In the streets you could smell satay being prepared, as the sellers, squatting over the little charcoal flames, turned over the bamboo skewers of goat meat and chicken meat and poured the spicy peanut sauce over them; the smell of satay mingled with the aromas of fish and spices and vegetables from the food stalls now open in the night markets. Kids selling tickets rushed eagerly from one tourist to another. 'See dance, see Ramayana, see Legong, see monkey dance,' they urged, and were waved away. Groups of young men congregated outside the cinema, a rough and ready shed, defined and decorated by garish posters picturing sullen, bare-chested men with gargantuan muscles cradling machine-guns.

Ann Pavlou was doing the job she had come here to do, with all the zeal that had made it possible for her to come here and do it.

Outside the Pagoda restaurant by the lotus pond near the temple in the middle of town, the chic people who would not eat anywhere else were not always pleased to be waylaid, to have her leaflets thrust into their curious hands, their unwilling hands, their suspicious hands, their eager hands. 'Read this,' Ann urged them, 'it's about tourism in Ubud, read this, it's about us, it's about being here, read it, it's really interesting, it'll make you think.'

'I didn't come here to think.'

'What are you selling?'

'They're trying to ban cameras. Aren't you?'

'No, thanks.'

'No, I've got one already.'

'No thanks, I'm not interested.'

'How you going?' Damien asked Ann, wandering up with his own bunch of leaflets under his arm, from the position he had taken further down the road. It was his first night working with the group. 'Not that many people are interested, are they? But as long as you reach someone. You do occasionally reach someone,' he added, having to provide his own comforting assurances, as Ann's eyes were popping at the sight of a tall black guy walking up towards the restaurant. Ann went straight for him.

'Hello! *Selamat malam*!' she said to him. 'I'm Ann and this is my friend Damien. We're just friends.' She thrust one of the leaflets into his hands. 'Where you from?'

'Hi there Ann, Damien,' he said, a polite kind of friendly, slightly wary but apparently not too unwilling to be invited into an exchange of views.

'What's a gorgeous guy like you doing in a place like this? Ha ha, just kidding.'

'What Ann means is . . .'

'What I mean, we're giving out this information, it's important.'

'Any questions, we're here,' Damien offered, a kind of parting shot as he moved away to resume his position at a distance and resume the campaign to capture the hearts and minds of the tribe of visitors.

'So what is this, you selling something?'

'No,' she said, 'not something; you could say we're selling a concept. What we're about is responsible tourism.'

He looked at the paper she had given him. '*Think About This*' in large letters over one page; '*What You Can Do*' headed another; '*Being A Good Visitor*' on the back.

She turned her full attention on him, for a moment neglecting the other people who could benefit from the information she offered them. 'Let me tell you . . . you got a minute?'

'I got a minute I guess. *Mañana*—they must have a word like that here. I'm going in there and eat.'

'Feed your head, that's what it's about,' said Ann, thinking, my affirmations are working, I'm empowered, I've got heaps of practice and tons of conviction. 'I notice you don't carry a camera.'

'Not this time.'

'Which means you experience rather than observe or gaze.'

'I'm not here for experience,' he said, not meaning anything personal she hoped.

'So you are totally in this experience of being here,' she said, talking over him. 'That's what we're all about.'

'You got something against cameras?'

'We want you to think about the whole thing of cameras,' she said urgently, tapping the pile of leaflets, 'the way people travel with cameras, what they do with cameras.'

'They take pictures with cameras.' He shrugged, as she continued, 'People say, we're only taking pictures, but we say, what you're doing, you're distancing yourself, you're carrying not a camera but a sign, right, a sign that your relationship to the experience is one of distancing, exploitation.' As she spoke she could see his unease; he wasn't interested in what she said and wanted to get away, without being rude, but not before he had asked her something; she wondered what. '. . . A new sort of colonialism,' she continued with an intensity that was making him back off, as much as she wanted him to get engaged in her cause and, actually, in her self. Then she was interrupted.

'What you people are doing is wrong,' a woman was saying. 'If you want to get involved in politics stay in Australia. You've got no business interfering with politics here.'

'Hey, can we talk? Don't just go off,' Ann called after the indignant woman. She made a sound of exasperation, and the black guy gave her an amused, sympathetic look. 'I want to tell them, it's not a matter of politics, we are all connected, our behaviour as visitors . . .'

'No argument from me,' he said, holding out his hands to display them camera-less. More out of indifference to her polemics than empathy.

'So you new to Bali? Holiday, business?'

'A mission, I guess,' he answered.

'I can relate! So what's your mission, what did you say your name was?'

'Tyler. I'm looking for a friend. How long have you been in these parts?'

'Not long. I came over to work with this group, we're networked with this group in Sydney, so I knew a whole lot about it all . . . only eight days, but my eight days is someone else's eight months, honestly. Your girlfriend?'

'My old buddy.'

'Is he, er, American too?' Is he black, she meant. He nodded, watching to see if this sparked any recognition in her, but it didn't, and so his question was answered, and he wasn't going to get interested in her, or her cause.

'If you'll excuse me, Ann, I need to eat. Good luck.'

'I'll see you round,' she called after him hopefully. A threesome of Australian girls was taking her leaflets. 'Leave your camera at home,' Ann urged them with a fresh burst of vigour, 'and get to really experience *being* where you are. Why do we take photographs? To prove we've been there? To take something away? To keep foreign people as objects, as *other*, so they're not people, only camera fodder. It's appropriation, not appreciation. We steal souls when we photograph people that way. I'm not talking about happy snaps of your family and friends, posing, say cheese, watch the birdie. You know what I mean,' she said, high on the attention of her audience, proud of the way her voice rang clear with conviction, the way other visitors had joined the throng around her. If that Tyler guy had seen this. But he was probably threatened by strong women. She went on. And people offered her their views too.

'But it's the age of the image, the image is everything, people want the image.'

'That's tourists you're talking about. Travellers . . .'

'Visitors,' said Ann. 'That's the word we use, visitors, we're all just visitors in other people's countries.'

133

'You can't tell people not to take photographs. What's wrong with it?'

'Let me tell you about this time, right, I'm standing here looking at this whole scene going on in the temple, it's a totally spiritual thing, and this guy comes over, holding up his camera and he goes "excuse me".' Ann said the words like a command the way he had. 'He's telling me to get out of his way because he wants to stand where I am so he can get a picture, like, he's got the camera so he's got the right to get everyone to step aside, and me, no camera, only my eyes, "only" right. If he'd been there snapping his camera and I'd come up pointing to my eyes, like, move over I want to stand there to look through my own eyes, would he think he had to move over? You see it everywhere, that camera thing. The dominance of the camera. That's what we're on about. The thing we tell people, think about what the camera is, it's a mask: they hold it in front of their face, they can't be seen through it, they have to look through it, it changes the whole thing of how they present to the world.'

Most people didn't want to know. Some of them listened to her story and a few of them got her point and a couple of them might have agreed with it.

'But we all want our own pictures.'

'If they had better postcards around here.'

'Taking photos is all right as long as you're discreet.'

'We always ask someone if we can take their photo.'

'Take is the word,' Ann tried to interrupt, 'take not make . . .'

'Do you?'

'If we can, we do.'

'You can't change the fact that everyone's got a camera.'

'I love my photos! How can I tell my friends about it without my photos? How can I remember what it was like?'

' "Now all art aspires to the condition of photography." Susan Sontag. We did our final-year project on it. Don't tell me about photography.'

TEN

She wasn't sick. But she wasn't well. There was nothing wrong. But the rightness had gone. The days dragged. She woke for the dawn, but she never went to the markets any more—too far, too difficult. Before, exuberant notes had filled welcoming pages. Now they seemed to be the relics of another life. Now she stared at the blank page, unable to mark it. It stared back at her. What did she have to say?

'Laura?' Marla whispered. Nothing. There was no Laura. Before, for a while, Laura had seemed to exist, able to be known and directed by Marla. Now she did not exist.

Before, Marla had worked every day, in a way that she never thought about, but was the only way she knew. She spent some time alone writing lists of questions, then set out each day to answer any one of them. She went to visit people she heard about; she looked for books; she returned to the art museums and looked again at their paintings; or smoked a kretek or two with any of the attendants there, practising speaking in Indonesian, and encouraging them to tell her about the paintings or the people or anything at all. 'You like to sit, too,' they'd say to her, 'just like Balinese.' The Balinese compliment: you're like us. She wandered wherever she felt moved to go and spoke to other people if she happened to feel like it. And things came her way: information, invitations, inspirations. A picture of Bali, layered in the manner of its famous paintings, layered again with the confusing, contra-dictory things she was told. She didn't need to decide about or judge them yet, she thought, and let the layers shift and merge like layers of waves in the sea. Before, she was led by serendipity or, anyway, it worked for her to think of it like that.

It wasn't like that now. These days, things refused to be found, people refused to be met. She would be on her way and the directions were always wrong. It always took longer to get there than it should. She would get lost. The person she was looking for was not there. Books had disappeared out of the library. The days now seemed to be frittered away and it was stupid to think of days like that.

Marla stared at her schedule. Find the woman who has the book on the trances. Find the guy who had been around in the old days. Go to the temple with the peculiar frieze of carvings.

Before, there was always a someone it was great to meet and spend time with who was also staying at Katak Inn. Before her trip to Kuta, she had enjoyed the company of other people. There had been a nice guy, Michael; they'd gone on a couple of day-long walks—hours tramping through villages, jungles and fields, to distant temples, telling each other the stories of their travels; there had been a nice woman called Beverly and they had gone to see dances and then talked far into the night about the extraordinary changes they had undergone. But those nice people had left, and now there was no one around to play with. Carlo had shut himself away to finish a drawing before he had to leave Bali.

The trip to Kuta had been oddly unsettling. It was fun to run into Tim and rage around the bars for a night but it took some days to recover. She was glad to get back to the gentle ambiance of the sloping, snaking gardens around her riverside bungalow.

But the atmosphere at Katak Inn had become somewhat unsettled, too. There was a lot of cleaning up and preparation. They were trying to get the office into some kind of order. The member of the family who was the heir and the owner was expected soon. He and his Australian wife were to return for a visit. He was their son grandson brother cousin kin employer prince. Marla was invited to dinner on the night he arrived.

Tjokorda Gde was slight and boyish, looking younger than

he was. His eyes were very black, expressing much good humour, confident charm, affability.

'Are you able to come home often?' she asked him politely. 'You must miss it awfully.' Why would anyone live in Australia when they could live here?

Sure he missed his home. That was normal. He remembered that when he was very young and had first seen tourists, he used to wonder how they could travel so freely, whether they did not miss their homes.

But he had come this time not only because he missed his home. He had plans, plans for the development of Katak Inn. 'I want to make a convention centre,' he told her.

'Here? Oh no,' she said.

'Is good! Can make much money.' He talked about all the rooms that could be built on this site, rooms to stay in and rooms for meetings.

'But it's so lovely here as it is!'

'But you pay too little,' he teased her.

'If you built what you say, I would not be able to afford to stay here,' Marla said. She made it sound as if she were humorously exaggerating her regret, but she was truly dismayed.

'Oh, not yet,' he assured her. 'It takes time.' It would take time to make the plans and build the rooms. He seemed to think she was apprehensive of being forced out in a week!

No, not that week. But she had liked to imagine that this would never be different. And nothing was like that, nothing. The only thing you can count on is change. She used to *teach* that stuff: dealing with change, managing change, being a change agent.

'I can build a swimming pool,' the enthusiastic prince continued.

'But the river is just there! And the spring.'

'I want to see the girls in bikinis!' he said mischievously.

Alone and listless again. This horrible energy that had taken hold of her. Regret, disgust, grieving. All her choices that had led to being who she was and how she lived, all were based on delusion and self-deception, that was the only thought she could hold at present; her choices had been made out of pathology not out of wholeness. Her aloneness and her childlessness. And now it was really too late to be otherwise. Ten years ago she had been seduced by Tony Liotta and a philosophy whose basic corruptness was hidden by its surface idealism. Be positive, go for it, create material property as a manifestation of your spiritual power. Everything is better than everything else. The trickle down effect, they hoped for. The piss-on-'em effect is what it really was. What they called personal responsibility was really rationalisation for egotism, for refusal of any basic connectedness. Tony was very smart, no one could deny that, but his smartness had dazzled her and had stopped her inquiring too deeply about his other qualities and his lack of them. And don't blame him, Marla, you bought into it, you went along with all of it. You thought you were smart too, once. Zapping with the Zeitgeist. A year of it all breaking apart, your world, your delusions, your assurances; leaving nothing but a heavy load of sour ashes to drag along to the next year, a year of searching for healing: everything from a shrink you could claim on Medicare to a homeopath who gave you essences of flowers to drop on to your tongue; yoga classes to stretch ancient pains out of your body and Tarot card readers for the thrill of a pattern of pretty pictures telling you that you had lost your lover, your livelihood, your home and your sense of direction on the wrong path for you and that you were thinking of going far away and this was a very good idea.

It might have been a good idea, but she came here and maybe she was meant to keep on going as she had planned. She came here and fell right into another black hole of delusion covered over by pretty promises of a new and meaningful life. She would have to leave here in a few weeks and continue her journey and make a *real* new life and get a job. There would have been work in Amsterdam but it was probably too late now. She was too old to fuck up like this. She and Tony were supposed to have had this mature, non-compulsive relationship. What that meant was they didn't make love too often and used work as a substitute for intimacy. They competed with everyone else who got up early and worked late every day of the week. They had a lifestyle instead of a life; the champagne was always French and everything else matched; and the rest of the money went on high risk investments that Tony took care of. Care was something he knew nothing about. Care was something she thought she should give herself and never ask for. Making love was always going to be better one day, when they had more time. All Marla's so-called strengths—her emotional self-sufficiency and so on—were expressions of her essential fear and distrust. That's what Tony had been mirroring, not an own-your-power ability. Marla thought with sour rancour of her upbringing, for that must have created this pathology. You weren't supposed to blame your parents but she did. They might have done the best they knew how but that had left her deeply and essentially convinced she wasn't good enough. This bitterness was immature and unenlightened but she was damn well wallowing in it and no one was around to stop her. Now she is in this beautiful place, this garden of tropical flowers. What's wrong with this picture? There's no one in it but her, and she can't put anyone else in it. She wants, she so much wants to rearrange the patterns of her life. Let the kaleidoscope turn! If only she could pray, she would pray for protection and guidance, pray to some Divine she barely knows and barely believes in. If only she had some faith. What is faith? The answer, the question, the challenge, the great deceiver. The substance of things hoped for, the evidence of things not seen. She didn't know how to picture her hopes, what she wanted to see. It was delusion to insist on living as she was doing. She really wanted to write this story, she believed in it, she could not leave Laura's story untold. But. But but but. You can cry, you can try to pray.

Carlo didn't want to go to Warung Ibu Suci. Suci was the Jewish mother of Bali, he said, she wanted you to feel guilty if you went anywhere else. 'I'll go wherever you want,' said Marla amiably. Carlo had dressed all in white, and wore bone and shell jewellery, a white turban on his head, a white scarf he pulled across his face. It was clear that he was rather agitated. He had so much he wanted to tell. He didn't know what was going on. In the house in the rice fields. The boys come and sleep with him and then they just disappear. He gives them money and then they don't even say thank you, they don't ask how he is, they don't say *Permisi* when they leave.

He had given Kadek the equivalent of $500 so that he could go to English classes. 'That's one and a half year's wages,' said Carlo, telling her all about it as they walked up the main street. 'If you look at it that way. But it's one deal of grass. Did you have any of that hydroponic grass that was around last year? Wasn't it fabulous? That was $500 for a deal. Look at it that way. I'd much rather pay for Kadek's English lessons. I said to him, all I want, the only thing I want, is to come back here and be able to talk to you.'

You can't always buy what you want, Marla thought.

'Come in here,' said Carlo. It was the Restaurant Tantra. 'They have the best chocolate cake in Bali.' The sort of food you never get in a house in the rice fields.

He ordered the cake and told Marla about going to the village with the boys. 'The men were around the television, playing cards. The women sat apart doing their nits. I went and sat with the women. The men waved at me, like this—' Carlo pantomimed the men: amused, scandalised. He had stayed right there with the women. He went into the kitchen with the women. Earlier, the woman who cooks at their house, after doing all the cooking and then cleaning up, had put a big bucket full of the empty plates and pots on her head to carry it all down to the village. Carlo helped her, and the boys laughed at him. 'Learn something, boys! I told them, you want jeans, you want computers, you want bank accounts and business—well, learn some other values too, respect the women's work, do some women's work.' Carlo had picked up the bucket and put it on his head. 'Oh, Bali style!' they all said. 'Yes Bali style,' he had told them, '*And* India style *and* Africa style *and* South America style!' He complained to Marla, 'They don't think of other parts of the world.'

They're peasant boys, Marla thought, what can you expect? 'It's normal,' she said.

Carlo went on. He had spent a lot of money buying piles of towels for 'all the Ibus in the village'. But when he went there he didn't see a single one of his bright new towels in use.

'They might be keeping them for special occasions,' Marla suggested.

'When I come back here,' Carlo said, 'no one gets *nothing*. I'll see who my friends really are. I'll go and live in the village. I won't have the kind of money I've got now. I'm going to live on twenty dollars a week.'

'You won't be able to come here and have chocolate cake.'

'I don't *need* it. I can live like they do. I've learnt so much about myself. This is an *a*-mazing place for learning about yourself, have you found that? Isn't it though? I found that the very first time I came here.'

The first time he came here, he had to face his fear of death. He thought he might have AIDS. 'I haven't fucked anyone and no one has fucked me,' he said, 'for nine years. But it can take fifteen years to develop.'

'Fifteen!'

'It can take fifteen years.'

'Shit.'

'And I thought, what about it? I'm not going to go and get a test. For some doctor,' he said the word with contempt, 'to point the bone. I really thought about it. Does anyone know how long they're going to live?' With that question, apparently, his fear of death, of AIDS and of uncertainty had been conquered.

'Doctors really are . . .' Marla began, but Edie was suddenly there at their table. She was a tall, highly charged

141

American woman. She ignored Marla, sat on the other side of Carlo and started ranting at him. Her precious beautiful house in the rice fields, the *best* house, the one with the . . .

'You've seen that house, Marla.'

'I've seen it! That beautiful house.' Marla had seen it on the way to Carlo's. He had told her this mad rich American Edie lived there.

'You've seen my house,' Edie ranted, momentarily acknowledging Marla. 'I have rented that house for four months of the year, occasionally longer, year after year, for . . . oh . . . *years*. And he comes to me, he actually says to me, that he is going to put the rent up. Because he was offered a higher rent by that German couple. Lola put them up to it, they wanted my house. I wonder what Lola got? Do you know how much they offered him! Just guess how much they offered him!'

They couldn't guess so she told them.

'God,' said Marla, 'you can get a flat in Sydney for that, a nice one.'

'A new flat with a harbour view,' said Carlo.

'It's a very nice house,' said Edie. 'It is a great house. But I do not pay anything like that now, not even nearly, believe me. I said to him, once upon a time in Bali you people did not all have this greed for money and it was a much better place. If he rents it to those Germans they're going to find they have trouble with Immigrasi!'

'I've never heard anything so heavy,' said Carlo when Edie had left. 'Trouble with Immigrasi. That was a threat. I can't believe she said that. She was obviously very upset. You would be. But that was too heavy. I'm really sorry. I don't actually know her that well, I only met her with Cherry.'

They were back on the street. 'I'm going to go jalan-jalaning home,' said Carlo. 'Sometimes I think it is really all going to disappear,' he said. 'When the old people go. It's like with the Aborigines. When the old men go, there will be no more aboriginality.'

'Oh Carlo,' Marla sighed, 'it's meant to be paradise here.'

'It is,' he said. 'It still is. But it's a paradise on earth.'

'Tainted by earth.'

'And I know it's me. It's me keeping myself sort of on the outside.'

'The edge of paradise.'

Marla didn't want any dinner that night, she didn't want to go anywhere. She sat on the verandah and looked at the darkness. The river lulled her senses, and for a moment she felt again its peacefulness.

She surrendered. She had been trying to force her work and it was the kind of work that couldn't be forced. She surrendered. She had been trying to direct the story before she knew enough about the characters. She surrendered. She had been trying to exert too much control altogether.

Laura refused to have romance invented for her. Laura refused to be known. Laura would not have experiences forced on her.

All right, Laura, said Marla, I give up.

I am not you, Marla, Laura said. I am myself. You are referring to yourself to know me and that is why you don't know me. If you listen to me I will speak to you. If you watch me I will show you what happens to me. If you can empty your mind you can know my thoughts. You can see me in your dreams or dream my dreams. Laura said, take me away from here. Let's go away.

Marla was sweeping her verandah when Tjokorda Gde came up the stone steps that reached her bungalow.

'*Selamat pagi*,' she called.

'You can ask someone to sweep for you,' he said.

'I like sweeping,' she said. Earlier that morning an arrogant American academic had come over to try and get to know her, which in her bad mood wasn't too sensitive of him anyway and then he had walked all over her verandah in his dirty shoes and had even put his feet on the table. '*Saya suka menyapu.* Is that right?' Her Indonesian was uncertain.

Tjok Gde laughed and came over and, stepping out of his shoes to step onto her verandah, said, 'Do I disturb you?'

'No! Please! *Silakhan duduk.* Do you want a drink? I'll get you a glass, and open the other bottle, I've been drinking out of this one.' She felt like talking to him.

'So polite!' he said. 'Just like Balinese. How you know these things?'

'Are you inspecting your land?' she asked him. 'Dreaming of high-rise hotels?'

He laughed. 'You happy here? Already staying a long time.'

'Very happy here. Happy, but . . . lately, feeling not so happy.'

'Lately not so happy,' he repeated thoughtfully. 'Have you seen the rest of Bali?'

'I've been on various day trips—Besakih and all that. I'm going on a two-week trip around Bali in ten days.'

'Why ten days? Why not now?'

She stared at him, lights flashing in her head. For the first time in days, she laughed. 'I made this schedule, this timetable, a plan. I planned it.' They both laughed, as if this were the best joke. 'What is this plan? I made it, I can unmake it, right?' Tears came to her eyes and not only from laughing. 'I had this idea I had to stick to my plan.'

'In Bali,' he said, 'we don't have so many plans. More important to feel when the time is right. When I am back in Bali, I am Balinese again. My painting cannot be planned. When it is right, I paint. I paint all day and all night. My wife brings me food and drink and places it by my side and I don't see it. When I stop painting, I eat and I sleep. And maybe no painting again. Inspiration, isn't it?'

'Inspiration,' Marla repeated. 'What is the word?'

'*Ilham.*'

'*Ilham.* Inspiration. This is inspiring. I'm going to pack, and go. But I will come back. You won't be here. I hope I can come back to this bungalow.'

'Of course you can,' he said and she believed him.

Eleven

She woke into a dream and woke into a dream and woke into a dream. Dream after dream opened, doors in a long long corridor, opening, opening. She was on a bed in Bali and woke to find herself on a bed in Bali and woke to find herself on a bed in Bali, in a dream. But the dream was not of lying in bed asleep, dreaming of love, but of love sending her into a dream. It was love: tender, romantic, exciting, soothing. Love of another, loved by another. She was gliding through bright green fields, perhaps on the back of a motorbike, holding fast to the waist of someone who completed a circuit of love. She was warm and wet, she was melting and flowing, it was love as it should be, love as it is dreamed of. The beloved lover was there, was more there than she was there, loved her and knew her and dreamed her too. That is what the dream was, and yet the dream was that she only dreamed of this.

TWELVE

The pools of Tirta Gangga lay below. Holy water of the Ganges. The old palace was in ruins but its pools had been maintained, and you could visit them or even swim there. Marla preferred to stay right where she was, high above, up the hill and up a hundred steep steps. The lovely new bungalows were set in a row, a glorious dress circle over some of the most staggering panoramic views this earth provides. The pools of Tirta Gangga. Brilliant terraced rice fields fanning out, extending for miles and miles. The sea and the island of Lombok clearly visible to the east. The waters in the paddy reflecting the colours of sunrise and sunset, both of which she could behold from her bed, her private verandah or the dining pavilion. She could be alone, peacefully alone, or she could go over and hang out with the other guests or the family. The boys of the family, anyway. The girls stayed in the kitchen out the back. They did not want her coming in there and they did not want to go out. 'How you like panorama?' the boys asked her whenever she appeared. 'Good panorama?'

'Great panorama,' she complimented them. 'Can I get a drink?'

'Why the hell not?' they sang. The hill was so steep they had only to reach over and pluck from the tree tops the young coconuts she loved.

Days passed and she lazed about, painting her toenails, reading novels she swapped with whoever came by, contemplating the panorama. She observed sunrise from her bed and allowed herself to drift back into sleep, not quite sleep, and not awake, but the edge of asleep, the edge of awake, her eyelids sometimes fluttering open to add the gorgeous sights before her to the drift of images patterning her memories and fantasies.

'Never been called mate so many times in my life.' That was Mac, a softly spoken blond boy from Santa Barbara, telling Marla about his first hour in Bali, at Kuta. Mac was alone too and they talked all through one dinner and met again for breakfast.

'When I first heard about Bali, what I heard about was the surf. I wanted to come to this part of the world for the surf. I started reading all about it and planning the trip. I started in Irian Jaya. I went to Komodo.' Both were marvellous places full of rare experiences. Mac told her about some of them. 'By the time I got to Kuta, there was the surf, but I took one look around and left in an hour.' He went up to Ubud and found a room for a night in the Monkey Forest Road. There was a sign outside that said 'Rooms, Breakfast, Sunset'. 'I liked that: they offered you sunset too. It was real nice: sunset over the rice fields, tea in a thermos left early in the mornings, breakfast as soon as you appeared, real nice people.' Then he came here and now he was going to race through the rest of Indonesia, figuring he'd seen the best, and he could meet a friend in Bangkok in a week.

'We loved Kuta,' announced a Canadian couple who swapped some books with her. They got Somerset Maugham's *Borneo Stories* and she got a Tom Robbins. 'The docket is still in that one,' they said. 'If you take it back to the bookshop in Kuta you'll get half its price back.'

'I'll probably be swapping it for something else right here.'

'Kuta is great. Bookshops. Cappuccino. We'd been doing some rough travelling so Kuta was like our real holiday. We stayed much longer than we expected to.'

'We walked from Kuta to Tanah Lot,' boasted a couple of hard-core trekkers, tight-muscled Aussies with peeling faces and well-organised backpacks. 'We bicycled to Singaraja. We're climbing Mount Agung in the morning.'

'Be careful,' warned another backpacker. He had run up the hundred steps to check the view but was staying at a much cheaper place below. He was very scornful of anyone who spent more than five dollars a day in Bali. He tried to haggle

147

with Wayan over the price of a glass of tea. Marla caught Wayan's expression and laughed. The guy said that people got led into the volcano by guides who then demanded more money to lead them out.

'No guide,' said the trekkers scornfully.

'Yeah well watch out,' said the cheap guy, aggrieved. 'Some bloke never came back out of there. You know what they're like.'

They were on the lower slopes of the holy mountain of Bali, whose volcanic depths were rumoured to be ready for another ignition, another explosion, about to explode and devastate the land; it was the wrath of Kali, punishment for the lessening of devotion and dutifulness. In the meantime the mountain lured groups of trekkers and climbers. Marla had heard that before somewhere, that some people never returned, they disappeared.

Maybe they only fell asleep. You could sleep forever on this moutainside. People don't disappear from themselves, do they? Disappear is relative, isn't it? The disappeared are gone from someone to somewhere. Or maybe they really do disappear. Marla felt that she had disappeared. She had sent only postcards. She hadn't done anything about the bag of clothes in Europe. She hadn't been working on her options.

'Good meditation?' the boys said when they came by, tending the garden or sweeping the paths. 'Good place for meditation?' It was so amusing, which words they had learnt. Panorama. Meditation. Why the hell not.

The boys—there were four of them and as far as she could tell they were brothers—though such things were never clear, here—helped her with her Indonesian. After dinner they sat with her so that she could help them with English. Wayan showed her the textbooks he was given at school.

All basket can be filled only the basket of knowledge never full when it allways filled up

The timit man his death is again and before his last death

Success with study no because cleverness but get from hard desire

Every page in the book was filled with this kind of thing.

'You have to learn English from *this*?' she asked, incredulous.

'Book from school,' he confirmed. 'Not good book?'

Not good? She couldn't begin to tell him how not good it was. This was their school textbook? Could there be schoolchildren all over Indonesia being told their future depended on their being able to master English, and then being handed books like this? Who the hell was responsible for this? Whoever got the job to produce this book shouldn't have. They had maybe translated Indonesian idioms word-by-word with a dictionary, not too carefully, not too good a dictionary, knowing little or no English. 'I'm sorry, Wayan,' she said, 'it is not a very good book. The way we talk English is not the way this book is written.' She repeated that in Indonesian.

'Please,' asked Wayan, 'what means this?' He pointed to the first line on the page.

'Wayan,' she said, 'if you want to learn English, do this: talk to people, listen to them, write down things you want to remember. This book will not help you.'

'*Pusing*,' said the older son another night, shaking his head with a doleful expression.

'Why are you confused?' Marla asked.

'Please,' he asked, 'what means this?' He showed her a letter from Germany, written in English. The girl explained that she was sorry she had taken so long to write but she had been very busy looking for an apartment. She found an apartment and then she was very busy looking for a job. She found a job so she has very little time. She doesn't know when she can come back to him. She misses him but it is so far away, so expensive to get to. 'I wish you blessings,' she concluded, 'for new experiences, new realities.' Marla didn't feel quite

149

right about reading this sort of letter. 'What means?' Gde asked. 'This my girlfriend.'

'Your girlfriend doesn't know when she can come back. Maybe a very long time.'

'*Pusing*,' he said again.

He did indeed look confused, as if he were having a hard time getting the hang of any new realities yet. He showed her the letter he had begun to her: 'It is nearly three month I am not see you. I am want see you. I am wait for you in September or October.' He watched Marla read it. '*Lama*,' he said.

'*Lama*,' she agreed. 'A long time. Maybe you will meet someone else before then.'

'Maybe I already meet,' he said, putting a certain kind of look on his face.

'Oh don't flirt with me, Gde,' she said crossly, in her most spinsterish manner. 'Don't practise on me, I'm too old for that.'

Ktut would read through his little dictionary, looking for words to try. It was only an English to Indonesian dictionary, and many common words did not appear in it. 'Plucky?' asked Ktut, looking up his book. 'I am plucky. Can say?'

'It's not usual,' said Marla uncertainly, '*Kata yang tidak biasa. Kata tua, Ingerris*. It's a strange, old English word.'

'Brave?'

'Yes, brave, you can say brave.'

'I am brave.'

'*Bisa. Bisa.*'

'You have plan? Can say like that? Have you plan today?'

'Yes, you can say that.'

'Do you have plan?'

'Yes. Have you a plan for today? Do you have any plans for today? Any plans?'

Ktut took her on his motorbike to a nearby secluded bay, a tiny, perfect arc of a bay, fringed by palm trees, with clear clear water. A myriad tropical fish in astonishing colours darted among marvellous coral reefs. Ktut had brought some snorkelling gear. There was no one else around. It was glorious.

When they got back, she wanted to give Ktut a couple of thousand. He didn't want to take it. She pushed it into his hand. 'Use it for petrol, for your motorbike,' she said. He seemed embarrassed and she hated to embarrass him.

She spent a couple of days going out alone to tour the district's markets and monuments. That involved dutifully entertaining crowded bemos over and over by telling them in Indonesian about the price of bananas in Australia and the many women who chose not to marry.

Suddenly that was no fun at all. She didn't want to do it one more time, she had a bad case of pre-menstrual tension coming on, she thought, as she left the last bemo at Ujung, the ruins of an old seaside palace. The inevitable boy appeared. I want to be quiet here, Marla explained as he walked along beside her. The boy however kept up his chattering and questioning. Marla stopped. It was hot. It was one pm. She was tired. Shut up and go away she wanted to yell at him. She did not yell. She explained slowly and carefully in Indonesian: I do not want to talk, I do not want to hear talking, I want to be quiet, to feel the peace, to hear only the wind. He understood, and walked silently along beside her. She sat herself on a stone ledge on the side of a mossy pool among the ruins. She became very still and heard only the wind and the sea. When she got up, the boy had gone, but he rejoined her as she approached the entrance gate, and accompanied her to the nearby beach. A line of fishing prau was drawn up on the black sand of the pretty little bay. Such stillness. No one about in the heat. 'Om swastiastu,' Marla sang. The boy chanted some other Sanskrit mantras and she copied them. Much better than the usual conversation. They chanted. She paddled her feet in the water, splashed around a bit, got her skirt wet, sat by the water a little while. Tiny patches of *paddies* were cultivated even on the small space between the beach and the road. The boy said she could go back to town by motorscooter for 200, same price as the bemo.

As they approached the gate a man on a motorbike drove out, stopped and handed her a helmet. She hopped on behind him and enjoyed the ride into town. She gave him 400 and the next adventure was going to try on underwear in a shop for women.

It was a hot, dark, stuffy little room looking on to a carpark and a busy road. She stayed right in the centre of the town of Singaraja. Tourists usually stayed at the beaches stretching along the north coast on either side of the old port. It was here, then called Buleleng, where Laura first saw Bali. No cars, no billboards, no electric lights. But a lot of things would have been the same.

Why couldn't Marla just go to the beach like everyone else? It was as if she had to ritualise her journey in order to achieve knowledge and prescience; as if she could not have done a thing unless it was part of the realisation of a previously conceived project. That's the kind of tourist she had turned out to be.

There was an old library and it might have some clues to the scholars Laura had met, cultural discoveries she might have made. It took longer than planned to find the place. A courteous gentleman showed her the books held there that were in English. There were studies of the contents of old lontars, the palm-leaf manuscripts that held all the written knowledge. Very few people were able to read them.

There was only one hour to closing, he informed her. Today they closed at eleven am. Open again tomorrow.

The man left Marla to look through the books. Bother their hours, she thought. Fancy closing just after I get here. What will I do? Is it worth staying another day so I can come back tomorrow? Will these books help me at all?

When the man returned, she asked him about the lontars, and he told her about some of the scholars who came and worked with them. There was still important new work being done, he told her, there were still old lontars with ancient texts in old Javanese. Most of that work was done around here.

But some of it was done elsewhere. And now if she would be so kind as to excuse him, he had to close up the library.

Elsewhere like where? she asked him.

Some Europan scholars came not only here but to a village quite a long way away, he told her. But most of them came here. Here was his card. She was welcome to come and talk to him tomorrow.

Marla was left to wander in confusion out into the heat. The streets of Singaraja were wide avenues. It was a town different from any other part of Bali. She remembered where she had heard of the village before, the one the courteous library man told her about. It was the place Cherry had marked on her map when Marla had said she wanted to see a genuine trance dance. It was quite a long walk back to the port. She would have some lunch at the first place she thought looked all right.

THIRTEEN

A large black rock, a jagged black spire, rises out of the sea, lashed by waves. It is a solitary cliff. The waters swirl and darken around it. It is a formal composition, a large dark carving of rock.

She wakes from this dream, cold, feeling so awfully cold. She has period pain, that cold, cramping pain, that dragging inside her abdomen and thighs. She might have been able to lie still, to sleep again, if it were either the cold or the pain. But both. She switches on the lamp, and pulls on the rest of her light, tropical clothes. Now she is layered in her entire temporary wardrobe. She lies back with her knees bent, the soles of her feet pressed together: the *supta-badakonasana* position she had learned in yoga: good for period pain.

Not every menstruation is this bad. The last one was trouble free. Sometimes it comes like this, with the pain. Like the first menstruation in Bali, but at least she was warm, and rested, and Agung Madé sent her grandmother to give her a massage, and she drank *kopi arak* at Ibu Suci. It wasn't always this bad. Only sometimes. Only now. It would be. She was unprepared.

She should have known it would be this cold by the side of the lake, someone might have told her had she asked. Up on the hill, earlier that day, after she had checked in at this lakeside resort, she had gone for a walk and discovered some very chic bungalows that actually had hot running water and bathtubs! She planned to go there the next day; it was an extravagance but it would be worth it. She would move up there after she had gone out on the lake with that dear little boy she had met, Sam. In the day it would be warm again and please please she won't be in such pain.

She turns off the light again, and attempts to concentrate on conscious breathing, sending sensations of soothing warmth to her poor cold ripping abdomen. There is absolutely nothing else she can do. She should include a hot-water bottle among her travel necessities. Maybe not. Period pain pills? Definitely. The strongest kind. *I promise, I promise.* She'll never be without them again. Hasn't she promised this before? Haven't there been other such ghastly nights, cold, remote, helpless, her blood scraped from her womb by sharp, ice-hard knives. Breathe. In. Slowly. Hold. Out. Slower. Warmth. Slowly in, hold. Sink, sleep.

Waves foam and swirl around the cluster of black rocks rising out of the sea.

FOURTEEN

This was the place to be! Was it ever!

Marla woke yesterday morning and gave into an unreasonable impulse that made her feel even more unwell after an almost sleepless night, pain and cold.

She forsook the bungalow high up on the hill by the lake, with its private bath and hot water. She woke and thought, there's probably no plug for the bath. Also, even if she could have a hot bath, she'd end up sulking because she hadn't brought her silk pyjamas. And she'd still have to keep warm by wearing all her layers of clothes—clothes that weren't made to be all worn at once let alone slept in.

She rose early and packed her bag before meeting Sam at six-thirty, as arranged, for the boat tour of the lake.

It was sweetly tedious, hour after hour, being rowed around its lovely shores. Shores where a dense jungle grew on a steep bank. They stopped to look inside some scarily dark caves that had been occupied in the time of the Japanese. Shores from which rice paddies stretched and farmers walked behind their cows pulling ploughs. '*Seratus tahun yang lalu*,' Marla was moved to remark, a hundred years ago, a thousand years ago, this might have looked the same. Sam was quite unimpressed by this conceit. Of course, farmers now wear shirts over their *kain* and other anachronisms might be found. How we love to imagine changelessness! They rowed past the shores where people came to bathe and to wash their clothes. Marla sat in *badakonasana* on the narrow plank, trying to ignore the subsiding but persistent pain in her belly, and concentrated on what she saw.

As he rowed, little Sam asked her about India, and the Ganges. He had heard it was a very holy river, was that true? What did she know about it? It is the most holy river of India, she told him, and many people go to it to bathe. I want to go there! he said, and he said it as if this were a precious wish he had long held. 'I want to go there,' he said surprisingly, 'and wash away sin.' 'Sin!' she said and looked around the clear lake, everything fresh and soft and perfect. Here? There could not be any sin here. Whatever did the boy mean?

They got out of the boat again at a lovely water temple with a curious Buddhist stupa nearby, and drank coffee at a warung. There were also a number of tourist restaurants there, which might these days betoken greed, competitiveness and covetousness and might represent the sin Sam mentioned, if he had meant anything at all.

Back at the hotel, Marla wanted to lie down again, sleep away the rest of the day. But the night would be cold. Her bags were packed, her room vacated. She paid her bill and carried her bags up to the road. Now she had to go somewhere. Somewhere hot, somewhere she would not need any hot bath, plug, pills. She knew where. It was marked on her map.

The rain began as she left the lake. The journey involved several changes of bemo. In one town she sat waiting, waiting, waiting, while the bemo filled up. It was as full as could be and it sat and waited longer. She felt so ill, so wretched. The bemo was stuffed full but the window had to be kept shut against the pouring rain, so the inside was packed tight; stuffy, hot, damp, smelly. She already had a headache, which grew steadily worse. She had the strangest feeling about her sudden journey—all that planning she had suddenly abandoned, setting off in quite another direction for no reason. Obviously, having her period had caused her to follow some irrational and self-destructive impulse. It was her chemicals, those hormones, to blame. Perhaps it was the start of an early menopause and she was about to become seriously deranged. She only wanted to reach somewhere she could rest, recover and rectify. She didn't want to talk to anyone but had to ask directions, and that meant a lot of talk. It had been the hottest part of the day for a long time.

Hours later, the final bemo deposited her at the gates of the main palace. In the teeming rain she walked into a large grassy area enclosed by high stone fences. A long pavilion down one side had been newly decorated with palm-leaf banners, and a man was sitting there. He hurried across to her, took her bag and led her through a maze of pavilions and courtyards.

Then she was in a courtyard with flowering trees and birds in cages. A beautiful plump older woman appeared. Her polite smile became relieved and welcoming when Marla spoke to her in Indonesian. Marla hardly needed to ask or to tell a thing, it was clear that she had come to stay a while. The woman showed her straight to the room she was to occupy. Tonight, she told Marla, a few hours from now, there was to be a special night for some guests who will come. There will be dances, the Cholonorang, the famous trance dance.

'That's fantastic,' said Marla. '*Nasib baik.*' How lucky I am. The woman smiled, and went to order some tea.

Marla felt welcome. She felt she had arrived at her destination. She felt she was exactly where she should be.

She sat on the verandah of her new room and drank her tea, looking at the courtyard with its various separate free-standing rooms, the flowering trees and the birds. Now I want, she said, to have a bath, and to eat, and to rest.

How easy it had become to know exactly what she wanted, to ask for it and to know it was hers.

No water had ever been sweeter than that she poured over herself in plethorific ladles in the spacious bathroom. Her aches and weakness and disturbance were washed away, and then she was as clean and fresh and relaxed as she had ever felt. The rain had stopped. She was led to the dining pavilion, and several dishes—rice, of course, and other delicious things—had been placed on the table. She felt as if she had entered a fairy-tale world, where genies appear and make your every wish come true.

She wanted to sleep for a while, and lay down on the comfortable big bed in her new room. She sank into a state of deep relaxation. She experienced sensations so strange she would have believed she was dreaming but she knew she was not asleep. She got up, washed again, and sat on the verandah.

In Bali, only sit on the verandah in front of your room and somebody comes to you, usually bearing whatever you most desire or need.

Marla stood as an elderly man approached her, dressed in a kain and neat shirt, very thin, very erect. Her host.

He sat with her and accepted some tea. They made polite conversation. He spoke excellent English: heavily accented, slow, plain, archaic, but with precision and to great effect. He had a round face and high pointed cheekbones over hollow cheeks, big pointed stick-out ears, an expression of infinite humour, tolerance, curiosity, wisdom. He looked, she thought, the very figure of an oriental sage. Whenever she recalled this moment she would fancy she recognised him immediately as someone she loved and esteemed dearly.

She had been brought to the smaller of two adjoining palaces. The Head Prince in the main palace was his brother, her host explained, in fact a younger brother but of higher rank. The Head Prince had five wives and twenty-nine children. 'And the wives,' her sage said firmly as if pre-empting the inevitable question, 'live together in harmony.' Marla nodded. She wasn't going to argue. Why should she assume the wives would not?

'And may I ask,' he continued in his own good time, 'what has brought you here?'

'It is difficult to say. If I may say so, I came here to find that out myself! I only heard the name of this place, and when I heard it again, I felt that if I came here for a while I could learn something. Already I am taken with this atmosphere and I feel it is where I should be.' It was a strange speech, as if someone else were talking. He listened, punctuating her pauses with 'Nah, nah, nah,' as he nodded vigorously. This expression was his own way of saying I see, go on, I understand.

Encouraged, she went on. 'I have stayed in Bali longer than I planned to. But I don't know why.'

'Listen to these two words,' he said, 'and engrave them in

your mind. *Sakala* and *Niskala*. The visible world and the invisible world.' Each, he said, was important, each equally important. Each, she should understand, of equal status to the Balinese. Each vital to the existence of the other.

'That is why I am here?' she asked.

'Instinct,' he replied. Instinct. One word in English that from his mouth carried vast import.

'How should I address you?' she asked him. He told her she should call him Ratu Aji. It was a term of respect to a married man of high caste. His wife, the beautiful plump woman she had met earlier, was to be called Ratu Biang.

'Are you the first child of your mother?'

'Yes, I am.'

'Then I will call you Wayan. So, Wayan, now it is time to prepare for Puri Night.' Puri Night—an odd hybrid expression. Palace Night for visitors.

Ratu Biang came over to the room and helped Marla to dress. Marla imagined the older woman was pleased to see she had her sarong, kebaya and selendang with her. She helped her to make the folds of the sarong neat and exact.

Marla had forgotten she had her period and she forgot she had a headache and she forgot it had been raining.

FIFTEEN

It is an hour after sunset. In the large outer courtyard of the main palace lanterns have been placed around, creating soft lights and long shadows.

'*Tamu datang*!' announces Ratu Aji over his megaphone. The guests are arriving. A large coach is stopping outside the main gates.

The group of tourists alights. Japanese. They are led through the gates from the road into the courtyard, and look around, cameras at the ready. Click-flash-whirr: they begin snapping at once. Snaps of the arrival.

Along one side, to their right, chairs have been placed on the long pavilion with the palm-leaf banners. Here the tourists are led at once, to be seated in tightly packed rows.

Behind them, on spare chairs with a great deal more space around them, Marla sits with Ratu Biang and some of the other ladies of the palace.

Over on the other side people from the village are gathering behind the gamelan orchestra. The music began when the arrival of the bus was announced, its lively chimes brightening the balmy night. The fast-swelling moon floats low in a gauzy aureole. The sky is clear; all traces of rain clouds have disappeared.

The wife—*a* wife—of the Head Prince sits next to her, a petite bird-like woman. Marla thinks she is not the first wife nor the fifth but in between. She holds Marla's hand, and tells her, in English, that she listens to the news on the BBC at 6 am every day. 'I learn English from the BBC,' she says. 'Never too old to learn!' She's said that before. 'English saying, isn't it? I don't speak English well.'

'You speak it very well!' The wife does something with her eyes, flutters them and squints with them at once, an indication of a gracious acceptance of compliments due to her.

'What a beautiful night!' says Marla, and repeats it in Indonesian. A beautiful night. So warm. The sweet air. And the moon almost full, and look how lovely it is.

Yes, yes, the wife nods, looking very pleased, with that fluttery squint, as if it's herself she's pleased with, for having provided such a night and for being complimented on it. Then she nudges Marla so that she will notice that the first dancers have appeared. The gong rings loud and clear.

To their right, opposite the gates to the road, are high stone steps flanked by the stone *candi*—the elaborately carved divided gateway which leads to the palace compound.

At the top of the steps, young girls have appeared, gold cloth costumes, legong-style, wound tightly round their slender bodies. They perform the 'welcome dance'—fluttering about prettily with their fans, arching their startlingly flexible fingers, in this pastiche legong, a tourist-pleasing contrivance, and at the final flourish, a shower of petals is scattered over the group by the smiling golden dancers. The group evidently understands that this scented strew is the finale to the evening's overture, and rises.

Marla follows the group on The Tour, and her hands are held either side by the ladies of the palace, so pretty and refined, arrayed in their neat and lovely costumes, their sleek dark hair coiled and ornamented. She wants to stay here forever! She hangs around the back whispering with them. The group's cameras click-flash-whirr. Ratu Aji in Indonesian and the interpreter in Japanese explain that the temple has many pavilions—this one for tooth-filing, this one for marriage, this one for the dead; and in the local manner porcelain plates have been imbedded into stone columns. The meaning? One asks. 'For decorative purpose only, no meaning,' replies Ratu Aji gravely.

She follows through the maze of courtyards to the festively decorated dining pavilions. Platters of many different kinds of food are borne to the centre pavilion. The guests file past; their plates are heaped with food by a bevy, a flock, an exaltation, of women gorgeously arrayed, and then they sit in their set rows at tables on the platforms around. Marla is told to sit at one side with Ratu Aji. As they eat he tells her that tonight she will see the famous Tettetkan, and to pay attention, and later he will tell her about it.

A small gamelan plays some sedate pieces. Dinner music. And when the group has been given enough time to eat and none to linger, it is ushered out again, back to the outer courtyard.

Many more village people have gathered at the eastern side. The lanterns flicker. Unlike electric lights which obliterate darkness, these lanterns frame the darkness, draw attention to its shadows, its mysteries, its sheltering of Niskala the invisible world. It is lighting which accentuates the darkness of the night, which creates an atmosphere of intense theatrical anticipation.

The gamelan rings out, pacy, lively. They are different dancers now: lively, pretty girls who sweep down the steps in a wild rhythmic waving of fans and swaying of hips. Their movements are more lascivious than those seen in the usual dances, the rhythms of the gamelan more carnal.

'Joged!' the ladies tell her. 'Joged Bumbung!' The new, secular dance of Bali, the kids' favourite.

Balinese dancing is far too refined ever to be quite abandoned. But the Joged is as teasing as it can be, and breaks up the former mood of solemn formality. Guests and villagers are vitalised by its irresistible energy. The temperature rises. The bright, pretty girls swoop and shuffle.

And then a male dancer appears. He is dressed in the costume worn by the few men who have been in attendance at the tour and the dinner: a gorgeous brocade sarong covered with an apron-like sky-blue garment; a crisp white shirt falls neatly over that. On his head is a beautifully tied brocade headdress. The young man joins the girls in the Joged.

In one of those split-second life-long moments of recovery, Marla feels as if she might have been leaning forward with her jaw to the ground and her eyes out on sticks and each of her body's cells visibly vibrating.

In fact no doubt she continued to sit quite still and only watched with an extra intensity that put the new dancer in a spotlight only she could see.

Well, she thinks *Welllll*! My goodness, my goddess, my dear. Well, well.

He is one of those dancers you see only once in a while. He has the most extraordinary vitality, the most arresting presence, the most astounding grace.

He steps out this lively, provocative dance, in that crouching stance, long curved fingers fluttering in sublime yet careless precision: high artifice balanced with divine naturalness: Krishna dancing. He dances, he prances, he steps and he sways, his eyes dart from side to side and then are held in a momentary sudden freeze-frame and as suddenly, the head is shaken in an exact little chuckle from side to side. He is the personification of brilliant, exuberant talent.

She sits in her seat, smitten, enchanted. Part of her is absorbed in the dancer's being, part of her is watching her dive off the edge of the world. My God, my goodness. Uh-oh.

SIXTEEN

It was Marla's first night in the Puri.

She dreamt of the charming dancer. When she woke, all she remembered was that he had sat beside her, and held her wrist with the fingers of one hand. There they sat, in a soft silence, in the atmosphere of spookily sweet glamour she had floated in all night. She woke and he was sitting there, her wrist in his palm, encircled. Then later she really did wake up.

The birds were announcing the fresh lovely morning. A symphony. She was served coffee, fruit, and a plate of little cakes made of rice, palm sugar, coconut. She will have this every morning. It is the best breakfast she has had anywhere.

SEVENTEEN

'And now, Wayan, what about the dances you saw last night?'

'So many questions!'

'Nah nah nah.' It was mid-morning. Her host had come to join her as she read and wrote her notes on the verandah. Seated opposite her, he accepted some tea, nodding his vigorous encouragement. Today he did not hold the staff to his belly.

'The trance dance! That was amazing. At the beginning, with the figures in white, around the tree, they were leyaks? What exactly is a leyak, a magician?'

'At the beginning of the play the leyaks learn black magic. The condition is that they steal the bodies of dead children. *Neleyak*, that is the verb, to practise as a leyak. It is practised generally by women. The women who will get the power to become a black magic person, must get the grace of Durga, the goddess in Pura Dalam. What is the aim? It is not good, according to the teaching of the religion.'

They spoke for a while about magic, black and white, the left-hand path and the right-hand path. Ratu Aji asked her about western magical traditions, and said he would give her written material about leyaks to study. There was a large collection of books and manuscripts here. This led to a discussion on healing. What a Balian is. A shaman, a healer, a magician. The different kinds of Balian. *Balian taksu*.

Ratu Aji said, 'Remember this word and engrave it on your mind: taksu.'

Taksu? She had seen this word in the books, heard it before . . . While she rapidly searched her memory, he went on: 'You have seen the shadow play, the Wayan Kulit, the puppets? Yes? Where have you seen? Nah, nah. The dalang is a common person of the village. He has not a good education, but when he plays the shadow puppets, he becomes

166

clever and wise: he has information about politics, religions, people. In his daily life, he is not so clever. Why? It is *taksu.* Some invisible power comes inside him and influences his brain. The dalang speaks automatically, without thinking, because there is something more than him—*taksu*—which is the invisible source of his words. When you see a dance, a player who receives *taksu*, the dance is more amazing than when not.'

'Is it,' she asked, playing her part, pupil to his Socrates, 'like inspiration, is it *ilham?*'

'A writer needs *ilham.* To draw, to paint, to make a carving, you need *ilham.* A dancer needs *taksu*, a dalang needs *taksu.* Sukarno, they say, was *metaksu.* You do not have such a word?'

'Charisma. Power. Possession. Channelling. Those things. And the trances?'

'Without trance the players would not be brave enough to stab. No protection. They do wear a talisman—a white sheet with holy drawings on it. The dancers are sprinkled with holy water by the priest; the priest is always there, to protect and guide. The player is influenced by the music, the audience, the atmosphere, the smell of incense, the offerings and the darkness of the night: all this help to get into trance. They have a belief in God, they are self-convinced; and suddenly: trance. Bali knows many kinds of trance. A pure trance is unconscious. Last night it was mixed, conscious and unconscious trance, and full of emotion. Did you notice that they stopped during the stabbing, and the priest came to them again? After the prayer was said, the Witch said the stabbing was too soft, not hard enough. The players said, but we are so angry, we do our best, we stab as hard as we can, we are angry. They stab hard, but they do not feel it. Only after the dance is over do they feel pain.'

He watched her as he spoke. 'I believe this is so,' she said. 'I have seen people walking on fire, and there are many stories of similar things.' She silently wondered if by conscious and unconscious trance he means acted and real.

'What is trance? For me, a non-educated man in Bali, it is a transition of mind. The mind is emptied and filled with an outside power. For example, a young girl cannot dance, but in a trance, then she can dance. You already know this, nah nah nah. Before they get trance they are no dancer and suddenly they do dance. Why is this?' He smiled at her—a beautiful smile—as if in pure joy at the ineffable ways of the world. Of Bali.

'It is a mystery,' she said.

'In the west, I think, you do not have this.' He was alert, wanting to know what she would say.

'In the west,' she said, 'it is possible to believe only in the visible world, and there are philosophies which say that this is right. Many people do not want to believe in the invisible world, or in mysteries; they do not trust them or do not think them important. Here, I think, such mystery is a normal and accepted part of life. Where I come from it is perhaps a minority interest.'

'Nah, nah.' He was not, of course, ignorant of western philosophies. He was a widely read man, and to call himself uneducated was a kind of irony, or conceit. He had exchanged views with scholars for decades, and she doubted he had anything to learn from her. Yet he treated her as if what she told him was interesting and valuable to him.

His work was to translate, or transliterate, the old lontars. They were mostly in the Old Javanese language he said. They got on to the topic of the influence of India and whether both Javanese and Balinese dance are derived from India.

'Javanese dance is more polite, the eyes do not move, for example, because they think that is more polite. Balinese dance is different, it is based on spirit, the moving of the spirit, to let the spirit do what it will. We think that clever dance is below a graceful dance; to be graceful is more valuable and attractive than clever. To dance clever, you can learn, but to dance graceful comes from inside, from the spirit.'

Finally Marla asked: 'And before the Cholonorang, the dance before that?' She had been waiting to ask. 'The Joged?'

'Joged Bumbung is perhaps like your disco in the west, although not as sexual, more polite. They shake their hips and so but it is not as sexual as the disco. The Cholonorang is dedicated to the invisible world—to Niskala. It is consecrated. Did you notice the priest? The dance is consecrated. But the Joged Bumbung is not dedicated, it belongs to Sakala.'

'And the dancers of the Joged,' she asked, 'are they from this village?'

They were not. They were from a nearby village, on the coast.

'All of them? First there were the girls dancing, and then they were joined by a young man . . . ?'

'He is from this village, from this family. You saw him help with the welcoming of the guests? And after, he joins in Joged Bumbung. He dances the way it should be danced—very graceful, no? The way he dances?'

'Oh, so graceful,' she said. 'So very graceful! Oh yes.'

'That is how. The way he does it, how it should be—the pauses, the eyes.'

'Oh he was very graceful,' she said again. 'Very graceful.'

She would have liked to go on saying this for the next few hours but desisted.

Eighteen

In the afternoons Marla went walking around the village and the villages close by. Notice, she told herself, notice the three main temples of the village. The Pura Desa at the northern end, the Pura Putuh nearby and the Pura Dalam always at the southern end. Notice the household temples in the north-east corner. North was the traditional direction Kaja—the direction of the mountains, to Gunung Agung, auspicious; Kelod the direction of the sea, wherein dwell demons. Notice the carvings on the roadside; especially notice the splendid ones at the crossroads, where evil energies dwell. They were not only curiosities, ornaments, but functional constructions. Yes, as well be reminded that every crossroads has the mischievous potential for taking the wrong way. Notice how supremely important direction was to the Balinese. 'Go east a little way', they say, or 'the shop to the south of the temple', or 'sit on the northern chair'. At the palace, her bed was placed with her head to the north and if she lay the other way she would be suspected of black magic.

Black magic! That turned out to be as normal a topic of discussion here as the weather was elsewhere.

'When my mother-in-law married,' Ratu Aji had told her one morning, 'she needed protection from a person who did not like her—a talisman. She went to a village far away and asked for a talisman from the priest who gave it to her. A secret she had to carry.

'A year later, she felt strange. She liked to see ill persons. If a neighbour is sick she likes to come at night and see, only to watch the person who is laying in bed sick. Every time, she is attracted to come and see the ill neighbour. She comes there very easily. Balinese compounds are surrounded by walls, and she stepped over the walls easily and hid under the lamp and everybody could not see her! Though she could see

170

everybody. Many, many times it happened like this. She thinks: what am I now? What have I become? A leyak? But I do not agree. She was attracted to see her ill mother in the house of a prince. There, she touched her own hair: wet! So she was convinced it was not a dream. Later she made a decision and she gave the talisman back to the priest.'

'It was the talisman, then?' Marla asked, feeling stupid. There must be a lot she had missed. Probably to want to go and see sick people is an extra creepy thing in Bali.

'The result of the talisman is to become a leyak.'

Talismans, leyaks, magic, rituals.

A person is not allowed to walk under things that are not pure. On certain days a person has to wash their hair under a certain kind of building. A person has to lie on the bed contrary to custom, with the head to the south or west rather than the north or east. A person collects bones from the graveyard and wraps them in a cloth. A person can turn into an animal at three am. A person has to persuade someone to accept certain foods. A person has to sweep the Pura Dalam at midnight. Such things are part of the black magic practice.

If a boy loves a girl and she does not love him the boy goes to the witch doctor. 'He asks for the power so that she loves him. The witch doctor gives him a talisman, a sheet with drawings on it, and certain formulas to speak, and to consecrate and keep her name. He must wait for the chance, and on a good day to be close to the girl and to touch her hand. If you can do like this, with all the conditions told, suddenly she changes her mind—now she loves him. Very strange. When the power, the talisman, does not still survive strong because the boy is lazy, the girl begins to look. Now she does not love him. Divorce. Balinese are very good but also they sometimes do black magic. Strange!'

Did he himself think it strange or was he only reflecting or encouraging her inevitable tendency to find these well-known things strange? Marla loved the mornings of intense scholarship, but no wonder that, after lunch and a midday sleep, she needed to leave the palace alone, and walk until sunset, through fields and villages and sometimes to the coast.

'Hello,' the people constantly called out to her, as she walked and noticed; 'Hello, tourist, where you go, hello hello.' This became a fearful bore. Very nice of them to be so friendly and all—the smiles were enchanting, although the hellos from the teenage boys had a sly quality as they egged each other on to ask her more, try out some English, get her to pay them attention. But over and over and over? Now, what you going to do? It would be so rude to ignore it completely, but if you went along returning every hello—like every few seconds sometimes, really—you would be like some visiting dignitary on parade, on show, bowing from side to side all along the road, and you'd feel really stupid, and walking would be no fun. 'Hello, tourist,' they called out, 'hello, where you go?' If you ever pause, for a rest, a drink, a look, people surround you. Hello, where you go, where you come from, where your husband, ohhh! you speak Indonesian! clever!

Grumpily she imagined telling them this:

You want to be nice to tourists? Then listen to this. We mind our own business in Australia. If a person is walking alone we think that person wants to be alone. We respect that. We don't ask strangers if they're married and how old they are the minute we see them. Don't yell hello at me for chrissake, don't ask me at every step where I'm going, don't come to practise your English when you only know two sentences. Think for a moment, just think, what it is like to be yelled at every step for six kilometres and asked every time you sit down where your husband is and how old you are. Friendly friendly friendly, that is the way we are, friendly, that's what you say—can't you think for a moment and see it is not friendliness we experience but harassment. I *know* you're being friendly but I also know why some tourists ignore you or just snap 'Don't know' at you all the time. I feel like saying None of your business! I feel like saying, fuck off, jerk!

I mean I know we should all live in the eternal now and so on but can't you think for a moment that every single time I sit down in a warung and ask for some tea I am asked exactly the same questions in exactly the same way and it gets tiresome? Haven't you heard of companionable silence? And would you just stop being so aghast puzzled or pitying because I am walking alone? Where are my friends? My friends are all far away each doing their own thing and I am glad. Haven't you heard of having something new and interesting to tell people you like? You want to be friendly, you want to get on with tourists, how about some consideration?

Of course she never said any of this.

She learned to smile vaguely in all directions while remaining self-absorbed. She draped a long scarf over her straw hat to hide her face, and when she sat down she managed to retain her privacy behind the barrier of a self-induced trance, or else, what the hell, hello, I'm going for a walk, hello, I come from Australia, hello, I am forty, hello, my husband is in Australia, my husband is waiting over there, my husband is in Denpasar, hello, I have one child, two children, three children, all grown up and in Australia, hello, I'm walking only walking only going for a walk only to look hello hello hello.

When a Puri Night was scheduled there was much toil in the palaces all day to provide the feasts. At nightfall villagers gathered in the large grassy courtyard in front of the *candi* of the main palace. Like the traditional ceremonial theatre, these nights were an occasion of socialising and provided the only opportunity for girls to meet boys. Pseudo events become real events. A busload of tourists would arrive, and the welcome dance would start the evening's program, always the same program.

Always, too, she waited with special anticipation for the Joged. He danced again: brilliant as fire, fluid as water, charming as blossoms, how could she say it?

173

In the finale of the Joged Bumbung, the dancers asked members of the audience to come and dance with them. The girls tugged at the hands of the reluctant guests most prettily. Being good sports, most of them, they let themselves be persuaded. Naturally this caused great hilarity to guests and villagers alike, these lumbering foreigners trying to adapt to the chimes of the gong and the mannerisms of oriental dance. The charming dancer, having persuaded a stout Japanese matron to get up and have a go, was able to dance as well as before, and also to be a perfect, attentive partner to the woman twisting artlessly before him.

On Marla's first night here, the Joged girls had come over, past the tourist group, to ask her to join in. Urged on by the palace ladies, she could not refuse. You would inevitably feel foolish, that unfamiliar music, those unfamiliar clothes, the expectation that any non-Balinese would look foolish. She escaped back to her seat as soon as she felt she had obliged.

'I listen to the BBC,' the bird-like wife told her, taking her hand. 'Every day. Never too old to learn.'

At the end of the night, they always held some silly good-bye ritual. The villagers all left, and the tourist coach appeared at the gates. The palace people arranged themselves in the pavilion to sing a farewell song and to provide a photo opportunity. The Head Prince posed with some of his wives and children. Flash-click-whirr. 'Five wives and twenty-nine children!' the tourist group was told. It probably got a reaction every time. 'One wife is enough!' sniggered one of the men in the tourist group. Someone said that every Puri Night. Joke.

The charming dancer appeared at her side. Was she staying here? he asked her in awkward English. Oh, she spoke Indonesian! Was she married? No one had asked her that here! She took this as a personal question. No, are you? she replied, feeling as awkward as a schoolgirl.

Remembering that, she reflected that it was an outdated simile. The schoolgirls of today could have taught her some poise no doubt. She felt as awkward as when she had been a schoolgirl. She hurried away, and went to sleep in her new room. To sleep and to dream.

The second Puri Night, when it was time for the feast, Marla offered to help. Ratu Biang looked pleased and put her on the central pavilion, behind one of the trestles laden with food, to help the other women to serve. There are a hundred guests tonight! Ratu Biang whispered. A hundred times 50,000 rupiah! She told Marla to tell the hundred guests that she was her sister-in-law, that she lived here. Tonight's tourists were from an international conference of travel agents held in Nusa Dua.

On her fourth night at the palace, there was a third Puri Night. Ratu Biang had taken her to the markets to order a new kebaya and Marla thought it suited her quite terrifically. Ratu Biang came again to help her to tie her sarong correctly and then returned to lend her some of those trembly gold flowers for her hair. Other white women often said they looked 'silly, stupid' in this costume but Marla was one of those who said she felt transformed, feminine, lovely.

'Beautiful!' everyone said as they made their way through the maze to the front courtyard to meet the guests. Marla thought, they tell you what you want to hear, here. 'Beautiful!' they all said. She felt beautiful. The guests arrived, the welcome dance was performed, and the tour commenced. As usual, Marla trailed behind with the ladies, and hung back whispering with them as the usual explanations progressed.

'Beautiful!' swooping over to her, taking hold of her hand. 'You look beautiful!' It was the charming dancer. The ladies smiled and stood aside. He stood there, at the steps to the temple, holding her hand, in the most natural manner, telling her she looked beautiful and she told him he danced beautifully and he told her that an American woman had once wanted to take him to dance in the States but he was married or he would have gone. Remember that one, the American? he asked the ladies, who smiled at him, God knows what they thought. Marla basked. This sudden demonstrative warmth, she just basked.

Yesterday's novelty was today's tradition and she took her place on the central pavilion serving food. The charming dancer swooped again and took her hand and said, 'This is my wife,' taking the hand of another of the ladies, one Marla had noticed as she was so petite and lovely. 'Beautiful,' he said, 'the same,' and they all smiled at each other, God knows what she thought, she smiled with shy grace, and he seemed quite guileless. 'The same,' he said, 'both beautiful.'

When the dances began again and the Joged dancers pulled out people from the audience, he came for her. She would have loved to dance, really dance, but felt restrained and restricted, and returned swiftly to her seat.

It was all forgotten during the Tettetkan. The more she knew of its story, the less she knew. Myths combined with history, explanations were contradictory, descriptions confusing. The drama was always intense. She loved to see the masks of the noble beast, the Barong, and the fearful Rangda, queen of the leyaks, the witch-widow of black magic—terrifying, her long sagging breasts flailing. The two were locked in eternal battle and neither ever won.

Neither ever won. Good and evil were locked in eternal equilibrium. Neither ever could win. These were the stories on which Balinese children were bred. While our stories tell our children about the goodies beating the baddies, the dragons slain, the rival dispatched, the witch is dead, the happy-ever-after. They don't tell them that here. They leave good and evil in eternal equilibrium. Think about it.

The moon was round and high—a mere sliver removed from the recent perfect sphere. The shadows flickering, the dancers leaping, their curved blades flashing.

After it was all over the photos were being taken. The charming dancer came and held her hand and asked if she had been to Tanah Lot. Did she want to go? With him? Yes! With me? he repeated, making sure they were talking about the same thing. Tomorrow? Yes, she said. It's like this, he told her,

I have to go to the office at six and tell my boss I want a free day and then I'll come back, so I'll pick you up at eight . . .

The others were calling him, looking amused that he was talking to her and hadn't noticed he should be back in his place by then leading their touristy farewell song.

NINETEEN

Marla drank a coconut and he smoked kreteks. They waved away the hawkers until one offered, 'photo?' She agreed. They posed. He with his arm around her. They watched the Polaroid fade in. The temple of Tanah Lot, surrounded by sea water at high tide, rose behind them out of the ocean like a strange black rock, the waves slapping around it, and they were there, their bodies touching for the first time.

They walked hand in hand and soon turned away from the cluster of shops and restaurants around the fantastic temple. Down the coast a little they stopped and looked at another temple, a small, empty one, a regular temple to Dewi Sri, the rice goddess. Further along, they turned off the main path; a smaller path led to a little stone table-and-seat arrangement under shade. There they sat, passing the bottle of Aqua back and forth. He didn't seem to mind drinking from the same bottle.

He was dressed in his work-day uniform: brown pants and blue shirt of narrow cut and unprincely fabric, the garb of a third-world employee. Oddly, her heart expanded at the sight of him thus attired, or masked. Here he was, himself, or another self, not only the aristocratic other-worldly dancer. She asked about his job. He had studied at a college in Java so that he could get this job in agriculture. He went around to the farmers to tell them of new methods. New methods sometimes bring poison and pollution, Marla suggested. Yes, he knew, but think of the farmers who ploughed their fields with a cow, all day, maybe in one day two hectares. If they used a machine, in one day many hectares. See? Hmmm, yes, she said. They sat silently a moment, she thought about why the farmers needed to plough more hectares these days. And things she'd heard about their perfect, ecologically balanced system being interfered with by ignorant development agencies.

178

They said things slowly, mostly in Indonesian. Marla used English if she had to, he used English if he could. Please repeat, they kept saying in Indonesian, please repeat slowly. They mimed and acted and gestured. They looked up words in her dictionary. And sometimes there was immediate comprehension of a lengthy utterance full of unlearnt vocabulary.

Suddenly he kissed her. She was startled. They drank some more water.

Are you angry, he asked, because I kissed you without permission?

I am not angry, she replied. If you had asked permission I would have said no!

They looked at the sea.

He held her wrist, his fingers encircling her wrist. Later, he suggested, after 2 o'clock, there is nobody there at my office and we could go there.

She hesitated.

'Problem?' he asked.

'For me, yes,' she said. 'Problem.'

'OK,' he said, almost singing it, 'oh-*kay*,' affirming that he would not ask for anything that was a problem for her. He was not going to plead, or persuade. Only to offer, and to accept her wishes.

Eventually he kissed her again. '*Pusing*,' she says. He is a pretty terrific kisser, and it's already the hottest part of the day.

He did not want to make her confused, he said, and they talked of other things. She felt she had slipped through some science-fiction black hole or down some fairytale well. Sitting at this private headland over the sea, suddenly being kissed by the charming dancer, going on sitting, feeling calm and happy . . . that did not happen in the world from which she had just abruptly been removed.

Episodes of their lives were implied in a single sentence. 'I from kingdom family,' he explained. She could not understand every word as he told her the history of the family. It was an old noble family, she already knew that, and she

179

had known that as he was called Anak Agung Alit something he was of high caste. She had also gathered that in Bali as elsewhere some people's families had acquired this title rather too recently, and those who had had the title for a very long time appreciated the difference being known. He told her how old the family was, its history, its present large size. There was the huge palace area she is staying in and smaller palaces nearby, such as the one he lives in. He told her of the relatives who had gone to other parts of Bali, other parts of Indonesia, other parts of the world.

When I saw you, he said, the first time, in sarong-kebaya, with colour on your lips, I thought you were still young and beautiful. You are old! he said. In Bali to be forty is already old. But you are like young. You are old, but still beautiful.

She could not explain why she laughed.

Why, he asked, why did you never marry?

'I did not want to marry.'

Why did you never marry? he asked again.

When men asked me to marry, she explained (if explained was the word), I never wanted to. I never felt ready, and then I felt I am happy alone. I like to work. I have many friends also not married. In Australia many people do not marry. Although here in Bali that is not usual.

Why, he asked her, did you never marry?

Once, she said, I lived with a man, almost like married. But I found out that he wanted a life different from the life I wanted. I am more happy living alone.

Why, he asked her, did you never marry?

'Karma,' she said. You are Hindu, she said. I like Hindu ideas. Maybe my karma is not to be married.

In which case she was admitting to unspeakable sins of a previous incarnation. In Bali you had such a strong sense of being *wrong* to be unmarried. She felt as if she were becoming defensive. Maybe was better to be married, she had thought that before, maybe they were right about that.

Why wouldn't she go to the deserted office after 2 pm? He was so lovely, and such a good kisser. But she did not want a hasty, furtive episode in a strange shed. If she had never done that kind of thing it might be good for her. What problem could she have on a beautiful island, a place for lovers, with a charming and graceful young man eager to taste her compliment her discover her. Her problem was maybe that she had developed strange scruples she could not explain. She did not want to go home with a guilty secret. She felt that the adventure he offered her was not good manners; that it would betray some trust. He understood. And besides. Sex, she told him, should not be quick and secret, not for her, not hasty. A long time, no hurry, many moods. (She needed the dictionary.)

She knew she could amaze him with more than the timid taste of pleasure, that taste of experience, that he wanted. She could in fact make quite a disruption, quite a passion quite a drama out of this, but she said no.

They walked further and sat again, at a more remote seat. More kissing. Her loose, tunic-like top, red and gold cotton and tied at the shoulders, loosened and revealed the straps of her stained once-white bra with its patina aquired from a daily saturation of sweat seeping though coconut oil and daily application of ineffectual laundry soap. Gazing at the swell of her breasts, he said, big, white, good! Glad you like it, she thought, amused, but hope you never wish I were younger.

They left the stone pavilion and that was the end of the kissing episode. They left to travel miles of hot, bumpy roads on his rickety little motorbike. He took her to a monkey forest and she bought peanuts for the nasty little creatures to grab at. There were bats high in the trees. There was said to be a monkey graveyard nearby but no one knew for sure. There were only bottled drinks available from the tourist stalls. They went to a glorious temple, situated in a curve, or loop, of a river, surrounded by water and ablaze with a profusion of highly scented trees in blossom. It was one of those places where you feel there is an angelic presence. She was delivered back to her palace in the sweltering mid-afternoon. They shook hands and thanked each other formally. She bathed, ate, and rested. Today she had learnt the words for permission, trust, kiss, moods.

I'm so glad he's at home with his wife, she thought, I prayed he had a wife, thank God for his wife, she thought. She didn't want a hasty sneaky screw between siesta and dinner. She didn't want drama or disruption. She didn't want a boyfriend. She was leaving the village in four days.

She was leaving the village in two days. She sat in the darkness outside her room, listening to the sound of a single flute shimmering through the silence; an occasional chirping and croaking from the gecko.

He had brought the bicycle around to her. Go now, he told her, I'll see you there. She set off. They couldn't be seen cycling together. She pedalled down the road, lightheaded. If he arrived at the beach, OK, and meanwhile she was enjoying the road. It was six kilometres to the coast. She had walked this road several times. He arrived at the exact same moment she did; pulled up beside her as she stopped at the end of the road, and she laughed. It was almost the end of the day and people were leaving: boys who had been playing ball on the beach, and girls and women who had been washing there.

They walked along the black sands. There was a temple on a cliff. They walked past it, further. A jungle path and then a little bay, rocks, cliffs; no one there but an old woman gathering salt. They took off their outer clothes to swim: her dress, his shorts and T-shirt. Her underwear was hot-pink. His was baby-blue. The bay the empty beach the soft sky the palms. They rolled in the shallow waves the warm sea the foam the kisses his skin like silk. Afternoon was changing into evening.

'You want?' he asked. She told the truth: she did want. But not here. Only if they could have had more time.

It was not she who suggested he could come and visit her in Ubud.

'But you are married!' she said.

182

You cannot be hurt by what you don't know, he said.

It is always known, she said, and she knew that still she would welcome him because she could not resist. This silkskinned goldenbrown angel rolling around with her in the roiling foam on this Bali Hai dream beach black sand white foam green palms lavender sky firework kisses hot pink blue golden brown her white belly marked red by his teeth. Someone might see, doesn't he care? No one sees, he says. An old woman at the bay's edge scrapes salt from the cliff. As if you can have secrets here! I will come to you in Ubud, he said, and if I sleep with you there, no problem? What the unearthly soft sky did she know about problem?

On the way back to their bicycles, they drew maps in the sand, repeating the directions. 'And on the right you see Warung Ibu Suci and you turn . . . ' But that was not the way to give directions. She thought hard, and remembered the setting sun over the hill over the river. It must have seemed strange to him that she took a while to work out that the main road goes westward and that he must take a turn to the north-west. They walked carefully apart when they returned to the main beach. 'Many people!' he said. There were maybe a dozen. He left first, while two adorable young women approached Marla and had a bit of a chat about dance.

Hours later, she sat alone in the soft warm dark. She got ready for bed and the sound of the flute changed to the sound of an Indonesian sit-com blaring with unusual ferocity from a television somewhere nearby.

TWENTY

'Lee Sale is a very good friend of mine. She and David Sale became divorced, and now live separately. Lee Sale now associates with a Balinese.'

Ratu Aji has joined Marla on her verandah. He came every day, to talk to her. Associates with, she thought, now there's a fine phrase. She knew who he was talking about: David and Lee Sale had made documentary films about Bali. She hadn't seen the films as when they had been shown she had not known she was going to be interested. She didn't know they'd broken up, either.

'He is a healer, a dukun, you know dukun? He is married, and five days of the week he lives with his wife and two days of the week he lives with Lee Sale. She has settled in the village of Tegal Suci. She is not happy. The community does not accept her, and does not invite her to their meetings. She asks me, what must I do to be accepted? I want to be accepted, and to be part of the community. Is it because I am not marrried? I said to her, if your problem comes from not being married, why don't you marry? And she says, perhaps then I will no longer be happy with him. He has one formal relationship—with his wife, and one informal relationship—with me. If we were to marry he would have two formal relationships and I would not feel I occupied a special position, and perhaps I would be no longer happy. That is what she said to me.'

'I can understand that,' Marla said. She wondered if this story had a special point, a warning perhaps, or an inquiry as to her intentions. Had someone seen her with Alit on the beach? No, she decided, that wasn't it. It was just the way significance suffused the slightest thing in these parts.

'What can she do? She wants to be accepted but she is afraid that if she will marry she will no longer be happy. Difficult, Wayan, so difficult.'

'I wonder, I don't know,' Marla says, 'about foreigners who come to Bali and buy a house because they want to live here. They can do it because they have enough money. And then they want to be accepted into the community! I don't know if I would feel it is my right to be welcomed into the community only because I had enough money to buy my house in the place I fancied.'

'Who can know, Wayan? So difficult.'

It was mid-morning. The day was very bright; every day was very bright. The rat-tat-tat sound of typewriting had been heard all morning. That was Ratu Biang, just out of sight on her own large verandah, sitting at a large table, transcribing the results of her husband's work on a large old manual typewriter. Marla's verandah looked on to the courtyard, with its formal garden enclosed in neat squares. A bird in a cage sang at odd times.

Understanding the western mind, Marla figured, was one of her host's projects. And for now, she represented the western mind. To understand the Balinese mind was hers, and he, with his command of English, his scholarship, his wisdom, was her ideal sage. She was all the more convinced of his wisdom by his frequent conclusion: 'difficult, so difficult'. That is a conclusion you could trust. She'd seen too many guys who think the answers are easy.

More than anyone he reminded her of the character in *The Leopard*. 'Should he come to terms with the forces of change or resist them?' She remembered that written on the blurb of an old Penguin paperback. Ratu Aji, she imagined, wanted first to understand these forces, before deciding the attitude he would adopt or recommend. But what did she know?

Marla imagined that Ratu Aji was well aware that the effects of the west, carried on the vehicle of tourism, were approaching even here.

He may not, indeed, any longer be in a position to recommend. People no longer look to their princes. 'Puri'—palace—was no longer a source of *noblesse oblige* but a commercialised word tacked on to any hotel or consumer emporium.

There was talk, he told her, of some tourist development in the area.

'Oh no,' Marla exclaimed in dismay.

At the coast, six kilometres away.

'Oh no,' she said. 'It's so lovely, so unspoiled.' She sighed. 'I am typical, you might say, of a certain kind of tourist who wants to be the only one to see the lovely unspoiled places.'

'The people here are very poor. They would like to make carvings and paintings and other things that tourists will buy.'

Poor? Poor? The people here? All this beauty, these bright and fertile fields, their dances, their ceremonies, the languorous rhythms of their ordered, timeless life? Good heavens Marla, you have been romanticising, haven't you? It's all right for you, wandering round on an extended vacation, noting certain details of certain temples, lapping up stories of leyaks and spells. The people here watched her go by and wanted something she had.

As usual, at noon Ratu Biang called them to lunch and they moved over to the dining pavilion, where rice and a range of dishes were always provided. Such good food! Ratu Biang did not speak English; Marla had to use Bahasa Indonesia, so the conversation was slow, until they finished eating. Then they conversed as before, with time out for translation.

Ratu Aji asked her about the place she stayed at in Ubud. Gossip, thought Marla, he wants the goss. on the other princes. She described the room, and told him how much she paid. There, they had had access to the tourist dollar for decades, and now they wanted more. She told him of Tjokorda Gde's plans for development.

'And his Australian wife?' he asked. 'How is it, a Balinese man and an Australian wife?'

'I got the impression,' said Marla carefully, 'that Tjok Gde is somewhat divided. He likes the freedom of the west. Yet he feels dislocated away from his family and the regular practise of his religion.'

'And the wife?'

'She liked Bali but it was difficult for her to live there, in the palace. She said it was nice for us to see all the offerings but it is extremely tedious to sit for hours with the women and to make them. I can understand that. I find the offerings charming, but could not spend hours making them.'

'And the children?'

'They are Australian kids, but half-Balinese. They've stayed in Bali many times. They come back for ceremonies. I think they've both been back for tooth-filing.'

Ratu Aji nodded away, thinking about it. 'Nah, nah. Difficult.'

'Yes,' she said, 'but in Australia there are many, many people—most people—from other countries who live there now—refugees, immigrants. And, often, they, and their children, feel divided . . . It's a typical experience. Of course, it may be more pronounced for a Balinese, whose . . .' she stopped and thought. 'Whose culture is more . . .' More what? 'Stronger,' she said uncertainly. 'Whose sense of belonging to a place is more . . . is also stronger. Than western people's.'

'Please excuse one moment while I translate for my wife.'

Marla's parents had migrated to Australia. 'After the war,' as they used to say when she was a child. Now they say 'after the Second World War'. Actually, it is all no longer mentioned. At that time, here, the Dutch had not yet left. The Japanese were yet to occupy. Such violent upheavals, bloodshed. Yet in this village it was as if history were a stasis barely disturbed, and only recently, and only by motorbikes . . .

When they spoke of the Dutch, Ratu Aji said, 'The countries which were in the Empire of the British formed a union, isn't it? They wanted to keep an association with Britain? They felt they had something in common that was worth to hold on to?'

'The Commonwealth,' Marla admitted. 'The English language.'

'Language. Your country and the other countries keep the English language. Also, aspects of the British system, isn't it?'

'I am actually against imperialism. Absolutely. But it is confusing when in India they point out its many benefits.'

'The countries of the Dutch colonisation *do not*,' said Ratu Aji with an emphasis she hadn't heard before, 'want to keep any association with the Dutch, none at all, and we feel no bond with other former Dutch colonies.'

She felt she should not ask for more than this glimpse of a bitter vehemence. 'No,' she said. 'I believe the Dutch were even worse.'

When Ratu Aji came to her another morning, Marla was immersed in a book on Walter Spies. They talked a while about Spies and the Pita Maha and his Saturday school for artists.

'But there is another side to that. Walter Spies liked to associate himself with men. You say "homo-sex". For the Balinese, it is something bad. For the westerner, it is nothing.' He watched her, attentive to what she would reply.

'There have always been such men, always,' she said, 'so we say that it is natural that some people will prefer their own sex. It is often said that many artists have been homosexuals.'

'Nah, nah.' He thought for a moment and then told her a story. He had a friend, a Dutch man, who was homo-sex. He had, Ratu Aji emphasised, 'no desire for women'. This man took his Indonesian lover to the Netherlands. The lover hated the cold and left. The friend asked for advice. 'Difficult, difficult,' Ratu Aji said. 'I say to him, you think more about your friend than your own soul. Come back to nature. Later he writes and says, you were right.'

Marla nodded thoughtfully, but there was too much left out of this story for her to understand it.

'Why are men homo-sex?'

'I don't know, I don't know if anyone can really know. There just always have been . . .'

'Are there now more men homo-sex than before?'

'Maybe more. Or maybe only it is more open. Men in the west have been made to behave a certain way. To conform to ideas of masculinity. That is changing. But to express the feminine side, it's as if men can't have that and also be heterosexual. Also, there has been a change in the way people think. Generally speaking there is more acceptance or at least tolerance for these things and so it can be more open.'

As she spoke, she was aware that she had adopted his careful, formal manner of speech. She was also aware that her own narrow version of these things would not win her any seal of approval as spokesperson for western culture. But she went on. 'And the kind of ideas that have influenced me see it as related to liberation. You tell me that *moksa* is the aim of life—liberation from the karmic cycle. We are not brought up with the idea of karma, some of us learn about it later, and we created the idea that the ultimate liberation is from ideas that prevent us from exploring the full potential of life.'

'Nah, nah, nah.' He was nodding, listening with great care. 'Men more than women?'

'I think so. Or perhaps only more conspicuously than women.'

He wanted to know why.

'I don't know. I'm not sure anyone can really know. But I think that in our culture women are allowed to be affectionate, to express their feelings, offer comfort to each other, feel intimate together. But for men, who are not allowed, these aspects of relationship suggest sex, and if they feel this, they think it has to do with sex. And men are supposed to be more sexual, so they will express their attraction in a more overtly sexual way. Perhaps that is universal.'

He wanted to know if it was true that more women were turning to homo-sex these days. (He had, of course, been studying the western mind long before Marla got here.)

'More. Perhaps because in this modern age in the west women insist on the same freedoms as men. Also because for many feminists it is part of their philosophy to have women

189

as lovers. Also because . . . because, in the west,' she said, 'it is a time when the relationships between men and women have been in confusion. There are so many different ideas about how people should behave, what they should want, what they should expect.'

The servant went by with trays of food, and Ratu Biang fetched them to join her. The conversation was continued at the end of lunch. He mentioned one of the famous Dutch scholars of Balinese culture whom he knew well. 'He said to me,' Ratu Aji informed her, 'I do not love everything about life in Bali. Two things I do not like. One is the caste system. The other, the position of women.'

'I see,' said Marla. 'In principle I agree, although in practice it is much worse in other places.'

'We have a kind of taboo about sex,' he said. 'When we play sex, it should last only five minutes, no more. The man has orgasm, but not the woman. Her pleasure is from the service and devotion to her husband.'

It was true that Ratu Biang, sitting there, smiling, trying hard to follow a conversation in a language she didn't know, waiting with patience and confidence for her husband to include her with his translations, did not in the least look like a dissatisfied woman. She looked like a happy woman. 'Perhaps,' said Ratu Aji, 'for my son's generation it is different, I don't know.'

I bet it is, thought Marla. 'We do have different ideas in the west,' is what she did say. He wanted her to explain. 'Especially in these modern times. Women now demand satisfaction and pleasure from sex. And we have the idea that sex should last as long as you can, be as varied as you can. Perhaps we have become rather out of balance, in fact I am rather sure we have. There is possibly too much attention to sex. When I was growing up, my generation had the idea that we wanted a great deal of sexual experience. We had philosophical reasons, liberation. Now, many people think it became unbalanced. Maybe we had to achieve our balance by going to extremes. I think so.'

'Excuse me,' he said, and translated. In spite of the topic, there was no difference in the tone of voice any of them used. They could have been discussing rice cultivation, tooth-filing or market prices. Funny how these abstract, carefully worded discussions seemed to have nothing to do with the realm whose vague distant images of rolling in the waves with a beautiful silken-skinned boy teased a distant horizon in her mind.

'In Bali,' he told her, 'a dancer can associate with many men. It is the same in the west? There is a famous actress who has had many husbands? Elizabeth Taylor? A dancer in Bali also has much opportunity to be admired by many men, and to associate with many men, so in Bali, usually a man does not want to marry a dancer.'

This was the first time she had heard anything of this kind. 'Oh we once had that kind of idea in the west too. But Covarrubias says that free sex is common in Bali.'

'He is speaking of the common people. Not the noblemen. Not the people of the triwangsa.'

Hmmm. The books told her that the three noble castes make up ten per cent of the population. Ten per cent who had a stricter morality. Maybe they had had too much to do with the Dutch and caught it off them. Somehow the topic of conversation shifted, and they were talking about *taksu* again. The dalang, the dancer, has a mantra, a formula, to summon *taksu* before a performance. 'You,' he says, meaning the west, 'you think that what you do is one hundred per cent your own. The Balinese says it is not.'

Marla said, 'Artists know that to create they have to . . . how to say? They do things they know are better than they really can do. They say "where does it come from?" But we don't have formulas or mantras. It is usually a personal discovery and one it is hard to trust. Artists are meant to be mad. Some of us think similar to what you're telling me but it's not the main idea, not the idea of the dominant culture. Here it is normal. That is why we are fascinated with Bali, our crazy ideas are your normal ones!'

'We live in a world,' he said, 'where three times three is

not always nine. Sometimes eleven.' He laughed, as if delighted. 'Now, Wayan, take a rest. Now you want to sleep.'

The caged bird sang, there were new blossoms on the tree, and it was her last hour at the palace.

Ratu Aji sat in his usual chair. One hand held the staff to his belly, and with the other his finger traced the dates on a printed Balinese calendar. Its patterns, its various conjunctions of the days of its seven-day, five-day and three-day weeks, its two-hundred-and-ten day years, held the code for a whole world, one she didn't, really, know the first thing about; it was a system of signs that she could not read, but more than that, it was a map of a cosmology's shaping of daily reality that he took for granted and she could not.

A day has several names, according to which kind of week you are referring to. When certain cycles coincide it is a special day, in some cases very auspicious. The priest is the one who knows about these things. Only leyaks are otherwise interested. In our culture we think this kind of mystification protection racket is not good. We're all for information-sharing. But here, to *mind* that these cycles are the priests' business is like minding that coconut trees point to the sky.

She loved the old man, she loved his wife, she loved the palace, she loved the village, she loved the books and the talks and the meals they shared, the Puri Nights, the neighbours' ceremonies—even when you sat for hours waiting for the right moment to begin; she loved the walks, the bicycling, every last little bit of it, even her irritations, her annoyances, her doubts. She wanted to cry because she was leaving, but that would have been so unseemly, and here she wanted to behave well.

'So, Wayan, you will come on this day.' He pointed to the date. It was just over two weeks away. She had sent a telegram to Katak Inn, and was on her way back there. She had a date.

'I will come,' she said, 'that morning.'

'You will have the other sleeping room,' he reminded her.

'I know,' she assured him. 'This one was booked a long time ago.' Someone was coming from America to be here on that date, one of the most serious of the serious visitors, one who had their own Balinese calendar, and could read it themselves. It was a date uniquely auspicious for ceremonies of purification. In this very village they would hold a three-day temple festival, and the full Cholonorang would be performed. Not the Puri Night version. No conscious or half-conscious play-acted trances. The real thing.

'And you will see,' he said again, 'the real trance of Bali.'

'I would not know,' said Marla, 'how I could ever say good-bye to you.'

TWENTY-ONE

It was midnight, it was three am. They lay close together on the bamboo divan on the verandah, a single sarong over both their naked bodies. The night air was warm. They watched the lightning; it flashed over the hilltop on the other side of the river, flashing in colours over and over, rhythmic soft blazes of lavender and white and blue, spectacular, silent.

They shared a kretek. Passing it back and forth, smoking the same spiced cigarette, was part of the single intimate act of every night he could stay with her. One night they counted the gecko's cries and talked about lucky numbers. One night there was the lightning on the hill. One night they watched a host of fireflies. When he was a child, he said, he'd been told that fireflies were created from the fingernails of a person very *sakti*. What was the word in English?

'A magician,' she said.

After the magician died, his fingernails kept growing and became fireflies.

Do you tell that to your children? she asked, but he had begun again to stroke her body.

The nights were soft and dark and they were in her bungalow in the highest furthest part of the steep garden curving its way by the riverside. Somehow he managed to stay the night with her, once, twice, three times. If there were lies he had to tell, he took care of them. Sometimes he came for the day only. All that way, all those roads, on that rickety little motorbike. She was humbled, she was exalted. Always he arrived dressed in the brown office uniform, that cheap imitation western dress. Disguise, camouflage.

Soon they were closing the windows and the door, soon were removing their clothes. She took off his clothes and he took off her clothes, but there wasn't much else that was new to him. 'How do you know these things?' she gasped.

194

'Porn,' he informed her gravely. 'I study the porn magazine.' She laughed. Thank God for pornography, then, she thought. In the absence of holy erotic temple sculptures, we need secular inspirations.

They knew so little of each other's past personality tastes history, they had little knowledge of each other's language, but if saying so began as doubt or complaint—and it did—it ended as only another way to express their pleasure, the improbable joy of it all.

'*Mau pakai kain?*' she asked, handing him one of her most beautiful sarongs. He tied it in the most graceful folds; second nature to him, a moving display of natural exotic grace to her. 'You look so beautiful,' she said. He was an apparition, he was from the invisible world, the other world.

They ate the fruit he brought her: branches of rambutan, revealing juicy white flesh when you twisted off the hairy coverings; golden-red papaya with its clean subtle fragrance; little fat sugar bananas.

It was all lovemaking: in bed, in the bathroom, on the verandah, kissing talking fucking sucking soaping massaging burning sandalwood finding words in the dictionary passing a kretek fireflies lightning eating fruit—all a single intimate act.

He took such care to give her pleasure, he made himself a gift to her. It was the kindest thing she had ever known.

It's all so non 'exciting', she would think, excitement had nothing to do with it. When she was alone again, and wonderful as he was it was nice to be alone again, then she could reflect, and realise and remember. Romance in the past had meant to her excitement, an 'exciting' person. Here it meant something calm and karmic to whose possession you surrender. Surrender? Surrender, submission—wasn't that supposed to be the wisdom of the east? Surely there was the wise kind of surrender and the weak-willed kind of surrender. There was no thrill in this surrender. But often she told him she was happy and she was.

For most men, sex is this build-up to a final crescendo and then it's done. This is so different. It's like the music, she thought, going to bathe in the river, wandering around the town, lying dreamily over a novel, this what do you call it, this romance, it's like the music, that absolute music, that feminine music, music without the western anticipations, without regularity, without climaxes, without resolutions, without finales.

When I first saw you. That night. When you wore. When you said. When you said that I thought. I did not know if you. I wondered if you. I wanted. When you asked. That time at the beach. When you said. I was shy, I was confused, I was ashamed, no not you, it was me. And you seemed. And perhaps. And I hoped. And remember when.

That day I first came here, he said, I hoped you are here, I hoped you are waiting for me.

I was waiting for you, she said. When I woke up that day, I thought, will he come? I will not hope too much. And I did not hope too much. I thought, I will wait till noon, and then if he is not here I will go out. Many other things to do!

I came and you were sitting here, right here, looking at your books. You did not see me come toward you.

Then I looked up and I saw you!

You looked up and saw me and you looked like this!

I was happy to see you.

I asked how many people live here.

'*Saya sendiri.*'

This house only for you!

Good, isn't it? No one sees, no one hears. 'Privacy,' she added in English, 'I do like privacy.'

When you make a noise like this.

You! You make noise, now it is you making the most noise. Like this.

The first time, he had put an alarmed hand over her mouth. But he had soon learnt that no one was around to hear. He's

196

taken to privacy, I've corrupted him, she thought. Now he will desire space and privacy. And the means to acquire them. I am sin, I am corruption, I am the start of the desire that causes misery.

That first time, he asked her, why . . . ? He drew his fingers down from his eyes. Why did she cry?

'Because I am happy, because I'm sad, because I love you, because I will leave Bali, because of this.'

'Understand,' he said. He wasn't pointing out how understanding he was, either.

He took her out on excursions he planned for her pleasure.

One day they stopped for a drink at a warung in a forest. The warung was enclosed by wire netting so they sat inside a cage and the monkeys roamed free outside, or shook the wire walls, looking in at the humans, as if they were animals in a zoo. She thought this was hilarious and everyone there laughed good naturedly at her mirth.

He aroused her lust, her imagination, her tenderness.

One day he borrowed a cousin's bike, a big, comfortable bike, and they went all the way to the lake, to the buddhist stupa on the water's edge. I stayed near here, she told him, just before I met you, and dreamt of a black rock in the sea.

He looked at her as if he knew every dream she ever had.

Love him? Whatever was she thinking of? I'm falling she thought, the oldest bloody cliché fall-for trip in the book. Saw him dance and fell. She, Miss Seen-it-all-done-it-all, Madam Never-again, Diploma-in-bullshit.

'Let's go, let's go,' she sang as she got on the back of his bike.

'Let's go,' he laughed. 'Fantastic.'

He took her hand to hold it closer around him and she kissed his neck; it was a moment where no one might see a moment through back roads through bright fields.

One night they went to the markets in Denpasar, and wandered around the gaudy stalls hand in hand. 'Many attraction here,' he informed her gravely, as if he had been trained for tourism. You're so adorable, she thought. This was where he had acquired the pornographic material which had so perfectly inspired his gentle, generous erotic imagination. She bought cassette tapes of Balinese music and they ate at one of the food stalls.

She felt light and lovely and young and free.

One night they went to a dance performance in Ubud. The only tourist dances he had been to outside of his own village. She could not imagine what he thought. Did he have a vision of the total desecration of all that he had been taught was sacred?

Back at her bungalow, as usual she lit some incense. Do it like this, he said, and he told her what she should say, the ritual words for lighting incense. She had to have the words written before she could understand them. It means, he said, 'Oh my God, I put the fire here.' It's about consciousness, she thought, and it's something he's always known, it's about making your actions dedicated, it's the culture of offerings, it's about giving to the gods the essence of everything consumed.

TWENTY-TWO

Love may well be a mystery greater than death but it was love that prepared you for death. At the heart of love was pain, but love, like a lover, did not reveal its heart at once. You loved a person place or thing and then you faced loss. Not at once, but when the rapture subsided and some sense intruded into the fool's realm. Love and death were linked by the threat of loss, even though love conquered death in stories of romance and art. Believe the stories, or death is forever and love is only a fast-melting sugar-coating on the bitter pill of life.

Heavy, Marla. You're probably pre-menstrual. It will be full moon on the night of the ceremony and you're about to get your period again.

There is romance in this air but there are demons here too.

Her feelings of being tortured by this affair were feelings she surprisingly identified as guilt, or 'guilt'. She had not thought guilt was in her repertoire. Was it in fact guilt she was feeling? Examine feelings and they become evasive and mutable and chimerical, like dreams. She couldn't say it was guilt for sure. But it was a tortured feeling.

The feeling became known when she contemplated her return to the village. She did not want to offend her hosts, that was it. It was as if she were behaving badly by having taken up with Alit in this manner. She did not however have access to any reasonably reliable conjecture on their probable views on the matter. They might not have minded; they like their guests to be happy, no?

Who did it hurt? His wife. Married. Marla didn't like affairs with married men and not because she ever wanted to marry her lovers, she didn't. She liked, she supposed, for married people to make their best and most honourable attempts to live up to the promises they made. Of course she had no business telling other people they should be faithful, she wouldn't even try it. And of course marriage could be seen—here, especially—as a social obligation rather than a personal one. And his social obligations really were none of her business. What was? Only her own part?

For Alit it was all right to have this affair with her as long as his wife did not see. So, Marla, what's it to you? I could get all righteous, she thought, about not deceiving anyone. But that'd make it not just a matter between us as individuals. If I insisted on openness, and I wouldn't, I abominate people who insist on openness, then I am forcing it to become a matter for too many other people. Alit was, no doubt, being courteous, as ever.

The old *tabus* of sex in fact were not, as Ratu Aji suspected, part of the life of his son's generation. As Marla found, Alit's wife enjoyed sexual encounters of a prolonged and varied nature, lucky her. That might give her a desire for experience of other men, how would I know, thought Marla; she might not concern herself with her husband's doings as long as he continued to satisfy her—a doubtless pleasurable obligation that he intended to fulfil, I take it. What am I worrying, even thinking, about her for? This is *the world* that I live in, this is *life* I am living, smart women take their pleasure where they may, independent women limit their responsibility to themselves.

Alit's wife no doubt had not the freedom to have affairs. That's not my fault, Marla reasoned, what can I do, refuse my own freedom in solidarity? Marla was told that Balinese women were contented with their role. For all she knew, the wife might be every bit as content as she was meant to be. Marla was not the evangelical kind of feminist who enjoined contented women to become angry with their lot. That she, Marla, did not want the lives they had was her own business. If the women here had come to her and said, 'We want more freedom,' she would say, 'I'm all for it, how can I support you?' But she saw no sign of it and she deplored the thought she couldn't avoid: that they were not saying it because they were too oppressed. Besides, whatever freedom was, it wasn't a simple matter of being a citizen of a capitalist democracy.

Generally tourists came to have fun or came to perceive that the traditional way of life bestows more contentment than their own. Even though Marla was delighted to dress in sarong-kebaya and go with the women to the ceremonies, she could never be a Balinese wife. Sitting for hours making those fiddly offerings. She needed her solitude, her moods, her faithlessness. That was how she knew who she was.

Remember Laura. Remember the golden age, the thirties. This is how to know her. She is part of her culture's system no matter how separate she feels from it. In the age of colonialism, she can practise only her kind of colonialism, she can't *not* practise it. In the age of tourism Marla can practise only a version of tourism. Tourism with its roots in colonialism—quest and conquest—whether it's holiday tourism school of life tourism business tourism development tourism. Culture defines this relationship, but so does character. So does imagination.

'It would be better if you do forget me,' she said. She tried to translate it. Then if it is better, he answered, I will forget you while you are gone, I will think about you when a letter comes from you, and when you are back in Bali we will be together again. No one else, he insists, no one else.

'Are you serious? How could I? Believe me. Only you.' This doesn't need translation. 'In Bali,' she says, 'only you. When I'm not in Bali, I don't know.'

She doesn't think to insist 'only me' in return. He has only ever slept with his wife and with her.

Alit said that she might keep coming back to Bali whenever she could and then one day she would want to build her own house in Bali. *No!* she said emphatically, no. She doesn't see herself settling in Bali, not even for this romantic bedazzlement or she might find herself looking to him to cause all her happiness all her moods.

If he were not married, he says, they would marry. She thinks that is just sweet-talk, but it's appalling enough.

There had to be a last day and this was it.

Every other time he took her out they had easily been able to borrow a helmet from the office. Today, they had planned to leave early. No one was around. Then Gusti had to go search far and wide for one of the spare helmets and it took ages. Both the helmets had been taken already.

Ibu Suci had a helmet she used to lend people. They went down there. That helmet had just been borrowed for the day.

They leant against the big borrowed motorbike by the side of the road.

'What if I don't wear a helmet?' Marla asked. This was ridiculous. They had planned to be on their way by now. It was a long way to go.

'Maybe police. Big road,' Alit said. They were going far, to the lake, and had to travel on several main roads to get there.

'Hey, Marla.' The languid call came from Donna, an American woman who lived beyond Katak Inn. She strolled past them on her way to the market. 'What's up?'

'We're trying to borrow a helmet for me.'

'Buy one! Didn't you know you can buy one for under five dollars? Simplest thing, just buy one,' advised Donna, going on her way. There was always an easy solution in Bali.

She says to buy one. How much is a helmet? Marla asked him.

Maybe three thousand, four thousand, he told her. He seemed embarrassed.

That was cheap all right.

We'll go buy one, Marla said.

Sure?

'Yes,' she decided. 'Let's go.'

There was no right way to act in this situation. It seemed the height of vulgarity: she needed to use it only this once: couldn't borrow it, we'll buy it. She could easily afford it, so why not? She might never use it again but she could give it to someone. Alit could not begin to imagine being able carelessly to afford another helmet let alone buy one to use but once. But she could, easily, so what was she going to do? Would it have been in better taste to pretend it cost more than she could afford? She wanted them to be on their way, not hang around here.

Lots of people ended up living in Bali.

These days they travel back and forth easily; moving to Bali isn't the end of the earth, the earth has no more ends. Marla had observed several pleased westerners gaily announce their ultimate shopping discovery. 'We can get our own house in Bali! For only $7,000. We can design it ourselves. We have a very special relationship with a family here, who will arrange it all . . .' It is often said that what the Balinese are best at is giving the visitors what they want. You want your own little house in Bali? No problem!

But Marla had heard the other side of the story too. 'There are plenty of places to stay,' said those opposed to the increasing acquiring of dear little houses; 'you can rent a house whenever you need one.' For one thing, the argument went, Bali is a tiny and populous place, and every house erected for a westerner (who was actually there part time) meant that much less land on which to grow rice. For another thing, land and housing were traditionally matters for a community, and the Balinese who was arranging your own dear house was engaging in a western-style competitive individualism which was against the spirit of what the would-be house-owner was supposed to be so taken with, the spirit of Bali.

And Marla didn't have to know all that to know that she

would never seek to realise any dreams she might allow herself, any fantasies of not moving on.

Suppose they do build that hotel near his village—and that seemed inevitable—and of course he could be lured into many an easy adultery by white women looking for . . . what is it they look for? Be careful, she wants to tell him, guard yourself agaitn heartbreak or disease.

He would like, he tells her one day, to leave the work he does now.

That she understands. A government job, a salary, who would want that for life?

He would like to have a business with tourists. His family own some land near the sea. There they could build a place to stay. If they had more money.

Don't let me think it, she thinks, don't let me even think it, I know he wants nothing from me, he has told me so and it is true.

'Oh Alit,' is what she does say, 'be careful.'

'Of course!' he says. But he does not know what she means.

What could he be to her? He was a holiday fling, and she would leave, and there would be those letters: 'Sorry I haven't written for so long, I'm so busy here, so far away, so long ago . . .' How well could she ever know him? If you believed the scholars he had a life-long sense of a mystical connection to the placenta ceremonially buried at his birth, all the afterbirths were meant to be his spiritual twins and he was never to neglect them. In his world, history and mythology were inextricable and supernatural causes lay behind all events. He saw time as repeating cycles rather than a linear flow. His ancestors were more important than his proper name or personal biography as an index of identity. His consciousness was imbued with dualities and trinities that were only ideas on paper to her; four-fold and eight-fold divisions that were to her remote and novel abstractions.

He took his assumptions about her consciousness from his own sources.

What could she be to him? A white woman. A white woman who was friendly to him. If she is friendly she will say yes to sex. That is what many seem to believe, leading to unpleasant encounters—misunderstandings she gets furious for being blamed for, the kind where a guy thinks she's got to do whatever he wants. A white woman, an object, an experience long dreamed of.

Yet he has a perfect life, a beautiful wife, two sons. He has everything. He's got a place he comes from and returns to, where he belongs.

She wonders if what he knows about her, what he thinks about her, is anything she would recognise, anything she would recognise as insight. He must wonder *why him?* Does he realise what she saw in him at once? Does he see what it is about him that charms her?

What are they to each other? Is their symbolic value to each other greater than who they really are? Is that always a question, in any relationship?

It was only a matter of time, and she had better name the time, and it would be soon, when she would say *and now I won't see you again*. She found out what day it was, and worked it all out. She went to Sanur, to the airline office. When she left here, and it was only days away now, she would go back to the village for the ceremony, and leave from there for the airport.

We can do this any time forever, Alit would tell her, even when we are quite old. Maybe he was right. If you accept that you will be single always, if you accept a life that has long periods without love, that was not the worst arrangement in the world.

Maybe she feared that he would want to stop before she

did. Some chick could come along. Some rich lady could come along. It could all turn into a horrible game. They have a nice time together, then she leaves, saying that she will return. For all he knows, she might not return. For all she knows, he might not want her when she does. It would become a matter of, who goes first? Will she leave him? Or will she be hurt? But now she was about to hurt herself by leaving. Would she be more hurt if she waited . . .

Jesus, God, Christ, what was she thinking of, was she trying to plan not being hurt? You can't think like this. Just stop it. The day was very very close.

Are you sure, she asked him, that no one in your village knows that you come to see me?

Of course no one knows, he assured her. '*Biasa-biasa*,' he assured her, '*Biasanya*.' When we are there, we will be like friends only, like brother and sister, just like usual, he assured her. 'No problem.'

How could she believe him? When she had been staying there, someone came running over to her in the street one day and said: the postcards you took to the post office yesterday all went today: two to Australia one to Netherlands and one to America! Her informant had been very pleased to tell her this, but the astonishing thing he actually was telling her was that the villagers had gossiped about what she sent from the post office. There were no secrets here.

Alit, everyone knows everything, she said. When I return, we cannot see each other like this. I want to see Ratu Aji and Ratu Biang. I must go back to your village, but I do not go for you. I wish it were not your village. But already I promised I would go back. I promised to arrive on that day.

206

PART THREE

TYLER

ONE

Toko Rose was a large boutique near bemo corner in Kuta. Most of the shops around there were hole-in-the-wall style, but Toko Rose was a contrast: plenty of floor space, garments set out on racks—women's clothes and men's; large mirrors and glass cabinets displaying fashionable costume jewellery. The clothes looked pretty good. Better than any others he'd seen around here. Tyler picked out a couple of cotton jackets, took them off the rack, then put them back again.

A pretty young woman was sitting at the desk. She was watching to see if he wanted to buy anything but made no attempt to persuade him. Down at the beach and in the alleys a non-stop hard sell went on; a constant importuning until you didn't even feel like buying anything you wanted let alone wanting anything you didn't have. This was different: just a cool, disinterested gaze. The girl recrossed her dusky legs, as if to emphasise her disinclination to perform a selling routine. What was this place, some kind of front? But the threads on sale were fine—good copies of good designs. Neil liked to look good and the stuff he had bought here was probably for himself.

'Hi there,' Tyler said, approaching the desk.

'Good morning,' the girl answered without any pretence at enthusiasm. She didn't say, 'May I help you?' nor 'Try it on, looks good, be a fool to pass.'

Well, thought Tyler, here goes. 'Can you help me? I'm looking for a friend of mine. He came here a while ago and bought some things. It was quite a few weeks ago.' He took out the photograph of Neil. She looked at it blankly.

'This from you?' she asked in her pretty, lilting accent: *dis prom you?*

209

Oh great, he thought, we all look the same to them, they're all going to think I'm flashing a photo of myself. 'This is my friend. The one who came here. Bought something. Do you remember seeing him?'

'No,' she said. He didn't know if she were telling the truth. 'How long have you been working here?' he asked. 'If I may ask?' She looked more sullen still. She wasn't making it any easier. A couple had come in and were riffling through the clothes on the racks, calling out to each other. The girl got up to stand near them, although she hadn't budged when Tyler had come in.

This was not going to be easy.

The couple left and the girl busied herself tidying the clothes they had disturbed. I'll try again, he thought, once more, I can't just walk out now. 'Look,' he said, 'please excuse me. My name's Tyler Evers. Pleased to meet you.' She expressed no responding pleasure. 'This picture is my friend, Neil Bolderstone. I'm looking for him. He came in here two—three months ago. That's why I asked how long you've been here.'

Miss Inscrutable Oriental herself. She was very young. She didn't like being asked anything except *Where can I try this on? How much is this? Just looking, OK?* Her repertoire of reply was restricted to pointing to the fitting room or to the dangling price label or to the sign that said, 'This is a FIXED PRICE shop'. The extent of her English ran to *Good morning, yes, no, looks great on you.*

'Come tonight,' she said, as if speaking with reluctance, but he responded as eagerly as if she had put herself out to be especially helpful.

'Tonight? There's someone else here tonight? OK,' Tyler said. 'I'll definitely come by tonight. Thank you.'

Anyone selling on the beach needs the money they make immediately, it can mean the difference between their family eating that day, or not. People selling in the markets, the stalls, the smaller shops are often part of a family that owns that business. They're pretty committed to selling, and will try hard; the whole family's prosperity is their own. At least, they make a commission on each item, so there's an incentive. But the girl in the shop that Tyler went to—that's something more recent around here, that's a shopgirl on a weekly wage and it's a very low wage and it's the same wage whether she sits at the desk filing her nails or whether she busts a gut trying to get you to buy. It's the same as the shops anywhere, Melbourne, Paris, Montreal, what's the incentive?

This Tyler learnt from a guy with a deep tan, blond dreadlocks and an indeterminate accent—transAtlantic, trans-Pacific, transglobal, trans certain places certain people know. They had struck up a conversation at Bar Zapata. It was the first place Tyler had been to on the short list compiled by friends who'd been here before. It was his first day in Bali and it was good to get out of the heat and it was good to get started on his quest. They had been joined by two slouching, sunburnt Australian women who kept up their own counterpoint conversation alongside.

'The service in Sydney is really bad,' one of the women informed them, 'worse and worse, they won't help you, they don't know what service is.'

'The Japanese? They've got their own shops, just for the service,' her companion contributed in the same familiar whine.

'I thought it might be a front,' said Tyler to blond dread. 'They weren't that interested in selling.'

'Front for what?'

'Laundering money, drug money, whatever.'

'No way man, that's not the way it works. The owner of the shop is making most of the bread out of export and the shop here is a sideline. Retail on one shirt will pay a shop assistant's wages for a week and those are nice shirts, he'd sell a few a day without trying, not as nice as the ones I sell, but they're OK.'

'Rip you off,' said the first woman, 'soon as look at you, most of them.'

'Try telling them', added her friend, 'we have the one price, same price for everyone, it's a bloody good system too, try telling them that.'

'I should go back tonight,' Tyler said. 'Someone might remember Neil.'

'We all look the same to them but a black dude they might remember.'

The women stared at Tyler, as if suddenly given permission to notice his colour. 'At least you don't have to worry about sunburn,' said the first one as if consoling him for an affliction.

'You know the place well, right? Let me show you this.' Tyler handed his list to the other guy.

'Your friend went into the hills and fell in love with a beautiful Balinese princess,' the guy said. 'This joint is closed, this one's been taken over by Aussie piss-heads.' He jabbed a forefinger at the list. 'This is the trendy bar, laid-back, kind of civilised, Eurogroovers hang.'

'Neil wasn't into Asian women.'

The two Australians went off to the rest-room together, holding tight to their bags.

'Up in the hills they do magic, they cast spells, you never get away. I'm going up into the hills one day.' Blond dread sighed and called for another drink. 'Me, make my million then let one of them tribal women magic me right away.'

Mali 2000 turned out to be further away than he thought. He had walked up the road from Kuta, where a return visit to Toko Rose had yielded precisely nothing. All along the way he kept being told Mali 2000 was just five minutes ahead. Although it was night it was still hot. He walked very slowly so he wouldn't sweat. He was starting to feel that the world was engaged in a conspiracy to keep him away from the place. The final information that Mali 2000 was only five minutes away came when he was well within sight of the place, and his informant walked the remaining short distance along with him to make sure he found it. 'Want transport?' the boy asked when they arrived. 'I wait for you OK?'

'Don't wait for me,' said Tyler. 'No one should wait for me.'

'Transport,' the boy insisted. 'For next time.'

Tyler slipped the boy a few coins. 'Thanks for the directions. But don't wait. I'm on a mission.' He didn't care if the kid understood. He was at the right place, that was a sudden feeling he trusted, the right place for something. There was more to life than his mission.

Mali 2000 was a large place. Inside, there was a bar down one long side, and an area of rattan tables encircled by chairs and sofas covered in printed fabrics in rich, deep colours. There was a raised area down the back. The music was cool and Latin. Jobim.

Tyler hesitated at the door a moment. He took a swift, practised measure of the place. He could tell in three seconds which part of any room to head towards. He began to make his way to a space near one end of the long bar, and then realised he was being signalled from the other side, from a large table to his left, and the most vigorous signalling was being done by a woman in a hot pink skin-tight mini-dress, which was the first thing you saw, her beautiful shape in hot pink lurex, and the deep tan, and the dark hair bundled up into a kind of swirly pile atop her head. She wore lots of bangles, she looked Spanish, she was at a table with several other people who, at a glance, looked like an interesting bunch, they looked like they were having a good time, they looked like they were on holiday on a gorgeous tropical island, they looked like they were very pleased with the situation already, they looked like they were making a place for Tyler to sit and join them.

'Here!' they were saying. 'You must be with us! Hello, good evening, how do you do, hi,' they said. 'Join us. We're not drunk! Because you look lovely. And we are all lovely, aren't we?' said their several voices as they made room and welcomed him and laughed with pleasure as they drew him into the realm of their charming effrontery. He was seated next to hot pink Spanish lurex. 'You don't meet anyone? You come alone, isn't it luck?' she told him with irresistible assurance. 'No one knows more than one other person until now,' she announced with pleasure.

Tyler was caught in high-spirited cross-currents of greetings and names. He was urged to drink a daiquiri and it was already there. He forgot everyone's name at once, and very soon after he forgot his mission.

The girl in hot pink was called Anita and on Tyler's other side sat a young man who looked like her younger brother. Anita's travelling companion, she explained. 'We get along perfectly, we never fight over men.' He was having an uproarious conversation with an older man who looked Greek, gold chains, dark hair at his chest.

'We don't know each other until today,' Travelling Companion told Tyler indicating the man, as if this were an amazing confidence.

'We did not *meet* until today,' the man qualified solemnly.

'We had not met and we had not known,' T.C. corrected, beginning to giggle.

'We had not met and yet we had known.' The Greek slapped the table in delight, as if this foolishness were great wisdom.

'No! We had met, and yet we had not known!' They both erupted into hilarity.

'Mushrooms,' Anita began to explain.

'I heard about those mushrooms. Like mescalito? I never . . .'

'Me also not . . .' As this sounded like a refrain of the trippers' psychedelic dialogue, they laughed too.

There was a Japanese couple who were often here on business, an English girl beyond them, and a few others until the circle was completed with the white guy on Anita's other side.

'You're American, right?' he asked. 'I can tell. You're from California.'

'No.' Tyler didn't like being asked where he was 'from'.

'In fact I've been living in Australia for the last year.'

'No kidding! We've got one Aussie at the table then!'

These people recognised each other: they wore bold colours and were unafraid to dress with carelessness or deliberation; they knew the place to go, in any bright new location on the globe, they knew where they'd find each other; even on their first night in Bali they would not be at any place other than the Mali 2000 bar. They would stay here until midnight and then go to a place right on the beach where there was dancing until dawn.

Another daiquiri was already there and Tyler drank it. The girl in hot pink had skin like honey, and her teeth flashed and her bangles tinkled as she laughed. Tyler laughed too. They drank and they laughed and they ordered more drinks.

Two

'The way you want Bali to be!' the billboard proclaimed. Beyond the fenced perimeters lay the generous gardens of the most luxurious, highly priced hotel in the area. Tyler paid his chartered bemo at the gate, told the driver not to wait and began to walk down the wide driveway.

The American Express docket had been for 'lunch for two'. Tyler had no idea why Neil would come here for lunch but it wasn't that far out a thing to do. Even the fact that Neil, who didn't like paying for anything, had paid for the lunches could be explained. He might have put both on the card, and got cash off his companion. Or he owed someone lunch. He might even have paid for lunch, he might have wanted to impress someone. But why here?

Anything could happen in Bali. Last night had happened. Although it wasn't that far out either—Tyler had lived some wild nights of course—it was a night not too easily to be forgotten, least of all for the next two days. Almost he wished he had left this errand until he felt halfway well but no, there was not a good enough reason to postpone what he had come here for, not the heat, not the hangover, not the hesitation he had always visualised when planning to visit this hotel. Now what?

No one else was in sight. People didn't do too much walking at a place like this. A couple of gardeners turned and watched him. He called, 'Hi,' and was met with a blank stare. This wasn't the kind of place tourists called out hi to gardeners.

At the open lobby area some fat white old tourists were being herded into a large white new bus with the hotel's name displayed on the side. They also stared at Tyler as he leapt up the wide stairs. He caught a couple of eyes and essayed a greeting only to be met with faces in the range tentative to frozen. Well of course. He didn't fit the profile of the typical guest, who wanted to see only other versions of himself on the premises. Tyler crossed the expanse of shiny floor and designer decor: style troppo deluxe international, emphasised by carefully chosen artifacts: here was a giant wooden Garuda, carved and painted in intricate colourful detail in the local manner.

'Good morning,' he said to the receptionist. She was attired in a glamorous version of the national costume, gold and rubies glowing at her ear lobes and fingers. 'Could you please tell me where the restaurant is?'

'Certainly sir,' she responded, the formula sounding oddly accented on her exotic lips. 'Please take the pathway you see to your right.' She indicated its location. Her gesture was that of an airline steward mechanically revealing the location of emergency exits or oxygen masks. That gesture Tyler and Neil had had to know well, and had once adapted into a silly dance for the entertainment of their colleagues, with an improvised rap: when the plane crash you get a life jacket make no difference if you lack it, and get a whistle in your kit but ain't gonna help when the shark had bit . . .

Smiling at the memory, and at the easily resisted impulse to repeat the performance for the benefit of the robotic receptionist, Tyler, turning from the desk, didn't quite hear what the woman said. She stood in front of him, thrusting at him a guided-tour itinerary and a ballpoint pen, a stout white woman in belted shorts and shirt.

'I beg your pardon?' Tyler said, not sure his double-take hearing was correct.

'Your autograph,' she pleaded.

'Who do you think I *am*?'

She said, 'Well, I know you're *somebody*.'

Tyler smiled at her graciously and said, 'Pleased to oblige,' signed and went on his way. He got it; he knew from way back that he wasn't easily taken for an ordinary guy in these places. He had short hair, chiselled features and neat clothes. Sport or television, they thought; to them there were no other thinkable references.

Tyler made his way to the restaurant. This hotel was a gorgeous place—neat rows of bushes in brilliant flower, neat stone pathways you could eat off, neat little statues bedecked in neat little black-and-white check aprons, and then the restaurant, a commodious pavilion with a view of the sea. Troops of waiters in their own lavish, uniform versions of native dress were in attendance. It was eleven am and a few tourists—a small group and two couples—were sitting over plates and glasses partaking of—rather than eating—their holiday mealtime late breakfast or early lunch.

Now he hesitated. He had made no plans other than to find the place, and see if anyone there remembered Neil eating lunch one day many weeks ago. This idea never did bear much scrutiny and now that he was to put it into action it seemed futile, ridiculous, pathetic. His toxic condition added no charm to the prospect. So here goes. A waiter was approaching. Tyler had not been prepared for the solemn air of oppressive etiquette about the place. Everywhere he'd been so far in Bali was marked with the atmosphere of casual friendliness the place was famous for. If you had more money than most, this is what you got. Tyler dearly wished to have more money than most but this is not what he wanted. There was no time to dwell on this thought. The waiter was attempting to show him to a table.

'No, wait,' Tyler said. The waiter was a young man, slim and slight of build, as all the local men seemed to be. So familiar was the knowledge that he was conspicuous that Tyler felt rather than saw a few of the diners looking at him, on the margins of his consciousness, like the knowledge that it was day. 'I just want to ask you something.'

'You want to make booking, sir?'

'No . . .' Suddenly the heat and the threat of dehydration asserted themselves. He changed his mind. 'I will take that table,' he said. 'Just a drink, OK?'

He sat, he chose, he ordered, and the waiter returned with an iced Coke in a large frosted glass. 'I want to ask you something,' Tyler said. He had his photograph of Neil ready.

'Have you been working here long?' The waiter blinked at him. How long was long? Why was he asking? 'I mean . . .' said Tyler. As he showed the photograph and the AmEx docket, several other waiters came over, each demanding to have a look.

It took a while, but eventually they understood that the photograph was of his friend, the docket was the receipt for lunch here and had been signed by his friend, the date of the lunch was many weeks previous, Tyler was looking for this friend, and if anyone remembered serving Neil, and maybe remembered anything else, anything at all, like where he was staying, where he was going to, who he was lunching with, then he, Tyler, would be grateful for the information.

Perhaps, he thought, he had better put a price on his gratitude. 'There'd be a reward,' he said. Reward was not a word they knew. 'I would . . .' What could he say, that he would pay for any information leading to the whereabouts of Neil Bolderstone? 'I'd pay,' he said. For a moment he feared a deluge of intelligence.

As he drank his Coke and ordered a second—each one cost several times the price of a Coke at Zapata or Mali—and as every waiter in that restaurant took his turn in the small throng surrounding him, Tyler began to feel increasingly foolish, and he began to feel angry.

By the time he paid and made his way through the lush gardens to the beach, his displeasure was immense. He could walk back along the beach; surely that would be cooler. He wished he had brought his sunblock cream. Yeah, black skin got sunburnt too.

The hotel's farthest fence had a gate that led to the beach, and there, too, its billboard reminded you that inside it was 'The way you want Bali to be!' And eat your heart out, everyone else thought Tyler, because Bali isn't the way *you* want it to be, Bali has dirt and poverty and armies of hustlers trying to make a dollar, and if you can't get behind a big wealthy wall you can't miss it.

And that wasn't what was making Tyler bad tempered. It

was the realisation that he had no hope in the world of even finding out what had happened to Neil, let alone finding Neil. And he had kind of always known it.

THREE

Up to the day he had left Sydney, Tyler had dreams about Neil. He dreamt that Neil returned, bent with the weight of treasures, from imperative, magical voyages; he dreamt that Neil just showed up, in a normal way; he dreamt that Neil had been there all along and they just hadn't noticed.

Tyler hadn't known what to believe. It looked bad. What had happened? No one ever came up with a satisfactory explanation. As time passed, people began to suggest that Neil must be dead, or very sick, or in captivity, though it didn't make any sense, you couldn't imagine any harm coming to Neil. But nor did it make any sense that Neil would stop writing to his wife, never return from a holiday, and leave no trace or clue as to his whereabouts.

The day had come when Caroline decided she was really worried. She *knew* the mail was unreliable, over there, in those countries. But still. There was always a telephone. She *knew* it was hard to get to a phone in some parts of Bali, people told her every last thing about it, so she knew that, but Neil had called her from there the first week he was away. You could always get to a phone sooner or later. And it was later and later and later.

She got worried, even though she had dedicated her capacity for worry to large, awesome sufferings. She worried, and then she worried that she was too worried. After all, there had been a massive oil spill that would devastate ocean ecology for aeons, the Third World had been totally fucked by the World Bank and famines and floods laid waste lands that were already the victims of atrocious greed.

She got worried long before Tyler thought it was time to get worried. He had problems of his own. He left Australia for a while and took a trip to Fiji. There was his Australian visa. And he had some big decisions.

'Make a commitment, Tyler,' Lydia was saying, 'or say goodbye.'

'Give me time,' Tyler said. 'Just a bit more time.'

'Putting me on hold,' she said. 'Again.' She had looked bitter and scornful and sad. He usually loved the way she would tell him all about himself but not this part of it. 'For the last time,' she said, and she meant it.

He loved her voice: the mournful Black Sea cadences; he loved her body, its muscular, supple perfection formed by regimented gymnastics since infancy. 'My Russian android' he used to call her. She easily kept up with him in the gym, and she even had a sizable butt, round and firm. Most white girls were made with a piece missing. She was happy going to the clubs and she could dance all night; she was happy staying at home and she could cook a hundred excellent recipes.

'You can keep going to new women for the rest of your life,' Lydia said. 'If that's what you want. And always put a limit on how close anyone can get to you, limit how well you can know another person. If that's what you want.' What he wanted was her, then and there, but she wouldn't let him touch her. He was on fire for her and she knew it. Women were different, for sure. She had been ready to put him through that pain and herself too, so that it wouldn't be the same scene they had always had. It would have been too. Making fine love, feeling very close, then and there, nothing changed, putting off the showdown for another time. Was he going to make it this time?

No.

He told Lydia that he loved her but that was all.

Then he went to Fiji, and stayed away longer than he was going to. With his airline contacts he could alter his ticket and not lose a cent, and he met a nice girl or two, on holiday, anything goes.

No one had been home at Neil and Caroline's for a while after he returned. Lydia had left the sports store, left the gym, left her flat. She had gone away, that was all over, and he tried to pretend he hadn't decided anything.

He set about forgetting the things she'd said. He didn't want to wonder how close he was able to get to anyone. 'If not me,' Lydia had said, 'if not me?'

All Tyler wanted, all he ever wanted, was The One, the One woman he made the whole commitment to, the One he could love and trust and believe, without wondering if there was someone else waiting for him, someone more beautiful more exciting more loving more understanding more fascinating, someone else to meet, the real One. Which is what he always ended up wondering. Anyway, he wanted to be free to climb a mountain in case he ever heard of a mountain he wanted to climb.

He moved into a flat in Potts Point, a short lease, a sublet. When Caroline finally caught up with him she was sure that Neil really had disappeared.

'People don't just disappear,' Tyler told her.

It turned out the world was divided into two kinds of people, those who said 'People don't just disappear', and those who said 'People are always disappearing'.

There were stories. Someone knew someone who knew someone who'd heard about an anthropologist from Belgium or somewhere who'd gone to film some bizarre ceremony the natives had over in Bali and he had disappeared. He might have seen something he wasn't supposed to. Apparently the whole story had never been uncovered.

They heard of a woman who had gone to Bali with her fiancé. Her fiancé had gone for a walk and never returned. There had been something about it in the papers, but they could never find out any more.

Caroline had reported Neil's failure to return to the police, and to the consul and to the immigration people.

It was bad enough that there had been an earthquake in South America where thousands died, each death a loss for someone. People still starved to death in Africa and in the street outside garbage piled up, a testament to the fatal indignities inflicted on the planet. And she was out of her mind

223

about Neil, and reporting it to the authorities did no good. 'It's like they don't believe me,' she told Tyler, and started crying. She told him everything. It was true that she and Neil had started having a few problems. It wasn't only because it was a bad time to leave her work that she had not gone with him. They had decided to have some time apart. Tyler realised that he was not surprised. 'Don't tell *them*,' she insisted, meaning all the officials. Marriage difficulties: they would only be confirmed in their opinion—held, she was sure, for its convenience to them—that Neil had merely neglected to keep in touch, either because he was having too much fun, or because of some quarrel back home.

'Most reports of disappearances,' the guy at the consulate informed Tyler, as he had previously informed Caroline, 'concern people who haven't written for a while . . .' Mothers, wives, friends, they get worried and report a son, husband or friend missing. Always, the officials tried to reassure Tyler as they had tried to reassure Caroline, turns out there's nothing to worry about. The traveller shows up somewhere and is amazed to find that back home they've been getting worried. Of course, the officials continued, we do everything we can. Local police have been notified. Have you been in touch with his bank?

Neil had not cashed any more traveller's cheques after the first ten days in Bali. Caroline had put a trace on his credit cards. He hadn't used his Visacard at all since leaving Australia. He had used his American Express card over there, but it hadn't been used in the last two months. No one else had tried to use his card. The postmark on his first postcard was illegible. The postmark on his second and last card was 'Ubud'. This was a town inland.

Caroline had even managed to get through to both the American and Australian consulates in Denpasar. She had rung Neil's mother in the States, and without revealing her own concern, found that Mom hadn't heard from Neil. But Neil never did write many letters. 'He's away on business,' Caroline had told her. 'He must be busy. I'll tell him to write. Or phone. When he can.'

Tyler talked with Caroline long into the night. Caroline was still obssessed with vast, intimidating, insoluble troubles that were not her own. She had just found out about a new, spreading affliction, she had read all about it in a magazine, it was called compassion fatigue, and that's what she had. It threatened to crush her soul, she had all the symptoms: she could no longer feel pity deeply enough, she had worried herself to a standstill and she was numb, she was overwhelmed by the awfulness of everything and it had damaged her, she sometimes forgot about Tibet when she worried about the rainforests, when news of an erupting volcano horrified her, she could no longer think about nuclear waste. There was another civil war somewhere and she was unable to care. But she cried again, as she confessed. And now Neil. He might not feel the same way she did about everything but he would never never just disappear, and Tyler knew that.

'I'll go,' Tyler promised before she left. 'I'll go as soon as I can. If I can get on a flight tomorrow I'll go tomorrow. I've never been there,' he said, which was true. 'I want to see the place anyway,' which was a lie.

Tyler made the arrangements to go to Bali while he thought new, troublesome thoughts.

He had been thinking new, troublesome thoughts for a while. It was because of turning thirty, he told himself, it was a crisis. He was soon to have his thirtieth birthday and thirty was the age at which he should know where he was going. Where he was going was back to the States and back to the airline. He wasn't going to marry Lydia, he wasn't going to stay in Australia, he wasn't going to be another Neil. He had had a great year off anyway. He hadn't become a star or anything but he hadn't really counted on it. He wasn't going to make enough of a living from modelling either in the States or in Australia, and anyway he was getting too old for that and anyway he wasn't sure it was what he wanted. He had a good job to go back to.

He hadn't thought a few things through, of course. News was that they tested everyone for drug use now—even for use outside working hours. Tyler never did drugs at work and not too much outside anyway, and it shouldn't really be a problem. But he had to admit—because his Australian friends insisted he take a position—that he thought it was wrong. Living outside of America had forced him to think of these things. There were a lot of wrong things that you had to live with though and there was no way out of it.

He wanted some security, he guessed, he wanted some guarantees. Australia had seemed really appealing at one time and he had played with the idea of staying there, an idea that was vigorously encouraged in Sydney, a town in which Tyler found himself to be someone lots of people wanted to know.

'How does it feel to be a symbol of the exotic and desirable?' his voice coach Fay Barry had asked him. Tyler's agent sent her more promising clients to Fay because modelling can lead to acting. She was a chain-smoking old woman with a tenderly ravaged face and traces of bohemian glamour of the crushed-velvet and feathers kind, and she took a mild, friendly interest in him. He only took a few classes, though, as really his voice was fine, and if he ever needed to work on it he'd do it then. 'It isn't me, I know that,' he answered Fay. If people reacted to him a certain way only because he was black and American, he said, that was their problem. There were some places he could go and be a symbol of everything fearsome and degraded. That was especially not his problem. He had learnt that formula: their prejudice is not my problem. This he knew to be true. But there was negative prejudice and positive prejudice. Some people reacted to him a certain way because they had Mandingo fantasies, some because he was tall and handsome, he listened well and spoke entertainingly, he went to the gym daily and had a smile that could ignite a swamp. In truth, he took credit for it, for the swing to the positive side of response he found from people when he got to Australia. Perhaps to most people he was a blank screen on to which they projected their dreams. People were mainly women.

Australian women came from all over and they were frank, bold, spunky and game. He had a good time, but to stay there began to seem like the end of the line; Australia was not enough; it was a little death. He missed energy. He needed to go back to New York. He needed that energy.

'But things are really bad in America,' his Australian friends suggested. 'If you live there,' they qualified. 'The race situation,' they insinuated. 'Perhaps not in New York,' they proposed. 'New York is fabulous. New York is terrifying. New York is amazing.'

He listened to people too much, he thought. He listened for who he was and for what he really thought. When he didn't like it, he stopped listening. Lydia was no android for all her perfections. She had a bruised delicate heart and he had hurt her. It might have hurt him too. He was not ready to realise this, he was not ready.

New troublesome thoughts. Big decisions were once and for all. Courage needed renewing.

Neil was important in his life. Meeting Neil was the major consequence of the first big decision he had ever made, and that had consequence aplenty. The decision was to leave the firm where he had been incredibly lucky to be placed in their trainee program as soon as he'd graduated. A career path was laid out before him. His strict, bourgeois parents were gratified. He had been brought up to go this way. A lot of people were trying to convince him that what the world needed was another black yuppie, that 'his people' needed all the achievers they could get, that he had a duty to make it in that world, that he had taken a considerable few steps on an exclusive ladder and the ceiling was out of sight. Tyler worked there a few years, and eventually figured that he had had his time proving he could fit into the world of achievers and role models, and it was something he could never prove, cause he got a lot of acceptance and he got a lot of unacceptance, and eventually he knew he didn't need to stick around to see which way it would swing in the end, if there ever was an end, or even which way it would swing tomorrow.

He listened when they told him to make his people proud, and he thought about it, and he figured he wasn't in the pride-making business. He had felt aged and freed by this knowledge, and amazingly able ready and willing to take a big risk or two, he, who had never needed to take a risk in his life. He wanted to see places and meet people, he wanted that a lot, and he didn't want to wait any longer.

He made his decision, he left the firm, he joined the airline and he met Neil. Neil had gone the same road and knew all about it. Neil became a good buddy, an older brother figure. 'Have a good time, Bro,' Neil would say, 'that's what it's all about. There's no one you have to prove anything to. Live your life. Stay free, climb a mountain. Enjoy. Live.'

Four

He really should have got a chartered bemo, Tyler thought, as he changed from one crowded, uncomfortable bus into another for the third time since leaving Kuta. At the bus stations the hustlers shrieked and thrust insistent garish packaged confections at him, never taking no for an answer; inside the bus he had to sit with his chin on his knees, a giant among pygmies; the road was hot and dusty and rough. Memories of tight-packed, rattling buses on pot-holed roads in poor countries were being shaken to the fore. This was worse even than the time he was persuaded to take the local buses in Mexico, and he had vowed then, as he vowed now, that no amount of saving money or gaining authentic travel experience was worth this much discomfort. Pain is forgotten when the injuries are healed so you do some stupid things over and over. Tyler was not the kind to claim his right to hardship in foreign places. He was the kind to luck into the easy way. Mostly. Except for these toy-size Balinese buses. Call it a learning experience.

If Ubud led to nothing as fast as Kuta had led to nothing, he could go back to the beach for a few days before returning home. Lydia—he could think about her now that it was too late to turn back—would be gone. There were always new girls in town but maybe she was the best, maybe it could have really led to something. He allowed himself some twinges of regret. Whatever. He would still have fun. Once he had done all he could do. Before he left Kuta he had managed to phone Caroline—surprisingly easily, actually: the desk clerk got him the number, it rang, and it answered. He left a message on the machine: I'm asking around, and I'm on my way to Ubud. When he hung up, the clerk told him how to pronounce Ubud. Not 'oooo—bood'. He'd remember.

He could have stayed on in Kuta for another day, for the

fun, but one more day and he might never have left. It just wasn't the right timing to find a place that could be that much fun. He had come with a mission. He had a conscience. Women sang their siren song and flashed their Spanish eyes, goblets were filled with intoxicating fluids and music throbbed its carnal rhythms, but a man had to keep his word. He was pressed close against an old farmer cradling a cage with a rooster in it; and on the other side he was squashed by a woman with baskets full of bananas piled on her lap and under her feet. No one protested when the bus stopped for more passengers. Protesting was something they didn't do, these people, they were passive, they were fatalistic, they were used to these conditions, they were consoled by the richness of their colourful beliefs. In fact, Tyler reflected, he knew nothing about it. The people who had just been squeezed into the bus stared at Tyler with undisguised curiosity, as the others had all done at first, and then also settled down into an apparent state of deep reverie, calm acceptance.

'Hey, Neil!' Tyler heard. Someone was calling him! 'Hey, Neil!' He was sure he heard it. There were a lot of people milling around the bemo stop in Ubud. Tyler was about to cross the road to find the tourist information desk. Three bemos, bumper to bumper, blocked his way. When they passed, a Balinese youth was approaching him, smiling, one hand extended. Tyler was dazed: he was only a moment away from finding Neil! He took the youth's hand.

'Do you know Neil?'

'Of course!' the youth said.

Tyler wanted to whoop with joy.

'What you want, I can show you,' the boy said. 'I am very like tourist people.' He wore a new-looking Hawaiian-print shirt, old-looking brown polyester pants and rubber thongs on wide brown feet.

'OK, let's get this straight.' Tyler took out the photograph. 'This is Neil, right? This is Neil and not me. You know this guy?'

'This your friend,' said the youth confidently. 'I already take him, I can take you.'

'I want to go to where he is. Comprendi?' This time Tyler extended his hand. 'My name's Tyler Evers.'

'Tahl—vis?'

'Ty—ler.'

'I am Wayan. I have motorbike. Must take.' He gestured down the road.

'Go take your bike, my man. I'll find a place to leave my bag.'

The information desk accepted his bag, and Wayan returned on a rickety little motorbike. Dubiously, Tyler perched himself behind the boy. His legs were cramped. This, after those Lilliputian buses! But all his discomfort was as nothing, minutes away from this reunion. His eyes pricked: he felt rage and relief to think that Neil was about to look up and see him. What the hell was Neil going to say? 'Glad you could make it'? Or 'What are you doing here?', or 'I can explain everything'? Or 'So that's who I am'?

They had taken the road back towards Denpasar for a while and then turned left on to a narrow dirt side road, bumped their slow way past a walled compound. Dogs barked and children came running. A little further they stopped. Some free-standing buildings overlooked bright green fields. It wasn't any kind of hotel or anything. He'd find out soon enough. Tyler leapt off the bike and stretched hard to relieve his aching legs and back. Wayan watched, then led him inside.

Masks. Masks all over the walls. It was a large white space and it was a showroom for carved and painted masks. Tyler's attention was arrested by the huge, grotesque visage in front of him. It was painted an angry red, with black, white and gold lines providing much fine detail. Huge round eyes bulged fearsomely, their gleaming, hyperbolic black centres emphasised by surrounding curlicues of red and white. Gold tusks sprouted from the sides of flaring nostrils atop huge protruding teeth. The whole fearsome artifice was crowned with coarse black hair.

'It is Rangda,' said a soft voice behind him. An older man, dressed in a blue sarong and a loose white shirt, had entered. His air of dignity and gentleness was reassuring. 'You know Rangda? The wicked witch of Bali.' Wayan was nowhere to be seen. 'Please,' said the man, indicating a hard wooden bench. 'Sit. Look. Take your time. No problem. Something you are looking for?'

Tyler did not sit. 'I was looking for my friend,' he said feebly. He felt he had to force his gaze away from the witch. He must have been staring at it for many long minutes. On another wall all the masks were as simple as the Rangda was ornate, simple features and simply painted white. He turned toward them.

'Neutral mask,' said the man. 'You are an actor? Actors know this mask.'

'Neutral mask?' Tyler repeated. Indeed these enigmatic faces could be seen as stern or smiling or expressionless, male or female or androgynous. In the corner stood a mirror on a stand; next to it, on another wooden bench, lay a couple of unpainted masks. They were neutral masks too. Tyler picked one up.

'Lucky mask.' The old man had glided up to him and pointed at the whorl of wood occurring right at the centre of the nose. 'This a lucky sign.'

Tyler held the mask in front of his face and turned to the mirror. The mask covered his head. It was a strangely horrifying sight. He held the mask up a moment longer, lowered it. It was another moment before he could turn from the mirror.

The man was watching him. His own face was neutral. He gestured round the walls. 'Many mask. Every kind. What you want.'

'My friend . . . did Wayan tell you?' The oddly unsettling sight of his body under the face of the mask, the peculiar realisation that he had entirely imagined that Wayan was taking him to Neil, the most unaccustomed disorder this caused, all this reverberated and on top of it all he was coming to his senses he didn't know where.

'The guy that brought me here on his bike. Said Neil—this guy in this picture—' What had Wayan said? 'I thought I might find him here?'

'You can wait for friend here.'

He had been lured here and would be hustled into buying something at some ridiculously inflated price. 'I don't want to buy anything,' Tyler warned.

'No problem,' said the man with infinite gentleness. 'Only look. What you want. Take time.'

The rapidly diminishing belief that there was a purpose to his being here slid entirely from his grasp. He had been brought here for no reason at all.

Tyler sat on the verandah of number three and looked at the wall of steep terraces before him. 'OK,' he said. 'OK. This is it.'

'Oh—*kay*!' sang the young fellow who had brought him up here.

'You very happy here.'

'It'll do. It's fine.'

He had looked first at a place where you walked through a family compound and past a pig-sty—the stench was abominable—to get to a few dingy little guest rooms in a dark corner. He had gone back to the information desk and explained more clearly what his needs were. It had been the hottest part of the day for a long time.

This time they understood him at once. A jaunty young man was called for, some rapid dialogue was spoken, and then Tyler was ushered on to another motorbike. This one took him down the main road quite a way, and then turned into the driveway of a hotel. The hotel looked OK, but the boy didn't even get off the bike, only called out to some guys working there who brought him a key. They left the hotel, drove back the way they'd come a short way then turned off abruptly into what seemed to be a long driveway, with a gradient approaching the perpendicular. The jaunty young man threw the bike into first gear, revved it to the max, and they made it to the top in a cloud of foul black smoke.

All it was, was five bungalows, set in a kind of dress circle formation. Each of them was entered through a verandah facing away from the driveway, and each was positioned so that one could not be observed by the other. Beyond the five bungalows was a hut or shed. Here, in the mornings, attendants made breakfast. There were no other staff quarters because these bungalows were a brand new annexe to the hotel where they had stopped.

'That Puri Maya. This Maya Bungalow,' Jaunty explained. 'This special for private.' He seemed proud to understand that this 'private' was something tourists valued, however impossible to know their reasons. 'Private, quiet, no one bothering. Good for honeymoon.'

Private was good enough. He wanted a place he could retire to: rest, read, think, do his exercises. Out there, oh boy, it was all you could do to stand upright. What was really good was the bathroom: it was brand new and included a bathtub as well as a shower, and hot running water. I'll take it, he thought. He should try and get the price down. What the hell, he could afford it, he needed something a bit special. He'd take a honeymoon bungalow even though he felt pretty sure he'd better stick to being alone for now.

'You wife can come here?' the boy inquired.

'I'm not married.'

'Oh,' said the boy wonderingly, 'not married.'

'But the bungalow is fine. Who do I pay? Can someone get my bag?'

It was a short enough walk uphill to the centre of town. Kids rushed at him. He took the sheet of printed paper from the first one, and then discovered it was a program for a traditional dance performance and the kid was trying his utmost to sell him a ticket. There seemed to be a whole bunch of different kinds of these dances on. It wasn't his kind of thing. He heard the music as he passed by a kind of hall with tarpaulin sides. One of the dances was to be held here. The most eager tourists were already lining up outside, cameras ready, for the best positions to take pictures. Tyler paused; there was something about the music—apparently a gamelan rehearsing inside. He noticed a tent behind the covered hall; a group of performers already attired in their splendid costumes were chattering outside. Then an ornate, red, masked head peered out of the tent. Tyler felt a thrill, partly recognition, partly some more indefinable *frisson*. After a moment he went on his way.

He was very hungry and he knew the Pagoda restaurant up by the lotus pond was the best in town. There it was. There were more pamphlets being handed out in front of the restaurant, but not by local kids. A red-haired, freckled tourist leapt away from her pamphlet-bearing companion at the sight of him and offered him one of her pieces of printed paper.

FIVE

Tyler had his head buried in a copy of *Time* magazine. The world was full of trouble; and trouble seemed for the moment to be controlled by the pithy summaries on the glossy pages.

The walled garden at Renuka provided some shaded seating. Tyler had spent most of the day enjoying his private bungalow, and then had walked up to town.

'Hello?' Tyler heard. Two voices, one unit, two bodies stopped before him.

One couple. Two people. Two Australians.

'You were asking about a friend of yours?' the guy said.

Tyler was all attention.

'I was asking about a friend,' he said. 'Friend who was around here a couple of months ago.'

'Right.' They studied him. They were going to decide what to tell him only after checking him out. He was being subjected to one of those rapid assessments: can he be trusted? He looked hard at them, too. This time he wanted to be sure what he was hearing.

'Neil Bolderstone,' they said.

They knew Neil! 'Neil Bolderstone,' Tyler confirmed. 'Tell me, what can you tell me? You seen him or what?'

'We know who he is,' said the woman. She had long lank red-gold hair twisted into a bun atop her head; her face was damp and ruddy from the heat. 'OK?' she asked, indicating the empty seats, and they sat. She fanned herself with her straw hat for a moment. Her companion was older than she was, with longish grey hair over an earnest craggy face. They were dressed the way most tourists were, in baggy wide shorts to the knee, T-shirts, sandals. They both wore those money pouches belted round their waists, the bulging pouch hanging over the pubis like an antique codpiece swollen with the suggestion of well-guarded treasures.

236

'You know Neil?' asked Tyler.

'Not know him . . .'

'Know about him.'

'Please,' said Tyler. 'I tell you . . .' gesturing, hinting at the hassle it had been, tracking Neil down. They didn't answer at once. 'He's OK, isn't he?' he asked, aware of prickles of anxiety, afraid of what they would say.

'He was OK,' said the woman.

'But no one's seen him for . . .' the guy paused.

'How long since you've seen him?' the girl interrupted.

'Before he left for Bali—about three months . . .'

'That's longer . . .'

Longer than what? She didn't say. Longer than the time since he was last seen around here.

A boy rolled over with two drinks on a tray. 'We came in for a drink,' the craggy grey-hair guy explained, 'and Ibu Renuka told us you'd been looking for someone. Ibu is a great lady and makes the best juices in Bali. You showed her a photograph? By the way, our names are—' he said just as Tyler said, 'I'm Tyler Evers.' As they went to shake hands a screeching sound nearby made them all start, then laugh as they realised it was a monkey chained to a tree, and then they exchanged rueful glances as they observed that the chain was very short and the monkey's life a brutal one.

'Poor dear little thing,' the woman moaned.

'Take him! Touch him! Take off chain!' challenged the boy who had just set the drinks on the table. Of course she would not, it was a bitter, vengeful little creature and would not understand a tender gesture. The boy laughed and walked away, as if having proved a point about tourists who always claimed a fellow feeling with a monkey and would never act on it.

'Milan, Caro,' the guy said, completing the introduction.

'Caro, Caroline,' she explained.

'Neil's wife . . .'

'Caroline too?' She nodded sombrely, as if in sudden possession of occult knowledge.

'So tell me,' said Tyler, 'who knows where Neil is?'

'Where do you think he went?' this Caroline asked.

'Here, Bali, he came to Bali, that's the last thing we know.' Tyler was starting to get edgy. If they knew a single thing more than he did, they were going to take their time telling him.

'Have you heard of Pelangi?' Milan asked, pronouncing the word carefully. Tyler looked blank. 'Pel-ang-i,' Milan repeated.

'Who or where? Or what . . . is that?'

'It's an organisation. An anti-tourist tourist organisation. To put it simply.' Caro put her drink down and started fishing in her basket.

'Not *anti*,' Milan corrected her. 'It's pro *appropriate* tourism. In simplistic terms.'

Tyler shook his head. 'I must be slow . . .'

'The Pelangi group . . . it's complicated, because it was one group, and now it's two groups,' said Caroline, scrabbling in the depths of her basket. As she gave him the basket to hold Milan said, 'We came in after the split, which happened around the time Neil was in the thick of it.' Caro produced a crumpled pamphlet like the one Tyler had been handed outside the Pagoda restaurant last night. Not for a moment had he thought that the freckled woman's propaganda might have been connected to his mission. Had he missed a clue? But what connection . . . ?

'Neil? In what?' Tyler suddenly had a notion they had better go back to basics. 'Hey, whoa, can we rewind? Neil—is not exactly a common name, but . . .'

'But a black guy is not all that common a sight around here . . . not a tourist, anyway. American, lived in Sydney . . .'

'Has to be Neil,' Tyler allowed. 'But this—er—Penalgi . . .'

'Pelangi—it means rainbow—'

'Organisation? Neil was here for a holiday, surf and sun.'

'There have been few people come to Bali just for a holiday, and something happens here, they get a new look . . .'

'They get a consciousness-raising . . .' she enthused, pulling her lank gold hair and retwisting it into a tight knot.

'They get a whole new outlook . . .' They were two people with one voice. They spoke as one, even the corrections, embellishments and qualifications added to each other's utterances were those of a single thoughtful person. They were two people who knew each other well, had known each other for a long time, did just about everything they could together, Tyler saw that much, they were a couple who had passionate causes like some people had children.

Could it be *Neil* they were talking about? Or not talking about. It was Neil they were keeping off the subject of. Neil was not the kind of guy to spoil his holiday by getting into political-type situations. He wasn't that big a greenie, even, more or less the same as anyone else: talk about it, care, honestly care, but to tell the truth not do much. When Caroline had started obsessing about plastics and dictatorships, Neil couldn't handle it.

They were telling him that Neil had got involved in this organisation that, he gathered, was like tourism-goes-green. This had never been Neil's area of interest, would never happen.

'I don't get it. But I'm listening.'

They maintained, then, that Neil had become involved in this group. What did involved mean? There had been some internal divisions. Milan and Caro had come over to Bali specifically to be with this group, which they heard about back at home. Home was Melbourne, Australia. They were both schoolteachers but, they said, 'We know some really interesting people.' He had long service leave and she had some leave-without-pay. 'A chance to follow our interests.' Professional greenies, Tyler guessed, ardent amateurs anyway. They knew about Neil, and they knew that he had gone missing. Neil had been with the group that had retained the name Pelangi, rainbow. Milan and Caro had arrived in Bali just when the decision had been made to separate. There was still some squabbling going on.

'Both groups basically have the same objectives,' Milan said, 'but there were some differences in terms of procedure . . .'

'. . . in terms of priorities . . .'

'. . . certain definitions . . .'

'I'm out of my depth,' said Tyler.

Milan and Caro looked at each other. 'We'll take you to Rainbow House,' she said.

'*Rumah Pelangi*. Talk to the group.'

'I'm a patient guy,' said Tyler, '*but* . . .'

'Tomorrow afternoon. Four o'clock. Meet us here at half-three.'

'Good timing. We leave the next day.'

'Singapore. Renew our visas.'

They would not be able to find anyone else before then, they said, so Tyler had to prove he was indeed patient.

'OK then,' he said. He had plenty of time until then. 'I'll get us another drink.' He looked around for the boy who had taken his order.

'Drink a juice,' Caro urged him. 'Healthy, local fruits, made right here.'

'Bottled drinks: multinationals—the people are being done over.' Milan's inevitable chorus.

An empty Coke bottle sat at Tyler's elbow, next to the *Time* magazine. He knew the point they were making, but he didn't happen to agree with it. People liked Coca-cola even if it wasn't a great health drink and people liked Coca-cola even if they didn't live in America and people had the free choice whether to buy one or not. If your diet is basically healthy, a Coke is not going to kill you. If your diet is not basically healthy, it's not the Coke that's going to kill you. He wasn't going to be made to feel like some big bad American, or dumb fool American, just because of what he drank. But he wasn't going to quarrel with these people.'

'Hey,' said Tyler, 'I'll have whatever you're having.'

'Best juices in Bali here,' boasted Milan, 'best arak too.'

'Local jungle juice, right? Not in this heat.'

'At night,' Milan conceded. 'Try it. Kopi arak. Arak madu.'
'I'll try it tonight.' Tyler was conciliatory too. 'Let me buy a round of juice.'

SIX

This was the main street, which he already knew well, and the map showed him that the town stretched out into other villages in all directions. It was a pretty little town.

He wandered through a large cassette store. They had most every kind of music, and the cassettes were really cheap. The new music section was the largest, and there were tapes of stuff that was very recent. They were all probably bootleg. Tyler picked out a few cassettes, then put them back on the shelves and wandered out again into the mid-morning glare. I should have bought the tapes, he thought, back on the street. He was not usually indecisive.

'Hey, tourist,' a young voice sang out to him. A pretty little girl, maybe ten years old, beckoned to him. She carried a large basket on her head and put it down, smiling at him. She was a vision of loveliness: both innocent and assured. 'Look at this, tourist,' she commanded him, beginning to lift piles of cloth out of the basket. He sat on a low stone fence, charmed by her childish feminine brashness; why should he wave her away and walk on? Where was he walking on to, anyway? He was just killing time till three-thirty.

'Which one you like?' the child demanded.

Tyler held up a hand: don't rush me, I haven't said I want one. 'I don't know.'

'Good price for you. You from America? You know Michael Jackson?'

He laughed. 'I know who he *is* . . .'

'You know Michael Jackson!' She was delighted. 'Number one! *I'm bad I'm bad I'm bad,*' she sang. 'Look!' She took out a patterned cloth. 'Number one batik. How much you want pay?'

'I don't know . . . not that one,' he said, suddenly deciding to buy a cloth. If there was a really nice one. A gift for someone.

That's what he'd do today, buy gifts for everyone, that was a very good idea. Plus, if he admitted it, he wanted to buy something from this child.

'For you wife?' asked the captivating little girl, shaking out another cloth, something different, something more like he wanted. 'You know Mike Tyson?'

'Yeah. Number one boxer, right?' Tyler mimed some boxing moves, to her delight. 'Show me this one,' he said, pointing to a folded cloth printed with huge purple flowers, troppo-deco.

'This one the best,' she announced, unfolding and shaking it out. 'OK, take this one. How much?'

'You tell me how much.'

'Fifty thousand only,' she revealed serenely. 'Quality number one.'

'I think that's too much.'

'What your name?' She was a shrewd little street-wise bargainer, taking her time if she had to, ready to wait until the customer realised that he was totally obligated to her.

'Tyler. What's yours?'

'Madé. OK, forty thousand only.'

'Do you go to school, Madé?'

'School,' she confirmed. 'I learn from tourist people.' He didn't know if she meant as well as school.

She fished in her bag, underneath the pile of batiks and sarongs, and found what she was looking for, a stack of printed business cards. She held one out to him. Astonished, he took it. It read *Madé Sri Amrita/Handicrafts Batiks Sarongs*; an address appeared below. 'My card,' she asserted coolly. 'Last price thirty thousand, OK?'

The Monkey Forest Road was a long winding thoroughfare lined with tourist businesses side by side all the way. The further from the main road, the newer the business. The crowded losmens behind walls nestled up at the main road end; further down, past the jumble of shops spilling their goods on to the road, were new two-storey hotels surrounded by open gardens. Tyler didn't like any of the clothes in the shops.

He made it all the way down to the end of the twisting road. The entrance to the eponymous monkey forest was marked by a blaze of gaudy street stalls selling exceptionally lurid tourist bait and bottled drinks.

It was probably cooler in there, in the forest, but at the entrance gate you had to pay a fee, and although it was a small fee he wasn't sure he felt like paying it. Tyler habitually calculated the worth of every purchase, and felt regret, looking at the ticket booth, that he was not able to spend money in a careless spontaneous fashion, just once in a while. These prices were ridiculous.

Two women rushed out of the forest in a state of agitation. 'Be careful,' they cried, 'be careful of the monkeys, one of them attacked us.' One woman offered her freckled arm so that he might notice her injuries. 'We have to rush to the doctor to get a tetanus shot!' she yelped.

'If they have them here,' her companion said. 'Careful, be careful,' they warned him feverishly and they hurried on, a frenzy of urgency. Tyler thought they might sizzle before they made it halfway up the road.

The man attending the entrance booth looked after them impassively. A few monkeys bounded out of the forest towards him.

Tyler turned and walked back the way he'd come.

Back along the Monkey Forest Road there was a café that looked good. Behind it was a small hotel and behind that lay some bright green fields on which distant figures stooped and toiled—peasant farmers providing a picturesque scene for the hotel's guests. They didn't get paid for that, Tyler remembered someone saying.

The open sides allowed the air to cool and circulate; the high thatch roof provided shade and freshness. Tyler was in no hurry to resume his wandering in the heat outside. He ordered another drink. At another table, two couples compared their purchases. Each item displayed or recalled was accompanied by calculations as to the degree of 'rip-off' involved. Eventually they packed up, paid, and left, staring at Tyler as they passed him without meeting his eye. No one else was left. Tyler stared out to the green rice fields beyond, lulled by the languid, timeless atmosphere. For the first time he saw why anyone would leave the beach to stay up here. He became aware of some flute music, without knowing how long it had been playing. He had no idea how long he had been sitting there, either, and felt reluctant to consult his watch and find out.

This momentary trance was broken. A young Indonesian man slouched up to Tyler's table, and sat down. Tyler felt a twinge of annoyance; all the other tables were empty—the youth was seeking his company. Why not? This was a friendly place, people kept saying so, and it didn't hurt to be friendly. The guy might have asked before seating himself, though.

'Hey, man. American? What you name? My name Doggie,' he said and held out his hand. He was dressed in ill-fitting blue jeans and a patterned green shirt with a black vest over it. He wore tennis shoes—no socks, and he fiddled with his sunglasses, pulling them on and off his face. His sleek black hair was oily, combed back from his forehead with a ducktail flip at his neck. He seemed to be trying for a 1950s J.D. image.

Doggie—where did he get his name?—called harshly to the young waiter who had hurried over with a thick plastic menu the moment Tyler had arrived, but had neglected to stir himself at Doggie's advent. Doggie yelled out an order. The waiter, a boy, questioned it. Doggie turned to Tyler, 'I have one beer, OK?' he said to Tyler.

What he meant was, you're going to buy me a beer.

Tyler arranged his features into A Look, just looked at the youth a moment. A moment to make it clear that he had a choice in whether to say yes or no, he was not impressed by the boy's chutzpah nor intimidated by his apparent poverty.

A moment, then he shrugged. 'Sure. Have a beer. On me.' He even grinned. And if he was going to buy the guy a beer he wanted something for it. He hadn't really spoken to anyone all day, and this third world hustler, minimal English, minimal style, was going to provide him with some conversation, at least. Maybe even some information, anything, like where was a good place to go for a drink after dark. Not that it was a drink he wanted. What he wanted was something to look forward to this evening, somewhere else to go besides the rainbow headquarters. In case it didn't lead to Neil. Plan B.

Doggie yelled at the waiter, then turned back eagerly to Tyler. 'I can help you,' the youth said. 'Something you want, something you looking for, I can help.'

'Well, my man,' said Tyler, 'how well do you know this town?'

'This town,' he said, putting on his sunglasses, 'is OK. You like Kuta?'

The waiter was there. That was *two* bottles of beer already opened on his tray. He went to put them down.

'No! No beer for me, I did not order a beer,' said Tyler. So, they were going to make him pay for two beers! For a wild moment he thought they were going to add a cover charge and a surcharge—but no, he wasn't in a Bangkok bar.

'Please,' said Doggie, 'take beer.' Tyler noticed that the waiter looked uneasy and was staring resentfully at Doggie. Great, thought Tyler, I seem to be stuck with a notorious jerk.

'I did not order a beer, I do no want that beer,' said Tyler, 'and I will be happy to buy you just *one* beer.' He tried to make it sound friendly.

Doggie and the waiter had a few words. Eventually the waiter took one of the beers off the table and departed with a few last words. Apparently Doggie had persuaded him he would take the responsibility of extracting payment for the second beer.

He would have to impart some immensely useful information for that to happen.

'So, tell me, my man,' said Tyler, 'what kind of work do you do?' It was probably a stupid question, or a sore point. Where were there enough jobs for everyone? What did people here do? There were the rice fields for the peasants; there were government offices for the well educated or well connected; there were tourists for anyone with, probably, the initiative. Or the stomach.

'I help tourist,' said Doggie. 'I hap very good stuff for you.'

Sounding like some TV thug offering drugs or guns or women. Probably wanting to show him some paintings or carvings that he got a commission on. The carvings were too heavy to carry but maybe a couple of paintings would be good presents—ask for the traditional style ones, he remembered being told. 'I'd have to see them first,' said Tyler.

'I can show you, I have here,' said the youth. And patted his pocket.

For a moment, Tyler wondered what kind of handicraft souvenirs were that small, before he reacted. 'No,' he protested, 'no way.'

'Get high before you die,' Doggie hissed at him. 'Best number-one shit. No hope without dope.'

Tyler rose from the table. He wasn't going to be talking to a guy who was holding, not in this kind of country. 'Please, sit,' said Doggie urgently. 'Is OK. I very good stuff this, no problem. No police, only get high.'

Tyler had gone to the desk at the back. 'Give me the check for my two Cokes and one beer.' The waiter was looking with venom at Doggie.

Those silver bracelets were really very fine. Those rings. Those earrings. It looked good, all of this. Tyler was looking at the elegant display in the large window of a shop that was three times wider than the other shops along here, with a tiled verandah in front, and a spacious area with glass display cases inside. It sold only silver: silver jewellery and silver trinkets. He entered. Several fans cooled the air; this place was opulent.

A sign read, 'Wholesale Enquiries Welcome'. He could get presents for his mother, his sister, Lydia, everyone, here; this was the best stuff he'd seen.

But he needed to choose fast. No, actually there was no time.

'Excuse me,' he said, approaching one of the attentive young men keeping an eye on him, 'where is . . . do you have . . .' Tyler *knew* there was a point to learning a few phrases in the local language. He could have asked in Spanish.

Another Balinese man suddenly appeared and said something to the concerned-looking assistant; he was a small slender man; authority and confidence were the first thing you noticed.

'Of course,' the young assistant said to Tyler in clear English. 'I will show you. This way, please.'

It was a western-style bathroom, with gleaming, spotless tiles. There were paper and a mirror and towels.

'Take your time,' said the authoritative man when Tyler returned. 'Sit, look, no hurry.'

'That's a big house coming up out there,' Tyler remarked; he wanted to say something friendly and he had noticed the construction under way on the land behind the shop on his way back.

'That's my school!' the man announced. 'I am building a school. Opening very soon.'

'A school? Regular school? Silver school?' Tyler was happy to sit here for a while, choose some stuff, talk to this guy. Guy had a good set-up. Interesting to know how it worked. Western partner?

'School of silver craft, also of English and of general studies. I am building the school and I am offering scholarship system.'

'So, this's your shop.' The assistants had turned their attention elsewhere as the putative proprietor seemed disposed to attend to Tyler. Tyler kept on examining the displays. Cufflinks, swizzle sticks, tie-pins: they had everything.

'This my shop, I have a shop in Sanur, I have a factory in Celuk. Best design, best quality, best price.'

'Nice stuff. I'm looking for some presents.'

'Please. Here you will find suitable presents for all significant other friends.'

'You speak English very well,' remarked Tyler. 'Those bracelets? And that one?'

'Nice bracelets, all free size. This is a fix price shop. I taught myself English, starting at the age of ten years old.'

'No kidding. I think you had a better teacher than most.'

'I taught myself. All prices marked on all items. My friends laughed at me, they did not believe me. I said, you see, one day! Already I knew English language was the international language.'

This guy was ten . . . how long ago? 'I'll take these,' said Tyler, putting aside three silver bracelets, 'but I'll keep looking.'

'Thirty years ago. Now I am forty.'

'So, around 1960.' This time Tyler articulated his speculations; the guy obviously was a mind-reader, as well as a predictor of the future and a benevolent patron. 'How did you already know to go with English? Thirty years ago?'

'Already tourists were coming, but only very few then. Tourists looked like people having fun and happy. The other boys ran away from them but my ambition stopped me from being scared or embarrassed; already I have an honest heart and I believe. I mixed with tourists. I had to have an excuse so I became a salesman, selling anything. Statues, paintings, batik, many different thing I could sell. All I wanted was to speak English, so I was with the English-speaking. I had a good response. I asked myself, how long? I said, depending on myself, in two years. I learned more and more. It was my first idea.'

'Can I ask you something?'

'You can ask! Don't be shy!'

'You . . .' Tyler gestured to indicate a collective you, '. . . don't mind tourists?' A good living was made out of tourists, he could see that. Who else was going to buy this stuff? So why should the guy mind? But he was thinking of

249

Milan and Caro, who had said tourists outraged the local people. 'I mean . . . ?'

'You hear something?'

'I have been told that tourists weren't too popular with some people around here.'

'Some people from Bali don't want tourists. They don't want change. Also some tourists come here and want us to live like a hundred years ago. They don't want change. I went through many, many arguments and conversation.'

Tyler picked up a curved silver brooch enamelled with bands of rainbow colours. 'I'd like to hear about it.'

The guy seemed pleased. 'Many tourists always rushing, never want to speak. How can you learn if you don't speak with people? But tourists only learn from book.'

One of the attendants delivered a tray with glasses of tea and coffee for Tyler to choose. His belly twinged a warning.

'Balinese people sometimes can get jealous if someone is good at business. Jealousy will always come. If people do not like you, they never will, no matter what you do. Revenge is a waste of time. If someone give you shit, send a flower. Don't get your power from kissing others' ass. I say, money is not bad. Only bad if it's used to cover up your weakness. Don't let money play with you. If you believe, if you have honest heart, you can make good business and nobody hurt. I choose who works here. I believe in open management. I study management. Be honest, work hard, and you get benefit forever. This is what I will teach in my school. And to have a target. If I don't have a target, might as well die! Tomorrow must be better than today. Don't be afraid of business! Don't be a frog under a coconut shell!'

'Don't be a frog under a coconut shell?' Tyler repeated, amused.

'Frog under a coconut shell thinks the world is very small, very small. Everything the frog can know is under the shell only.'

'I get it.'

'Too many people here are thinking like that.'

'But not you.'

'People think according to freedom of mind. Not because Balinese or because tourist or because religion or so on. Only according to free mind or not free mind. If you have free mind, can be a hero. I want to be a hero. So I am building a school.'

'I'll take these, too. Did you ever see the guy in this photograph?'

'Next Wednesday at three pm the Governor of Bali will come to see me here, to talk about ideas on how to help the village people. Already many people coming to me for good idea. I can always help with business idea. You can bring your friend. If I am here, if I have free time, I can talk with you.'

SEVEN

'Here we are,' Milan announced.

'Losmen Samadhi,' announced Caro in turn, somewhat unnecessarily—the sign outside said so.

He hoped the bathrooms were clean, he hoped they had running water, he hoped they had paper. The bathroom was the first thing he was interested in. He would be very careful what he ate tonight. He might not eat tonight.

Last night he had gone to the satisfactory Pagoda restaurant once more—no demonstrations this time—and if he couldn't trust that, what place could he trust?

A narrow path led to a slightly wider long courtyard flanked by a row of rooms either side—guest rooms down one side, family rooms on the other. A couple of Balinese women were sitting outside, with flat round baskets on their knees, busy fingers performing some task Tyler couldn't make out.

'Rainbow House,' Caro added, as they approached.

'*Rumah Pelangi*,' Milan said.

Rainbow House was a room at the far end of the row. A couple of people sitting outside waved at their approach. Embarrassed, Tyler hurried past them.

The bathroom was clean, although the floor was wet. There was paper, though he couldn't find it at first. The flush on the toilet didn't work, which sickened him, until he realised he could achieve the same effect using the plastic ladle to throw water from the filled tub. The toilet itself was western-style, that is, it was higher than the Asian toilets, although it didn't have a proper seat. It could have been worse.

This time he noticed the room as he returned through it to the verandah. Two single beds provided seating. Ecology posters were gummed to the rattan walls—posters of wilderness, rainforest, national parks. A table held a couple of boxes of files.

A few of the people in the group were staying in adjoining rooms, and the verandah that ran alongside was used as part of the meeting room. Milan and Caro introduced him to two people, then there were four, then more, then less. The names eluded his memory.

'Have some tea,' Caro advised. Tyler looked doubtfully at the tray on the low table; it held a couple of large thermos flasks of hot water, glasses, jars of tea, coffee and sugar, strainers, and a plastic bowl in which to place 200 rupiah when you made yourself a drink. A pretty young woman with large dark eyes smiled at him with frank interest. She was dressed in bicycle shorts, a T-shirt and a vest of glittery Indian fabric. 'Go on,' she urged, 'you should. Drink a lot, or you'll get dehydrated.'

'Just don't take Lomotil or any of that western shit.'

'Janette's got a homeopathic remedy if she comes later.'

'There's a special leaf, if you can get a Balinese to show you.'

'Bruce here?' asked Milan, to Tyler's relief. The reason he was here was to meet the person who had actually had some contact with Neil, and going after that person was all he was interested in. The condition of his health was none of their business. Tyler had understood that some formal meeting was scheduled for four o'clock. But apparently four o'clock was only an approximation of the time that some of the people, including Bruce, might wander over to the room. Tyler couldn't imagine Neil staying long around people like this.

'Rubber time,' Milan said. '*Jam karet.*' His smile invited Tyler to share his delight in the laid-back tradition that taught schedule-dominated westerners not to be hung up on time, and invited admiration for his scattering of phrases in the local language. Tyler felt no delight and no admiration. He just wanted these people he was to meet to get the hell over here, tell him what they knew about Neil, and then leave him alone. Or maybe he would just as soon they didn't show, and he could forget this whole thing. Maybe he needed a doctor, not that he would go to a doctor here. He hoped to God this stomach thing was something he could shake off. He just wanted some straight answers to some straight questions, but these were not straight people, they were bent, green, rainbow people.

He swallowed his irritation along with a few sips of the weak, lukewarm tea. It gurgled as it hit his stomach. 'Tell me all about it,' he said, and they told him.

The Rainbow Group had been founded eight or nine months ago. Before that, local people had tried at various times since the late seventies to organise themselves to deal with the growth of tourism and its effect on their lives. For instance, they had tried to provide information to tourists about local customs. Tourists had caused grave offence by their obscene dress, rude manners, intrusive cameras.

These attempts however had variously foundered. One group of locals had begun an English-language newsletter, but this had been stopped by the government, and the group had split up. Local communities were divided. The greedy wanted to make profits out of tourism; the traditional wanted to be polite at any cost; the scared wanted no part of anything that might be construed as being critical of the government, which had promoted tourism vigorously since the 1970s and made the most money from it.

Foreign visitors had been coming for years, journalists, writers, interested people, from America Australia Europe all over, studying and writing about the phenomenon of foreign tourists interacting with indigenous culture. Some of them had been returning to Bali for years and were appalled at what had been happening. They began talking about eco-tourism, restricted tourism, alternative tourism.

In recognition of the compromising difficulties that were inevitable if tourists and Balinese joined forces, some people had decided that tourists should have their own group, and so Rainbow House was created, right here, at Losmen Samadhi, which is where those original people had always stayed. After several trips to Bali they felt a sense of responsibility to the place. They created the Rainbow Group, and they created the structure for its operation. They set up a network that ensured that there was always someone to take over the co-ordinating activities as previous members left Bali. Other people would come in through a word-of-mouth process and sign up for involvement in activities according to the amount of time they wished to spend on the group. Some people came here for two months and then renewed their visas; some came for only a few days. Some returned, some came only once. It was all rather informal, perhaps a little more informal than had first been planned, but that was how things worked around here.

So, was there anyone around now who had been around when Neil was here? Only Bruce, and Bruce hadn't showed up yet. Rubber time.

OK then, people signed up for activities. Like what?

The main activity was to produce and disseminate information on local culture and correct behaviour.

'Right,' said Tyler. 'I've seen some of it.'

Not all of it was written information—they also scheduled talks and video nights.

'Video nights?'

'In Peliatan. There hasn't been one for a while.'

Video night in Peliatan. Maybe Neil had gone along one time. Nightlife around here was limited. It was cultural dance shows or nothing.

Neil might have signed some visitor's book or something that would show when he had been there. Then Tyler would have a more recent last date sighted. What difference would it make? At least when he rang Caroline he would have something to tell her. 'I've got a question,' said Tyler. 'Do you have records of everyone who's been part of this?'

They all took a moment before they answered, and then all spoke at once.

'Sort of.'

'Not really.'

'Yes.'

'No.'

255

A little laughter acknowledged the speaking all at once and the contradictory replies.

'We've got some stuff and the others have some stuff.'

'The others?' Tyler felt as if he was being set up; forced to supply these inane prompts. In spite of that little ripple of laughter these people shared a seriousness that he was left out of.

What it was, there had been a split. The Rainbow split, they called it. Some of the people who had been in this informal network had decided they had their own ideas and they took off to do their own thing their own way.

What, asked Tyler, a last desperate grasp at a straw, what was this split all about?

'We deal with what is, and they deal with what may be.'

'We're into information and they're into confrontation.'

'We do things that are in harmony with the whole thing of being here and they bring in all this other stuff that divides people even more.'

No one who actually *knew* Neil is around. They *heard* about him. It was at the time of the split, when things got confused.

But what about Bruce? Wasn't there this guy Bruce who knew Neil?

'Bruce?' said a new arrival. 'He left yesterday.'

EIGHT

Neil. Neil whom he had known for years and years. Neil who had been with him at the airline ever since he joined. Neil who had preceded him as a drop-out from the life of approved respectability. Neil and all the holidays they had taken together, all the women they had met, all the bars they had closed, all the parties they had enlivened. Neil who had kept going back to Sydney, Australia, finally admitting that one sweet woman had a hold on him.

Tyler knew Neil. Once. He knew the Neil he had known. He did not know any Neil who would go to a place like Bali and do anything but take it easy, party by night and surf by day. He worked hard and played hard.

Tyler even thought that he knew Neil better in some ways, important ways, better than Caroline ever could. The way two guys know each other well, when they go way back, worked together, holidayed together, and sometimes they'd even let each other in on some deep feeling stuff.

He'd heard women talk about the fact that their conversation was just about always about the deep feeling stuff, and men didn't do much of that, especially not among themselves, and Tyler knew what they meant, and that they were mostly right. And he could talk to Neil about that a bit, too. Women talked about how men could get into deep feeling stuff with them and Tyler and Neil agreed that there were ways that they talked with women who they got close to that were different from the ways they could talk with each other. And that didn't make any one way right or wrong. They were good friends and there was trust there because they didn't intrude over the boundaries, didn't push past the limits.

Tyler had taken his first holiday in Sydney because of Neil—sure—but he had returned and then stayed for his own reasons. Tyler realised that Neil needed time alone with

Caroline when they got married.

A great place, Neil said. You can make your life whatever you want it. The girls are great, the weather is great, the opportunities are great. Australians don't know what work is. They get more holidays than anyone. When they have their annual holiday they get paid an extra percentage of their pay! He couldn't believe this at first either, but it was true. They've had it easy in the past and they haven't adjusted to how it is now. If you're prepared to work and use your time you can do well.

All this Tyler found to be true. Not that he had made up his mind about things the way Neil had. Neil was a bit older than he, maybe in more ways than one. He'd taken on two businesses—selling water purifiers and Peruvian rugs—as well as doing bar work and kept them up when he got his residency and started working for an Australian airline. For Tyler, it was different. He was still in a having fun and looking around stage of his life. Trouble was, he couldn't see when it was ever going to become a new stage. Neil was in a different kind of new stage.

The way it started with Caroline—first she wouldn't turn off the TV if it was one of those gruesome depressing documentaries about how horrible things were in far-off places no one could do anything about. Then she would start to look for these programs. Then she started telling everyone they should be watching them too.

'Did you see that thing about the African elephants?' she would implore. 'They're nearly extinct. Did you see what they're doing with nuclear waste? Did you see where the food didn't get to the people in Ethiopia? You should! It's so bad, it's so bad. We have it so good.'

She didn't have to watch that stuff, Neil would say. How did it help anyone else to make yourself miserable?

'How does it help anyone for us to be better off? How does it hurt anyone to care about them?' Caroline would retort with a passion formerly reserved for the finer points of fashion styling.

258

Neil said, 'This is how it helps. If I earn good money have a nice car and live well and I appreciate it, maybe someone will look at me and say, I can have that too, I can improve my life, I can work hard and have that.'

'That's so *American*,' Caroline wailed.

'What is that, that's so bad all of a sudden? You play American music, you go to American movies, you got you an American husband—hello, baby—and what? I'm meant to think like an Aussie? She'll be OK, just let me put my head in the sand, as long as I got the dole . . .'

'I'm only saying we should *care* . . .'

'All the good ideas here are American ideas,' Neil said. 'Remember?'

It was a stupid fight, not exactly a fight, not exactly a discussion, asking unanswerable questions, going round in circles and off on tangents, proving nothing, airing grievances . . .

It seemed to Tyler that Caroline had changed. Or had revealed her true colours.

Neil told him, 'Being married is different. It sure is different.'

'I can imagine,' said Tyler.

'More different than you can imagine. More different than I thought. You know how they say you have to work at it? Believe it. That's a true fact.'

'Work,' said Tyler. It had been a tense little conversation and he wanted to be very careful of what he said. He could have said 'Hope it's not *only work*', or 'You're not afraid of work', or 'I never did that kind of work'.

Neil didn't have to go into it; he would tell him as much as he wanted to, and Tyler never had a reason to push him. They trusted each other. He still thought he knew Neil as well as anyone, and now, here in Bali, two strangers who hadn't even met him were telling him he hadn't known Neil at all.

If they were speaking the truth.

There was no reason to doubt it.

If they weren't speaking the truth, the whole thing became

259

somewhat more weird again. They knew who Neil was.

Crazy snatches of old stories he didn't even know he ever heard:

He was a nice quiet person, we never knew . . .
He was a good neighbour, this is a shock . . .
He was an ordinary guy, this is not like him . . .
A person goes and does something out of character. A person is under stress. A person's marriage is rocky and he feels the ground shift from under him. A person goes to a strange and distant place and is attracted to a cause. A person had a secret life, a hidden self, a split personality.

None of these things sounded like Neil.

Those things have been known; Tyler has not known them but they sound like bits of familiar plots, familiar from who knows where, movies, urban myths, magazine features; stories of the kind where everyone knows someone it had happened to and you could never find an actual witness.

Tyler wasn't sure he was thinking straight. He had to get his thoughts back on track. There was some track he was trying to get on to. What was the damn track?

What was he, Tyler, capable of?

What would people who knew him say about him? Out of all the possible directions he could take in life, which ones would be:

Just like Tyler, just what you'd expect . . .
Funny, but when you think about it, yeah, Tyler would do that . . .
Totally not what you'd expect . . .
No way in the world, not Tyler, no way . . .

A year ago he would never have imagined himself here: behind him, those months of travelling and living in Sydney; ahead of him his uncertain return
and
around him
this

this private view
this bungalow
in this village
on this island

Where had Neil stayed? Why did Neil leave the beach?

Tyler felt he was submerged in the question of Neil. He was subduing some feeling about it that demanded to be recognised. Resentment. He damn well resented it. He resented the mystery of Neil. He resented having his whole trip run according to the search for Neil. He resented that he had to think of Neil like this. It was as if he hardly knew who he was any more. As if he had no purpose, no personality, no credibility except as the man looking for Neil. He resented that. The feeling seemed to be linked to experiences that were familiar but unnamed, unrecognised, and prevented any further thoughts on the subject.

NINE

The low bamboo table was covered with paper. Felicity and Jane always carried guidebooks, notebooks, maps, journals and textbooks, as others might carry arms or talismans. They were very serious visitors. They studied the books and made schedules for their eager visits to distant temples and shrines, which they recorded with sketches and notes. They told Tyler about some of these temples. One was very large and important. It was an hour's drive away. One had springs of holy water, and they had hiked to see it, two hours' walk through fields and villages. One had some very old carvings that were crumbled with decay, from which they had just returned. The Buddhist elements were of particular interest to them. They compared them with Buddhist elements they had already studied.

They had offered him their cheerful company when they entered the café Tyler was sitting in. Having travelled together several times, they made a point of speaking to other people. 'We can't just speak to each other all the time,' they said.

They had a well-bred English look, brisk, sensible, sporty. Late thirties? Fortyish? They had met in the Himalayas, where they both went frequently, trekking, mountain climbing, and seeking knowledge. They usually went to India and Pakistan, and had never been to Bali before. 'We weren't particularly interested, were we?' But they came. They had hair shiny from one hundred brush strokes a day, they wore denim skirts that covered their knees, and crisp, modest shirts in blues and greens. Intrepidness and decency blew in gusts off them like perfume. They wanted to know about him.

'I wasn't that interested either,' Tyler said.

'Where do you usually travel to?' asked Jane, her bony face and bird-like eyes bright with curiosity.

'Mexico, Brazil, Hawaii. I've lived in Australia for nearly a year. Sydney.'

'I'm from Sydney! Jane's from Melbourne. Are you liking Bali?'

Tyler paused, which made them all laugh. 'Don't be polite,' Felicity urged. 'Tell us the worst.'

'All it is,' said Tyler, 'is that I only came here to find a friend of mine . . .' Foolish as he felt, starting on the story, he had determined a while ago that he would talk about it at any opportunity, because you never knew.

'Someone who lives here?'

'He came over for a holiday and we never heard from him again. His wife got really worried, I got worried . . .'

Police? The consulate? Immigrasi? The airlines?

'Hey,' said Tyler, 'come on.'

Of course, he would have thought of those. How awful for him. How mysterious. Dreadful. Was his friend . . . unhappy? Was he mixed-up with . . . strange people?

'Not usually.'

Felicity had once worked as a trekking leader in India and one of the women in one group had been very safely delivered back to Delhi after the trek, but had never turned up at home. She had stayed on in India to do some shopping and ended up at an ashram which she decided never to leave. She had shaved her head, put on a sari, and renounced all former ties. Her parents spent a fortune tracking her down and finally they found her but she refused to go back with them.

Jane had been on a mountain climbing expedition in Pakistan that had found the frozen remains of earlier climbers who had actually been reported as having returned to base camp before they disappeared but in fact they had never reached it.

'Excuse me,' Tyler said, realising he would have to use the nearest facility, and he dreaded what he would find there. This wasn't a proper restaurant. The waiter didn't seem to understand what he wanted at first, then pointed to a door. The toilet bowl was floor level, the floor was wet, and the flushing was manual. He had better get used to it. He was used to it.

Back at the table, the women had been served plates of fried rice, and were spooning fresh chopped chillies over it. He nearly ran outside again, but contained himself. He wanted to leave.

'Excuse me,' he said, taking his seat again. 'I'm told they got a name for it. Bali belly.'

'Hmmmm,' they said sympathetically, their forksful of spicy rice poised mid-air. 'Eat chillies.'

'Huh, next week maybe.'

'Have you found out anything about your friend?'

'No. I don't know. Someone told me he got, um, met these people who have this thing, "Rainbow Group" . . .'

'Oh yes!' said Felicity.

'What?' asked Jane.

'The leaflet yesterday.'

'What leaflet?'

'When we were having the grilled tuna.'

'Oh . . . Not using cameras. I'm glad they're telling people. Ladakh? People with cameras pushing in everywhere, cameras right up priests' noses . . .'

'It is awful. If they have a camera they think they can push in anywhere. At least they're telling people. Jane! Tyler should meet Mario.'

'Yes! Go and meet Mario. If you're lucky.'

Mario was an Indonesian name. Mario was an incredible guy. He had once published an English-language newspaper right here. Then it was stopped. But it was written about in journals all over the world and Mario began to be asked to speak at international conferences on tourism and development. He had lived in Bali for a long, long time, but had been brought up in a town in Java; like Sukarno, his mother had been Balinese. He had been a bright young businessman, had opened the first disco at Sanur long ago and had made a lot of money. Then he left that and changed completely and came up here and had begun to work for the local community. Jane had wanted to interview him, for an eco-travel magazine a friend of hers published, but he had declined to be interviewed. But if you were lucky you'd get him at a time he felt like talking. Mario knew everything.

'So,' says Tyler, 'what were you, involved from the start?'

'When does it start? Tracing back, one thing back to another, back to another, there is no start.' This was Mario—laughing at serious questions, playing with you, offering riddles, teases, mockery. Tyler met Mario fifteen minutes ago. Strangely enough he liked the guy.

Tyler had found the tiny office behind the camera store. A stout Indonesian man was locking the door. 'I am Mario,' he answered Tyler's inquiry. 'Today I am Mario. If you can believe me. Yesterday I said, Mario is not here!' He had a broad wide face, a few strands of a wispy beard hung from his chin, his eyes blazed with a fiery intelligence and danced to an offbeat humour. He told Tyler he could accompany him. They went to sit at a coffee stall in the markets. Mario had exchanged greetings all the short distance. Tyler filled him in on the story so far, while Mario smoked the clove-scented local cigarettes.

'So,' asked Mario, 'what do you think of this Rainbow Group?'

Tyler paused. 'I think they're well meaning.'

'What is their meaning?'

'What is their meaning?' Tyler repeated. 'Is this a quiz? Do I win a prize? Their meaning—they're upset about tourism. Not upset enough not to be tourists,' said Tyler, surprised at his own sarcasm. He didn't think he had had any position on the group's upsets.

Mario chuckled. 'They come on a tourist visa, eat tourist food at tourist restaurants, then they say, I'm not tourist. So what is tourist?'

'I agree with you—I mean, I don't know. Look, I'm the one, I'm not really a tourist, I'm not at the beach, I'm not having fun, I'm not trekking to temples.' He took out the photograph and handed it over. 'This is why I'm here.'

A woman placed glasses of thick black coffee before them. Tyler hoped to hell the glasses were clean. How did they wash them? Just rinse them in the same used water all day long? The woman peered at the photograph, exchanged a few remarks with Mario and gave Tyler a curious look.

'You are looking for your friend. Are you looking for yourself too?' Mario chuckled again.

'I'm right here,' said Tyler. 'I know where I am.'

'Many Americans come here, saying they are looking for themselves. Why do they think they will find it in Bali? First they come and buy land, and build a house and find themselves that way. Now they come and pay big money for seminar with guru and get guarantee that they will find self. But you looking for your friend—I don't know who you can pay. Maybe no guarantee.'

'I'm about to give up, really. But I've got to have a clear conscience. As long as I've looked and asked wherever I can.'

'Everybody looking for something. What are these people looking for?'

On one side of them Balinese peasant women were packing up their baskets after a long day's trading. A few tourists wandered around. A blond couple sloped by attired in singlets, and untidy sarongs knotted around their waists. To the other side a group of young Balinese men clustered around a couple of motorbikes, shoving, smoking, joking.

'We ask tourists to wear Balinese dress to temple,' Mario said. 'They say they cannot wear because don't understand. First they must have a theory. These boys don't have a theory, they understand jeans by wearing them.' Mario lit another kretek. 'Some tourists are saying is not OK when Balinese are wearing jeans, not OK for electricity, not OK for telephone. Already there is coming computer and satellite dish. It is tourists getting upset. Coming here telling us how to be more Balinese.'

'Know what you mean. I've been told how to be more black.'

Mario laughed. 'They tell you how to be same like white man, they tell you how to be more like authentic African, isn't it?'

'Something exactly like that.'

Mario turned back to the picture. 'I think I see this man. But maybe not sure.'

'I'm told he got mixed up in this Rainbow movement situation, but I can't find anyone who actually knew him. I get told stuff I can't figure. I'm told the Rainbow Group split, and maybe Neil went one way. Tell the truth, I don't see Neil getting into this scene at all.'

'Oh, you discover the split!'

'I don't know the story though.'

'Did you ever see a split rainbow in the sky? Rainbow must have all the colours, isn't it? Can't split it long-ways. Some-time rainbow goes only on one part of the sky.' Mario laughed, as if daring Tyler to guess if this was meant to mean anything.

'I'm not actually political or group minded or anything myself.'

'What is the American song about the rainbow? Over the rainbow?'

'Somewhere over the rainbow . . . old-time song.'

'What is its meaning?'

Tyler sang a few bars under his breath to remind himself. 'All the good stuff's over the rainbow, out of reach. Maybe.' He thinks, plays a few lines in his head. 'Freedom and stuff.' He shrugs. 'It's just a song out of an old-time movie.'

'Lot of gold if you find end of the rainbow, there is a saying, isn't it?'

'Gold at the end of the rainbow . . . yeah . . . I haven't heard that since I was a little kid.'

'Here they tell little kid, tourist is the rainbow and gold is at the end of the tourist.'

'Yeah?'

'No tourist, no gold.'

'Right. Tourist bring gold and tourist bring trouble, right?'

Mario didn't laugh. 'Bring gold, bring trouble, bring many things. Many people'—he gestured around him—'asking me, Mario, why these tourists coming to Bali? They want to eat their own food, they want to build their own houses, they don't know our religion, they always wanting something different. Only thing they know is taking photographs.'

'I don't get it, what do you do here? You with some organisation or what?'

'I'm a one-man NGO.' Finally Mario handed the photograph back. 'You looking for Neil but is Neil looking for you?'

Tyler spreads his palms—look, no weapon, no tricks, no answers. 'He's my old friend. His wife doesn't know what happened to him. Look, if he wants to go, OK, it's his life. But I don't think so. I don't think he's just gone wandering.'

A second thick black coffee arrived.

'This is embarrassing,' said Tyler, 'but I need the john.'

Mario pointed down the road. 'Go to that restaurant. I stay here. I have work here. You stay Maya Bungalow?' How did he know? 'Go, get rest. If any news come, someone will find you.'

TEN

Tyler made his grim way back to the Maya Bungalows, praying, he who never prayed. Let me make it. Let this be over soon.

He reached his home at last—home is what it felt like, his clean clothes were there, and a bed he could lie on in peace, left alone. Curiously he was hardly sweating at all, though he was boiling hot. There were two mouthfuls of pure water left in a plastic Aqua bottle. Apprehensive as he was of the effect of swallowing it, he was thirsty enough to try. Immediately his stomach responded with searing contractions, and he dashed to the bathroom once more. Sitting on the lavatory he removed his clothes. Back in the room he found the purple-flowered sarong he had bought from the lovely little street urchin with the business card—it seemed so long ago. He shook out its tight folds and wrapped it loosely around him, collapsed onto the bed, and immediately drifted between an uneasy sleep and a semi-conscious state.

Occasionally he tried to grasp hold of any sensible thought he glimpsed among the memories, figments and dismay that ran amok in his brain. How long had he been here? Only a week, a mere week. Exactly a week. He'd leave in another week, he promised himself, no later.

He'd leave now. He was sick. There was nothing to stay for, nothing else he could do.

Yes, there was.

There was a loose end he had to tie up. There was a stone he had not turned. There was unfinished business.

One little thing. It was only a little thing, but one little thing could have the most momentous consequences. That had to be true. There would be no stories otherwise.

He could not leave Bali yet. He had to remember the one little thing he had left to do before he could leave in good

269

conscience; figure if it could be done and how to do it; then leave. No, *do it*, then leave. Whatever it was.

The maelstrom in his head would not be stilled; its gyrations mocked his attempts to grasp the elusive thought that would save his life, the elusive memory that he needed to survive. There was a clue, a sign, and if he did not recognise it he would die.

Was this how people died?

For whose sake was he to get better?

Later, Tyler spun out of sleep: clammy, troubled, his mouth thick, his mind struggling to make its way through the psychic turbulence, returning to an awareness of the messed-up bed and the sour, dirty odour of his illness.

There was a word for this unbalanced, dislocated feeling. Disoriented. He had to get oriented. Orient. He was in the Orient and he had to get oriented.

He had a momentary deranged sense that this thought was a kind of breakthrough but the only breakthrough was bodily. His bowels once more exploded, blasting their desperate, final squirts of foul green bile, ripping vast areas of tender, bruised, internal linings, leaving his anus bloody and painful.

He ran the shower and lathered himself into a tower of foam. The hot water tap did not work and it was after all unnecessary. Mild warm water ran from the other tap and, with the cleansing suds, washed away the stale sweat and the vile dreams that shadowed the edge of his mind.

Once more he lay on the bed.

The thoughts were ridiculous. But they took hold, invading demons. He was too sick to recover. He would be left here, alone, too weak to move, and might . . . he could not stop the thought.

The end of Tyler Evers, demised alone at a honeymoon bungalow in a third world village. He had more than an upset stomach. It was more than his bowel working too hard to expel some miniscule third world bug. It was a serious disease. It was the start of something that would be the end of him. No. He must not think this. He would rest a little, and then go out to find a doctor. Who would confirm that he had dysentery. Dengue fever. Worms. Cholera. He shouldn't go to a doctor here. They didn't have proper medical schools. They would stick used hypodermic needles into him and infect him with diseases even more hideous than the one killing him now. They would use old discarded medicines dumped on to the developing world. There must be a drugstore in this town, where they sold proper medicines. Maybe not. He might have to go to the capital to find that. The big town. Denpasar. He would never make it. He would have to send someone. There must be someone. Jesus and God it was awful to think. He would let himself drift off into unconsciousness, he would have to do that, and then, and then, and then.

'Hey, Tyler, old buddy,' said Neil. 'Is that you, Neil Bolderstone!' Tyler explained. Neil chuckled. 'You're late,' Tyler started to say, but it wasn't that, that wasn't what he meant at all, and Neil wasn't there any more. Tyler struggled into wakefulness once more, then gave up, and sank back down into the inchoate regions where hallucination, memory, knowledge and perception admitted no boundaries.

'It's too late now, Tyler,' Lydia said. He could hardly see her and tried to get closer to her. But he was pinned down and could not move. He had to tell her to wait, only to wait, but she faded away. 'Too late,' she said. 'Too late now, Tyler,' said Janet Leebold. She was nine and he was nine. She lived down the street and they played together but he had not taken her with him when he said he would and she would not let him say he was sorry and she would not agree it was all right now. It wasn't all right now. 'You *always*,' she said. Something unforgivable had happened, some line had been crossed, but she must forgive him, he must make her see that, it was so important that he be forgiven.

'I'm sorry,' he insisted.

'It's all right. Drink this,' he heard, a female voice in a familiar dialect, urging him to sit up. Who was this, some phantasm, some delusion? She had large dark eyes and wore a vest of shiny Indian fabric over a T-shirt and bicycle shorts.

He had seen her at the Rainbow thing and she had smiled at him with frank interest. He was at first more grateful for the lucidity of this fresh, certain memory than for the drink she had been stirring, and now handed to him.

He drank it, without tasting it, aware only of some tremendous relief in his body. 'You have to drink a lot of liquids,' she said. 'If you get dehydrated you'll be really sick.'

Almost he laughed. He was really sick already. 'Sicker,' she said. She smiled at him. 'Hope you don't mind,' she said. Mind? How could he mind? 'I heard you were sick.' She had found out where he lived, and came by, just in case, just to say hello. There wasn't any thing to drink here, and the door was open and he was sleeping and she thought he didn't look well. She found a Balinese guy in the shed and got him to boil some water. Steam rose from a large thermos flask on the table. 'Some guy called Ktut,' she said, waving towards the small hut past the farthest bungalow. It was twilight now, the sky glowing a silvery yellow. 'I got him just before he left,' she said with cheerful pride.

He watched as she stirred another glass of the pale tea. It wasn't only sugar. 'Salt,' she said. 'Salt and sugar.' Her tone did not invite any demurral. This was the best thing for him, and she was going to see he took it.

She smiled at him as she handed him the drink. He drank all of the second glass as well, even though usually he only liked strong tea with milk, and the thought of adding salt was nauseating. She was still smiling at him when he finished. She found him attractive, and didn't mind him seeing it. He didn't know what she was attracted to. Maybe it was enough that he was a black man. Maybe she just liked him. There was no way he could do anything about it.

'If you want anything,' she offered, 'just tell me. I can go and get it, I don't mind.'

'You're very kind,' he said. 'Really.'

'I'm used to looking after people.' She spoke in a high-pitched, childlike voice, in a sing-song rhythm. 'What are you going to do tonight?'

'I'll be staying right here,' he said. 'I'll probably be asleep in an hour.' He hoped she would not offer to stay. He was very grateful to her, and she was a nice girl. When she got up and walked across the verandah, he noticed that she had long, narrow legs that, although sturdy, were slightly knock-kneed in the most adorable way. He loved her knees. 'You want some of this?' he asked, indicating the flask. 'It's all I can offer you.' He wished he could say something funny.

Her name was Sophia. She was an Italian-Australian, and used to work as a home-care nurse. She had been travelling in the south of India and the south of Thailand. India was beautiful and Thailand was beautiful. She pronounced 'beautiful' earnestly, drawing out the first syllable. 'Beeaauu-tiful', implying all sorts of grave, rare virtues. Bali, too, was beautiful. 'Away from the tourists,' she qualified. She didn't know much about the Rainbow Group, someone only took her to see their videos and stuff. She persuaded him to drink a third glass of the strangely inoffensive liquid. She was due to leave Bali in two days. 'Only two days,' she said, in her sweet, thin voice, the words full, he thought, of meaning, innuendo, regret. 'Oh well,' she said, 'I'd better go.' Reluctantly, he thought, but firmly. Or was that his vanity. 'Hope you're better soon.'

'You've been great. Really. I was thinking I had some awful disease.' Dis-ease. He had to regain his ease.

'Oh no. You'll be right soon.'

'I don't know how to thank you,' said Tyler. 'I'm going to be laid up for a day or two, or I'd . . .' Take her to dinner, buy her a present . . . 'I would have liked to . . .'

'Oh, no,' she said. 'It's all right. Take care of yourself.' It was suddenly dark outside, and she had gone.

He straightened up his room, and his bed. He began to wash his clothes, but gave up and left them in a wet soapy pile on the bathroom floor. He was exhausted, and went gratefully back to bed, even though a merciless terror awaited him. What if he were not getting better? What if he were permanently damaged? It occurred to him that he had not had an erection in three days, a record.

Neil passed by the bungalow. Tyler tried to call to him but could not make a sound. He tried to go after him but could not move. Neil was there, covered in a fierce red-faced golden-tusked mask. No, it wasn't him. Everyone was there. The girl Sophia was there, stirring tea. But it was not she. There were masks and people and people in masks and people offering to cover him with masks. Everyone he had ever known in his life. It went on and on, malevolent, turbulent. If he woke, the shadows in his room were shadows of his dreams. Back into sleep, the dreams were full of the tastes and odours of actuality.

Someone was moving around on the verandah of his room. He had been half-awake for some time, vaguely aware of the sound of sweeping on the path outside. The art-house horror-movie dreams had tortured him through the whole long night. He felt he had lost at least five pounds.

A woman was placing something on the table. The thermos and glasses had disappeared, but a jar of sugar and one of salt was evidence that not everything he had experienced in the last fifteen hours was a dream.

She looked up. She was a fair woman with ash hair and yellowish eyes. 'I hope I didn't wake you,' she said softly. He shook his head, slightly bewildered. It was early morning. He had never seen her before, had he?

'I wasn't sure if . . . if you have everything you needed.' She had brought him some plain rice, wrapped in a banana leaf, and some yoghurt in a plate covered in plastic. 'Invalid food,' she smiled. 'To start you eating again.' She didn't say who she was, who told her he was sick, where he was staying, that he was alone. People talked.

Only an hour ago he had been sure that eating again was not a proposition for the foreseeable future. Now suddenly white rice and yoghurt where exactly what he craved. Invalid food. No valid food for him. He had to get valid.

'I was afraid of bothering you,' she was saying, backing off the verandah to show she was not going to stay, didn't want anything from him, and would have as soon not let him know who had done this for him.

'Oh, no, oh please,' Tyler said. 'This is great, you are great, really.' He wanted to be able to say he would repay her, but was unable to find the right words. He gestured his inability to say more.

'Charlie said, they'd look after him where he's staying, but I thought, I just had a thought.'

Her husband was hanging back at a little distance, and gave him a friendly half-salute. He was a big man, unmistakably Australian, a man who liked football and beer, but he had a gentle, shy quality, his wife's modest dignity. He's a lucky man, thought Tyler. And he knows it.

'ESP,' said Tyler, gratefully. 'This place, you *pay* for no one being around. I could die here . . .' and they wouldn't know, he was going to say, but his tone wasn't light enough, and he forced a smile. He didn't want to admit he didn't know who she was. 'Been in Bali long?'

She and her husband Charlie had been visiting a friend of theirs from Australia who was working in a town in Java as part of some kind of volunteer program, and were stopping off in Bali on their own way home.

'You're an angel. Really. Both of you. This is totally angelic.'

'Rest is good,' she said, leaving. 'It can be nice, just resting, letting go.'

'Take care, mate,' Charlie called.

'If there're any messages,' she offered.

Tyler couldn't think of any messages to send to the Rainbows. Only that he was still waiting.

It's nice just resting, she had said. It might be, but he hadn't come here to rest. If he had come to rest and relax and

275

recuperate, he would have gone to a beach. Maybe he would go to a beach. He'd go back to Legian, or to one of those quiet beach resorts he'd heard about.

A couple of mouthfuls was enough for now. Strange and amazing as it was, he could not stay awake and had to lie down.

If Tyler had been told that alone in a hut in a third world country, a native man had entered, taken off his clothes, and turned him on to his stomach, he could only have imagined an outrage, struggle, a fight to a final victory.

But it was nothing like that. Tyler submitted like a child to its mother. He didn't know the old Balinese man, he didn't know how he had turned up here, but he had not the slightest impulse to fight or question him. Was this how people died?

The man ran his hands down Tyler's back and Tyler felt at once the sureness, the expertise, the healing force. These hands went to work and bit by bit they stroked, kneaded, poked and pummelled Tyler's body, the puckers of distress were ironed out, the tensions smoothed away, all the way to the scalp, the fingertips, the toes.

While lying on his stomach, Tyler, acquiescent, glimpsed a little boy. The child seemed to be an apprentice; he watched the massage closely, and occasionally the man would mutter to the boy, as if explaining aspects of what he was doing.

When the old man turned him over, he began work on Tyler's upper body, and then moved towards his abdomen. Tyler tensed up in apprehension, but the man responded with an admonishing click of the tongue and shake of the head. His poor, tender, battered abdomen! If the man touched him there it would be agony. But no, the man's touch was extraordinary. He seemed to feel his way around each organ of Tyler's abdominal area, and to be massaging internally. Sometimes it was painful, but the pain felt like a healing pain rather than a hurting pain. Tyler opened his eyes and the man gave him a triumphant grin, his teeth loosened and darkened, red stains at his mouth.

The old man pointed to Tyler's penis and chuckled. He then pointed to his own, and held up his little finger, and pointed back to Tyler's, holding up a forefinger, and chuckled again, as if his bawdy comparisons were immensely comic. 'Big banana,' he said, and chuckled away. The old man pointed at Tyler's arm, the skin. 'Black!' he said. His own: 'Black! Same!' He cackled again, as if it were a great joke. Tyler couldn't help grinning back at him. Once more he pointed to Tyler's private parts. 'Big black banana!' and he shrieked with mirth. Those seemed to be the only English words he knew. His mirth subsiding, he continued to work on Tyler's body, kneading even his legs and his feet.

Tyler drifted off into a half-sleep, ineffable visions, a state of wise and mysterious submission. Sometime later, the man had gone and the boy was sitting there, as if waiting for him. 'Hi,' said Tyler. 'Hi,' said the boy, with a grave look. Tyler found that he had been covered with his sarong, and wrapped himself in it as he stepped off the bed gingerly. A moment's dizziness. He felt weak, and yet faintly, tentatively well again. He poured himself some tea, and stirred in a lot of sugar. The boy shook his head when Tyler offered him some, and sat watching him drink it. From the adjoining bungalow came the thin sounds of recorded music.

There was no way he could guess the time by any sense of what had been happening, how long he had slept, when his visitors—visitations—had come, the length of his dreams. His watch was lying where he'd left it but he didn't want to make the effort to reach it. But the coolness and the light suggested about late afternoon.

The boy said, 'Please put on clothe.'

'Excuse me?'

'Clothe.' The boy pointed to Tyler's jeans. Tyler put on his jeans, sneakers and a T-shirt. The boy waited, and then began to lead the way. Tyler followed. He wanted to ask the child his name, where they were going, a lot of things. His name at least. But the boy had passed the bungalows, led Tyler through some rice fields beyond and then began scrambling down a path in some jungle on their left, looking back only to be sure that Tyler followed.

They reached a spring gushing on to a rocky ledge. Below them was a shallow bay in the river, where a group of boys washed and splashed and sang. Tyler's companion looked at him. Tyler smiled at him. 'This is great!' he said. 'This is really great!' The boy smiled back, a smile of such pure pleasure that for a moment Tyler was literally dazzled.

The boy took off his shirt and shorts and, kicking off his rubber thongs, ran under the gushing stream. Tyler followed. He splashed and washed and sang and played with the boys under the spring and in the river. Their hoots of laughter filled the fresh dappled green air until his companion indicated that darkness was approaching and it was time to depart and go their separate ways.

ELEVEN

'I wasn't going to talk to you. Even though I heard you were
OK. But you're looking for your friend. Your only reason is
he's your friend. You came over here and you've gone looking.
That's a good friend.' The guy was looking straight at Tyler
as he spoke. 'I don't know who'd come looking for me.'

He could look anyone straight in the eye, Tyler thought,
this Dennis: facial lines set in both resignation and determi-
nation, long dirty-blond hair, faded denim shirt accentuating
the blueness of eyes that look like they've stared straight into
the sun a time or two.

Tyler acknowledged what he said with a shrug. 'I don't feel
too noble,' he said, 'if that's what you're saying.'

'None of us is too noble round here,' said Dennis wryly.
They were in one of the Balinese roadside cafés, the place
where Tyler had met Felicity and Jane. He even remembered
their names. It seemed like a very long time ago. He couldn't
work out how many days ago it was—many days, more than
he'd counted—as he was concentrating on Dennis. 'We've all
got mixed motives. But you're going to keep on looking.'

'No. I'm about to give up.'

'What's that make me, your last chance? Or your last ditch
stand?' Dennis and Tyler were still getting the measure of each
other. Dennis was another of those Australian guys that had
a lot of different influences mark their speech. He had an air
of manic energy subdued by a hard-won control and by a touch
of mid-life world-weariness. A surface stillness; unpredictable
currents beneath.

'You could say that,' said Tyler pleasantly. He could have
responded competitively to the tacit challenge Dennis offered,
but he felt that course would not lead to information about
Neil. He returned Dennis' eye-to-eye gaze.

'The people here, they think it's rude to look someone

straight in the eye, know that? They do a lot of things differently from us. Some things we will never totally understand. Some things just don't translate. Know what I'm saying. But you want to talk about Neil. Neil understood this thing right from the start.' Dennis looked at Tyler, taking in his speechless moment. 'I understand Neil went through some changes here.'

'That would have to be right. That would have to be an understatement.' It was strange how Tyler felt some uncertainty though he knew this to be true. 'Can you tell me about meeting Neil?'

'Yeah. I had a meeting with him just before he left, and that was the only time I met him.'

'He left?'

'Left here, not Bali, stayed in Bali. Went to a village up in . . . I'll give you all the details if you still want to know. First I think you should have some background. Neil went to do a job and he didn't come back. But we're in a situation here where no one wanted to go looking for him unless they already knew what had happened to him, Catch-22 type situation. Most people don't have a long-term commitment here, so they had no reason to go. If they see long-term, they have reason to be careful about going.'

'People in your—what is it? I'm way back in square one where the Rainbow starts. He did this job for you?'

'He did it for himself. That's how this thing works. Everybody takes responsibility for their own actions. But we get together for discussing action, who supports who, general feedback, bouncing ideas around.'

'OK,' said Tyler, though it was far from clear. 'So this is a breakaway from the Rainbow thing? So what was the split-up all about? Gang territory?'

'Territory, yeah. No. Basic politics. They're an information group and we're an action group, to put it simply. The people you met would buy anything that had a picture of a dolphin on it and think they're saving the world. At first we were all satisfied with just getting something started. You know the story here. These people are very polite, gracious, tolerant people and it's fucked them right over. They are also people whose land was red with blood when they were hunting Communists in the sixties. The land was red with blood when they committed mass suicide long before that. Bloodshed is like the shadow side of warrior energy. The right face of that energy—that's what we're on about. We think action goes way beyond nice little pamphlets and dinner-party debates on camera etiquette.'

There was an underlying thread of logic to this speech; Tyler knew that by now so he guessed he'd learnt something, even if it were the thread itself he wasn't sure about. 'So, what are you telling me, this thing is dangerous?'

'We are not a popular group of people and being unpopular in this country can be dangerous. But if you're not making enemies you're not changing anything. There are very few of us. Most tourists don't want to know. There're people who live here, foreigners, great life, decadent, easy, they don't want to know about us either. There're people making very big money out of development, and they have power, same as everywhere, and they would do anything to stop us. Then there's everyone else who gets paid by those people, or are scared of them, or don't want to see that anything outside of their own backyard is any of their business.'

Dennis spoke in a voice low enough for Tyler to think he was taking care not to be overheard. Tyler didn't think Dennis was deluded or manipulatingly signalling a non-existent threat, but he didn't know what he did think.

'So you see, you might be looking for Neil, but we still don't know how much we should tell you.'

'We' Dennis kept saying, but Tyler didn't know who else he meant.

'What I feel like,' said Tyler, 'is I came into a movie half-way through. There was something at the start that explained what's going on.'

'The thing that happened at the start,' said Dennis, 'was a few people asking themselves why they were travelling in the first place. Most people go not to see, but to take pictures. The Wishys got that right.'

'Excuse me?'

'Wishys—short for wishy-washys. And all they do is wish it were different.'

Dennis elaborated. At first everyone who got together over their concern about the effects of tourism on a developing economy and a traditional culture felt they were all on about the same thing. Then the arguments about what you actually did became more emphatic than their areas of agreement, which seemed to diminish. The people Tyler met before had decided 'information-sharing' was their main principle. It's the 'information age', they said. People with access to information made better decisions was their point. According to Dennis, and to the 'we' he mentioned, information was not enough, especially when it came too late. Direct action was the way to go. They were willing to actually *do* something that would make a difference, if only as a warning; something so passionate, theatrical and risky that people would at least have to *consider* what it urged them to conclude.

'This is my problem,' Tyler admitted. 'I don't see where Neil came in.'

'He was a very political guy.'

'He never, once, registered to vote.'

'Right. That was a political decision. Maybe not the right one, maybe he'd make a different decision now. Neil was a guy who liked to say what he thought?'

'Yeah,' Tyler replied swiftly, fleetingly aware that it wasn't that simple a question. Neil must have thought a lot of stuff he never said. But what did he say, he was very sure about. 'Yeah,' said Tyler again. 'Pretty much.'

'We might think we have limits on our free speech where we come from, but we don't, let me tell you, we don't. Speaking relatively. Places like this, this is where you don't take free speech for granted.' Dennis shrugged expressively. 'I've seen where that one thing is enough to turn someone's thinking right around.'

Getting into a discussion on free speech was like going back to college, Tyler thought, back to the classroom part of college. Which was not his favourite part. Or Neil's. 'OK, here's the thing,' he said. 'Neil was into having a good time. Neil liked his fun.'

Dennis laughed. He actually threw back his head and roared. Loud enough that the few people around them turned to look, smiling. Tyler, after a moment of sheer astonishment, gave a little laugh of his own, expressing more surprise than mirth. He didn't know what the joke was.

'You don't think we have fun?' asked Dennis. 'Man, I have led you seriously astray. We are serious, sure, I am very serious about this, this is serious shit we deal with. But. It's fun, believe me, there is more bloody joy and comradeship and heart-lightening bloody purpose in what we do . . . we have our laughs and we feel, you know, righteous and we feel the love of life that is felt when a warrior goes in to battle and that is fun. And we see the tourists trudging around looking for the next snapshot, the next western restaurant, the next bargain, and we do not often see anything near the degree of fun we have. OK, you see what I mean, but think about it. I've been involved in action for a long while and they think they can put you down by saying exhibitionism, vandalism, looking for kicks. As if any degree of play, or pleasure, taints the integrity of our purpose. I'm getting rhetorical here, but that's my training. All I want to say, a guy who is ready for deeper levels of fun comes to where we are and knows he's at home.'

After his illness Tyler had spent an unusual few days in his strangely quiet bungalow. He never saw more than a glimpse of the other guests. He slept a lot more than usual, he exercised on his verandah, he read at random from old magazines and new books; he ate at a clean, modest restaurant nearby, where the waiter would leave him alone at times, and then sit with him to practise his English and ask about the exact words of old pop songs, at precisely the times Tyler was likely to be approached by other tourists making a bid for his company. He could not remember wanting to be alone before, not for this long, not with this new unnamable state of mind.

He had gone back to the spring by the little bay of the river, but there were women bathing and washing there, and he retreated hastily. He would have to return at dusk, that must be the boys' time, but he hadn't done that yet.

He had had a fleeting but horrible thought that the illness might have damaged him but woke one morning with his cock near to bursting with hardness, and that was enough for now. He noticed women but did not return any curious, interested gaze. When this was over he would know what he was now ready for, what had changed. He was waiting but he was not impatient. He had time to think but there were no thoughts. And then on a sudden impulse he walked down the steep driveway and a guy in a faded denim shirt was waiting there. 'Good day, Tyler,' he'd said. 'I'm Dennis. Can we talk?'

Dennis reckoned they should build a BaliWorld. Like Disney-world, or Movieworld. It would contain everything ninety per cent of tourists wanted from Bali. Then no one would have to come here and these people could get on with their lives and prepare for the twenty-first century in peace. Even the tourists who claimed they weren't tourists, even those who sought the authentic, wanted swimming pools, international phone lines, clean sheets, cold beer, fixed prices, strict schedules, commentary. BaliWorld, or they could call it McParadise.

Tyler threw in a few arguments that he didn't even know he could have thought of. There was nothing Dennis hadn't heard.

After a couple of cold drinks they'd eaten some fried rice and some fruit salad. No one had any other urgent appoint-ment and Dennis had become somewhat warmed up. Tyler didn't think he was arguing with him, but Dennis was telling all the ways tourists didn't know what they were doing.

For instance, they often claimed that travel broadened the mind, but there was no proof of this anywhere. They claimed that when they had been to a place they took more interest in references to it if it ever got reported on 'The News', and if there was a TV documentary about it they watched it. This has never proved to do any good for the people whose lives had provided the subject matter. Tourists presumed that their dollars brought only benefit to the people whose country they photographed, even while they paid for everything from flights, accommodation, food and guides to multinational companies who didn't necessarily pay anything like they charged nor invest anywhere near as much as they profited. Some tourists claimed that travel provided them with character-building adventure and risk, but didn't consider that it now cost more and took a lot more imagination and ingenuity to fabricate travel risks than to avoid them.

'So, what are you saying,' Tyler contributed, 'people should stop travelling? I'd be out of a job. I work for an airline.'

'People aren't going to stop travelling. You'll keep your job. Some of us into eco-travel do suggest that the only totally sound thing to do is stay home.'

'That's kind of extreme, isn't it?'

'Exactly.'

If he had ended up sitting here listening to this, then maybe Neil had too. OK, then, this was the last wild lead he'd follow. All make a good story one day.

According to Dennis, Neil had learnt about a village near the north-west coast, that had up to now restricted tourism to a few buses that came to see a dance then left again. There were plans for a big new restaurant up there. Here was a chance to commit that dramatic, dangerous action. Now that was adventure, risk, fun.

Tyler recognised a rerun of an old feeling. That resentment. He resented that he was being forced to think of these things, he who was meant, he thought, for having fun and getting lucky. But the resentment did not flood his mind, it just made an appearance, let him remember it, and sat quietly to one side. He also recognised the old irritating bewilderment: he, who had learnt to judge people pretty well, he thought, had to make an urgent judgment, and felt oddly unpractised—him!—at realising what he knew. It was, barely, possible that Dennis was lying, and that Tyler was being set up. But what for? Could he figure it? If any of this were true, he had some place to go next. And then he'd be out of here. Somewhere, he had a life.

'If he did do something up there, how come you never heard about it?'

'If. If he did. Or if he were stopped. We hear about everything but some things, it's like they never existed. That's what it's like here.'

Finally, Tyler said, 'OK, I'm going to go to this village. I'll get a car to drive me there.' They wouldn't have seen too many black guys, he figured, and the sight of him would recall Neil to anyone who had seen him if, indeed, he had ever been there. 'I get to the village. Then what?'

'That's up to you, man. Not to be unhelpful, but there's no blueprint, you know. If Neil got there and did anything, you could sniff around, find the development areas, and you might find out. You might not.' Dennis shrugged. 'Sorry. I know what it's like around here.'

'You've never been there? Where do I stay?'

'There's a place to stay, old palace where they do the dance for tourists, some imitation trance-dance show. It's an interesting area for that, the trance thing, big purifying ceremony deal. Special occasions. Could be one coming up.'

That was the thing about the big choices you made: it was as if you had no choice. In little things you exercised choice, you selected, preferred, favoured. In big things you just know what you're going to do. Sooner or later. Tyler knew he'd follow any lead to Neil until it came to a dead end. Or, of course, until he came to find him, which he no longer could easily imagine. Always be prepared for the unimagined, it's something hard to recognise. At this point, when you accepted rather than made a choice, all the questions became practical ones.

'How long does it take? Know a good driver?'

Inner steadfastness, outward yielding. The darkest darkness is about to perish of its own darkness.

Persist, persevere. That's all he knew how to do any more.

The reasons for his actions would be revealed in their results.

HONK IF YOU ARE JESUS
PETER GOLDSWORTHY

Thursday's theatre-list—curettes, TOPs, terminations, pick a euphemism—was the worst of the week. Even a ligation or two—gynaecology's bread and butter—would have made for a little variety. I could have done the work blindfolded.

'Spin me three times, Sister. And aim me towards the patient.'
'Sorry, Doctor Fox?'
'A joke, Sister. A small joke. You must be new.'

At the age of forty-five, Dr Mara Fox, senior lecturer in obstetrics, world authority on *in vitro* fertilisation, is burnt out and weary of the human race. Offered a Chair in Reproductive Medicine at the new Schultz Bible College on Queensland's Gold Coast, and unlimited funds with which to resurrect her failed research projects, she makes the move—only to find herself entangled in a bizarre scientific nightmare.

A 'scientific romance' in the tradition of H G Wells? An Orwellian satire? Peter Goldsworthy, author of the internationally acclaimed novel *Maestro*, and a modern champion of the lost art of story-telling, has written a new novel that resists categorisation. A novel that is above all stunningly original and highly entertaining.

Honk If You Are Jesus is a contradiction in terms: contemporary literature that is unable to be put down.

INSIDE OUTSIDE
ANDREW RIEMER

On a freezing November day in 1946, Andrew Riemer, then a ten-year-old with mumps, left a bomb-scarred Budapest on his way to Australia. A few days before Christmas in 1990 he returned to the city of his birth where, amid the decay of a world waking from totalitarian rule, he tried to reconstruct the past from shreds of memory and family myth.

In the years between, his career had taken him from being an expert in French-knitting, a skill acquired when, unable to speak English, he was put in a class for intellectually handicapped children, to Sydney University, where he now teaches English Literature.

Andrew Riemer has written a classic. Witty, lucid, heartrending and wonderfully funny. No reader will ever forget his two worlds, or the profound questions he asks about them.
JILL KER CONWAY